CU00832297

Val Lewton was born in Yalta, Russia, in 1904. Aged five, he emigrated to the US with his mother, a sister of the famed actress Nazimova. Before entering movies in the 1930s, he was author of nine novels, several works of nonfiction, a portfolio of poetry and two pornographic titles, sold under the counter. He worked as assistant to David O Selznick - whom he tried to dissuade from making *Gone With the Wind* - before being put in charge of RKO's horror unit in 1942. As prime artistic mover behind the nine horror films created there, including *Cat People, I Walked With a Zombie, The Seventh Victim* and *The Body Snatcher*, Lewton transcended low-budget restrictions to restore darkness, melancholy, psychology and suggestion to the genre. Today, his films are recognised as classics. He died in 1951.

First published in 1932 by The Vanguard Press, New York City
Copyright renewed © 1960 by Mrs Val Lewton, as widow of the author
The moral right of Val Lewton to be identified as the author of this
work has been asserted.

First published in this edition in 2006 by Kingly-Reprieve
an imprint of Kingly Books, Glasgow
www.kinglybooks.com

Special thanks this edition go to Val E Lewton and his family,
Martin Scorsese, Freida Orange and Alison Stroak.

Layout and cover artwork by Marc Baines

Preface copyright © Val E. Lewton, 2006
Afterword copyright © Damien Love, 2006

Printed and bound in Great Britain by Clydeside Press

A catalogue record for this book is available from the British Library

ISBN 0953163962

NO BED
OF HER OWN

by Val Lewton

KINGLY
REPRIEVE

FOR
DONALD HENDERSON CLARKE

PREFACE

by Val E Lewton

My father's first successful novel might have been titled *The Education of Rose Mahoney*. But on reading a first draft my mother observed, "Rose seems to have no bed of her own," and the title stuck.

As a child I wasn't allowed to read *No Bed of Her Own*. It was considered far too racy for children - in a category my father's aunt, legendary actress Alla Nazimova, called "hot books." After my father's death in 1951, looking for a hot novel, I did read *No Bed of Her Own*. To a post-war teenage adolescent it didn't seem hot at all. At the same time, viewing his more famous horror movies didn't seem all that scary.

Now, more than fifty years later, *Cat People* and *I Walked with a Zombie* are highly admired noir classics. So, maybe there is more than a lurid title to *No Bed of Her Own*. If it's not a hot read, what is it? The first novel about the great Depression?

That was my father's contention. A book burned by Hitler as degenerate literature? Yet another dubious claim. Or, like my father's movie *The Seventh Victim*, a great story about New York, featuring a gutsy, slightly clueless heroine, trying to navigate an alien world?

Rose Mahoney, a cheeky blond typist, may lack the education or wit of other Lewton heroines, such as the courtesan, Nell Bowen, in the film *Bedlam*, but she shares with them an unwavering ethical compass. Sure, she's a tart, a flapper, a poster child for the roaring twenties caught up in the great financial crash of the thirties. Yet she has *her* standards. But her standards, admirably frank and genuine, don't cut it in a world without work. Like Micawber in *David Copperfield*, Rose keeps expecting that something will turn up. While waiting, she explores the dark corners of life in New York City, a world hidden to her before losing her job, her apartment, and finally her bearings. At novel's end, it looks as if she will have to sacrifice her scruples to survive. Before steeling her resolve to make it at any cost, she looks to the primitive social safety net of pre-New Deal America. She finds that compassion and help only go to those considered the deserving poor. Rose is too young, too pretty, too proud to be considered deserving. And so a hardened Rose determines to help herself...

There is a later, cleverer, deservedly more famous New York working girl than Rose Mahoney – the Holly Golightly of Truman Capote's *Breakfast at Tiffany's*. But even if, in the end, she is herself just as clueless as Rose, Holly is literally, and in literature, decades away from her. Capote's deconstructed novella is as discursive and graceful as *No Bed of Her Own* is stolidly traditional. The literary stylishness of *Breakfast at Tiffany's* is a perfect match for Holly's hipster façade. Rose's blue-collar scruples call for a more straightforward approach, and she gets it. As quick as cells in a comic strip, *No Bed of Her Own* rushes through twenty abbreviated chapters to a melodramatic conclusion. Similar to my father's films, the story abruptly moves from scene to scene without transition or dissolve. Open the book; begin reading. It won't take long. The book was written in several weeks and there is not a wasted word.

Val E Lewton
Washington DC
November 2005

"Man begs; woman sells."
- VICTOR HUGO: "LES MISERABLES"

ONE

"Go on, you'll be peddling apples if you get fresh with that guy."

Rose Mahoney wiped the bright lipstick from the corners of her mouth with a paper towel and kept looking into the mirror in front of her. Mary Schmidt, busied at the same task and looking into the same mirror, could see her warning had made no impression in the calm, smiling expression of Rose's eyes.

"Then I'll peddle apples," Rose answered evenly. "A depression isn't going to scare me into being yellow. I'll tell that Brayman dope where to get off any time he tries to pile on more than the traffic will bear."

It was five minutes to nine and the women's washroom of the Landsman & Miller Pneumatic Tool Company offices was warm and crowded. After the scurry from subway to office along gray, windswept streets, the steaming radiators and the tile walls, glaring white under the strong electric bulbs, seemed cozy. The girls were fussing and chattering as they fixed their faces, adjusted paper cuffs to protect their sleeves and smoked the last cigarette until lunchtime. This morning preparation for the day's work was one of the big features of the day among the Landsman & Miller stenographers.

Rose crushed the paper towel into a tight wad and tossed it into a container; then she began to brush the excess powder from her short straight nose and the smooth cheeks sloping away from it to high, clean-cut cheekbones. Looking into the mirror as she did this, Rose was pleased with what she saw. She could well believe Mrs. Feinberg, her landlady, who told her every time she went down into the steamy kitchen of the boarding house to pay her week's rent:

"*Nu!* Why don't they put you in the movies? With your looks -"

Her blue eyes, Rose judged, were her best features. They looked out impudently from either side of her short nose, and their brightness was enhanced by stubby, thick lashes. Her mouth was too broad and full, but a short upper lip made it seem eager and provocative. White powder, liberally applied, hid the freckles on the bridge of her nose and her once mouse-brown hair had long ago become golden blonde. Now she was contemplating another bleaching to achieve the current shade of platinum.

"How do you think I'd look as a platinum blonde?" she asked as she tucked her compact into her handbag, and then, before Mary Schmidt could answer, went on to ask, "Got a cigarette?"

"Uh huh!" Mary grunted in answer to both questions, her entire attention concentrated on the plucking of a stubborn eyebrow.

Rose reached over and took Mary's handbag from the washroom shelf and rummaged through it for a battered pack of Camels. She took one, lit it, and leaned back against the washbasin to rest as she puffed out the first, luxurious exhalation of cigarette smoke.

The girl on her left, mixing a bromo-seltzer in a dust-coated, finger-smeared glass, groaned.

"Jesus! What a head!"

"Beau night?" Rose asked her.

"Yeah. The boyfriend and I went up to Boogey Town. We got plastered. And, can you believe it, Rose, I danced with a nigger!"

"No!"

"Yeah!"

"You're kidding!"

"No, I'm not. I got terrible tight and there was this here coon at the next table - a big, black buck nigger - and for some nutty reason I got a yen to dance with him. I don't know whether he asked me to or not, but the first thing you knew we was dancing together. The boyfriend got sore and there was a helluva fight. I got pushed all around. No more Boogey Town for me. Let the niggers have Harlem; I don't want any part of it."

The girl, a muddy-complexioned blonde, with hair as light and frizzy as a china doll's, was the bad egg of the Landsman & Miller Pneumatic Tool Company's stenographic force. She had been christened Milka Pudniac in Milltown, Pennsylvania, but on her arrival in New York, after two arduous years getting through a six month's course in the Milltown Business Institute, she had changed her name immediately to Mildred Purdy. Her tales of gay debauch with her boyfriend, a small-time bootlegger, furnished the scarlet touches for the gossip in the women's restroom. Rose had slyly questioned Mildred, however, and had discovered she was still virginal. From this fact, Rose had drawn the conclusion that bootleggers must be more chivalrous and less demanding than clerks.

Mary finished pulling the one eyebrow which had disturbed the utterly artificial symmetry of her thread-thin brows. She looked apprehensively at her wrist watch.

"Nine o'clock Rose," she stated. "Give me a puff on your cigarette and we'll go in. Brayman says -"

"The hell with Brayman!" Rose interrupted. "Light a cigarette yourself. He won't fire you for being half a minute late."

"He might."

"The hell with him!"

"All right."

Mary opened her handbag and took out cigarettes and matches. A quiet girl, Mary lived in fear of breaking rules. She was devoted to Rose, drawn to her by the other girl's colorful dash and by her strong acceptance of life. Yet it was Rose who redoubled her fears by persuading her to break rules and declare rebellion against petty office restrictions.

Mildred, her hand shaking, finished her bromo-seltzer and put the unrinsed glass back on the shelf.

"Gee - was I plastered," she remarked in a curiously mixed tone of pride and pain.

"Bum liquor?" Rose ventured.

"Naw. Not now," Mildred informed her. "My boyfriend says so few guys are putting up dough for booze these days they've got to sell the good stuff. Besides - my boyfriend always has the best. He ain't in the business for nothing."

"It's a swell depression," Rose applauded.

"My brother-in-law is out of work," Mary said. "But that don't mean much; he's always getting fired. My sister's got a job. She leaves the two kids with mother - Julius is so lazy he don't even want to take care of the kids."

"Sure. It's the guys who'd rather play pool than work that are out of a job. Didn't I hear Brayman shooting off his mouth to Fanny Fishface the other day? He was telling her all about it. Any guy who really needs work can get it." Rose told her.

"That's about the size of it."

Mildred took Mary's cigarette out of her hand and took a long pull on it. Blowing out the smoke as she handed it back she said:

"I'm getting along; I want to be at my desk before Brayman comes in."

"Stick around," Rose said. "It'll look funny if you're at your desk and we're still here."

Mary took Rose's elbow.

"You and I had better get on too."

"Wait till I finish my butt."

"But Brayman said -"

"The hell with that pint-sized executive!"

Behind the closed door of one of the cubicles which lined the wall of the washroom, a toilet regurgitated with a loud, rumbling sound. A second later the latch clicked up and the door swung open. Fanny Wise, pulling her red woolen dress down about her wide hips, stepped majestically out of the compartment. Tossing her black hair back in a gesture employed by her favorite movie star, she crossed the room to the washbasin.

At sight of her, a silence fell upon the other girls.

"Hello," Fanny said to them in a thin, sharp voice that could scale the heights of clamor with shrill screeching whenever anything displeased her.

"Hello," they answered.

For a moment, as Fanny washed her hands and reached for a paper towel, Rose, Mary and Mildred kept silence. They felt ill at ease in her presence. Fanny wanted them to feel ill at ease. By hard work she had achieved a position of some trust as secretary to the advertising manager and felt herself far above the rest.

They, for their part, feared and disliked her for her airs of superiority. Rose could always get a laugh from the other girls by imitating Fanny with an armload of serious literature. For

Fanny never even stepped out to luncheon without carrying under her arm several fat books and a copy of the *American Mercury*.

Rose, especially, disliked her. An easy-going person herself, she could not understand Fanny's obsession to be somebody. It was easy to explain. Fanny's father, a mild-mannered, soft-spoken German Jew, with a warm, friendly smile, had been kicked around from job to job. Even while a girl in school, Fanny had been as a mother to him. Then, when she got her first salary raise, her father had retired and become a baseball fan, approaching this new profession with an ardor he had never displayed in any other business. Early responsibilities and the constant goad of her father's failure had made Fanny a careerist.

Fanny was in love with her boss, who scarcely noticed her. This passion she had tenderly nursed for the past six years, enjoying her own suffering, for it was easier to work hard, teeth gritted, when one was a martyr to a hopeless love. This frustration and her addled virginity had acidulated her temper. There were days when her temper was as sensitive as a nerve exposed by the dentist's carelessness. At such times the other girls were afraid of Fanny, but not Rose. She was just waiting for Fanny to get "fresh" with her, and Fanny, realizing that Rose would welcome a quarrel, treated her with more consideration than she displayed to the other girls.

Now, as Fanny washed and dried her hands, humming to herself, Mary, always apprehensive, made agitated signals behind her back to attract Rose's attention. She was trying to tell her they should get to work now that Fanny was there. Rose understood her meaning perfectly, but questioned loudly.

"What?"

"We'd better get in and get to work."

"What for?"

"Mr. Brayman said -"

"The hell with Brayman!"

Fanny's pudgy hands, a moment before busied in drying themselves on a paper towel, stopped moving in mid-air.

"But - we -" Mary began apprehensively.

"Aw, we don't have to mind that dope," Rose said loudly, her eyes fixed on the back of Fanny's head.

Fanny whirled round.

"Miss Mahoney," she shrilled, "there is a rule in this office: all stenographers must be at their desks by nine o' clock."

Rose blew two thin streamers of smoke out from her nostrils before replying.

"I've been here long enough to find that out, but what about you?"

"I'm not a stenographer."

Rose smiled.

"Of course you're not a stenographer. Our old shorthand teacher used to say that a good steno should be fast, alert and young."

Fanny paled. She was thirty and sensitive about her age. It seemed to her that as she grew older, her boss paid less attention to her. And this was true, but it was only because he found he could leave more of his own work for her to do, and no longer needed to supervise the doing of it.

There was a moment's silence as the two girls faced each other. Mary edged away a little, frightened. Then Fanny mustered what dignity she could, and said:

"Miss Mahoney, I'm sorry, but I'll have to report you to Mr. Brayman. The stenographic department is very lax. I sent down a letter two days ago, and it hasn't come back for my O.K. yet. That's because you loaf out here in the washroom when you should be at work."

She crushed the paper towel into a wad and with an airy gesture threw it into a waste container. Then she turned and stalked out of the room with long, swinging strides in imitation of her favorite motion picture actress, a lank Swedish person to whom such a gait was well suited. As Fanny Wise was short, thick-hipped and had long, pendulous breasts which Arthur, the office boy, had labelled "belly blankets" among his confreres, this striding walk made her ludicrous. It was as if a side of bacon had suddenly taken up aesthetic dancing.

When the door had closed behind Fanny with a definite click, like the period at the end of a short and angry sentence, Mary turned, white-faced to Rose.

"She'll tell Brayman."

"Yeah, I know. He's always sucking around her, hoping she'll ask Flynn to get him into the advertising department. Fat chance! Flynn doesn't pay any more attention to her than he does to the bottle of water on his desk. Fanny's filled it with fresh water every day for the past six years, and he hasn't ever taken a drink out of it."

"Mr. Brayman'll fire you."

"The hell he will! He can't fire anybody. He hasn't got the authority to fire anybody. Tim Kane is the personnel director; he's the guy that fires you. And I've got a heavy drag with Tim. I let him kiss me one day on the stairs when we were having fire drill. I've got a drag."

"We'd better get to work."

"All right."

Rose flipped her cigarette end into a toilet bowl and watched the damp paper disintegrate and let the brown tendrils of tobacco float out onto the clear water. Then she turned and followed Mary and Mildred out of the washroom.

As they turned into the main hallway an elevator door opened and Martin Brayman stepped out, his thin, stunted figure very dapper in a tightly fitted overcoat, and a derby cocked jauntily on his well-greased hair.

"Good morning girls," he said cheerily as he went past them with short, quick steps.

They chorused a half-hearted good morning, and Mary watched him as he went briskly into the office. She was afraid he would look at his watch and see how late it was. When she saw that he had forgotten to do so in his excess of morning energy, she sighed with relief.

Rose stuck out her tongue, held it tightly between her lips and blew out her breath to make an obscene noise.

"- that for Brayman," she said.

"Shh!" Mary cautioned.

Mildred laughed and then stopped abruptly as the jerk of her laughter sent a sharper pain through her aching head.

The girls went to their desks and sat down, pulled the oil cloth covers from their typewriters and settled back to wait until Brayman distributed the work.

Brayman was a short man with a cock-sparrow arrogance and conceit. Unfortunately, Brayman, although he had all the other qualifications for "big business" success, especially a flawless demeanour, had little grey matter between his thin temples. As Assistant Office Manager in charge of stenographic work, he had little real authority. There were five girls under him and he had only to distribute the work, look over it to see that it was correct and send it on to the department from which it had come. To this task he brought a wealth of memoranda on slips printed with his full name and office title, a great dignity and the manners of a harassed executive. There was always a serious and preoccupied frown between his heavy, black eyebrows. Actually he had so little to do that he spent his time rustling papers about his desk as if engaged in urgent business, in writing memoranda he never sent, and ruling lines on blank sheets of paper with the air of one who felt the heavy weight of the entire concern on his shoulders. These ruled lines of paper went into the waste basket. Brayman's greatest moments, however, came when a salesman called to sell him stationery. With what an air of seriousness did he lend an ear to the man's sales talk, and then with what tact and dignity did he refuse the man's product, pointing out some fancied weakness in the material. As a matter of fact, purchases of this sort were out of his jurisdiction. A purchasing department handled such matters.

Now, with great care, Brayman hung his coat on a patented hanger he kept for that purpose, flecked a speck of lint from his derby hat and put it carefully into a hatbox on a shelf in back of his desk, and then turned, with a great dry-washing of his neat, well-manicured hands, to his desk.

There was a memorandum in an inter-office envelope on the pristine aridity of the desk top. Brayman seated himself, took a paper knife from a drawer and slit the envelope. With great seriousness, tilted back in his chair, he read the message.

"In view of the present economic crisis, the Landsman & Miller Pneumatic Tool Company has decided upon retrenchment. It is planned to decrease the staff. You will send the name of your least competent worker to Mr. Mudge of the Auditing Department before three o'clock."

Brayman smiled. This pleased him. An important decision had been put into his hands. A sense of power flooded his puny soul. He looked over at the row of stenographers, sitting idle before their machines. He could fire any one of them! Mary? She was slow, but then she never dared to question him.

Mildred? She always gave him a quart of Scotch at Christmas. Vivian? Her father was one of the biggest furniture store owners in Brooklyn. Ruth? His eye ran down from her face to her protruding breasts. Rose? She was the fastest worker, but she talked back.

It was hard to make a decision. He mulled the question over in his mind. It gave him pleasure even to think about it. If they only knew that he was sitting there deciding, weighing, their fates.

All morning long, as the girls typed, he busied himself with paper and pencil, writing down first one girl's name and then another, crossing lines through the names and turning the matter over and over.

At noon, when he was putting on his hat and coat, Fanny Wise came out from Flynn's office and perched herself nonchalantly on the edge of his desk.

"Going to lunch?"

"I thought I'd go to Childs."

"Wait until I put through a call for Mr. Flynn and I'll go with you. Dutch?"

"Fine."

Fully dressed for the street, he waited, fretting, until she was ready.

Seated at a table in the restaurant, Fanny took a cigarette from her handbag and Brayman leaned over to light it for her.

"Thanks."

"You're nervous. Your hands shake."

"Yes. There's so much to be done in our department, and the copywriters are so lazy. It's like pulling teeth to get any work out of them."

"The girls are getting that way too," he told her, to show that he also had responsibilities.

"Yes, I've noticed," she said.

"What have you noticed?"

"The girls aren't working as they were last year. Something's wrong. I sent down a letter two days ago, and it hasn't come back yet."

"I'll take it under consideration."

"I have my own theory," Fanny said.

"About what?"

"About the girls not doing the work they should. You have a bad influence in your department."

"How's that?"

"That blonde girl - you know -"

"Rose?"

"Is that her name?" she asked with elaborate unconcern.

"Rose Mahoney."

"She's too pert. I've heard her advising the other girls - making suggestions that were detrimental to business discipline."

"I'll look into it," he told her. "If she is a bad influence - I'll get rid of her pronto. I don't want anyone spoiling the girls. I noticed that they're not as hard-working since she's come."

He had made up his mind. Fanny Wise would see how he could hire and fire. Rose would be out that night. It would boost him in Fanny's eyes.

At two o'clock a memorandum was on its way to Mr. Mudge. It suggested Rose Mahoney's name for the list of those to be discharged in the retrenchment.

In the Landsman & Miller offices they distributed the pay envelopes just before the employees went home on Friday nights. A girl from the auditing department, trailed by a policeman, came down with a tray full of envelopes.

"Thanks for the insult," Rose said, taking her envelope.

The girl from the auditing department, who usually had a

wisecrack ready for such pleasantries, said nothing, and turned away. Rose did not notice this and calmly opened her envelope. There was a blue slip folded in with the green bills.

She took it out and held it up for everyone to see.

"Bye-bye little Rosie!" she sang out.

"Aw," Mary said. "Aw!"

"Jesus!" Mildred exclaimed.

Brayman, who had watched her from the moment she took the envelope in her hand, kept his face purposely blank to hide his satisfaction. Then he looked at Fanny Wise, lounging in the doorway of Flynn's office.

He was so pleased with all that had passed, that he did not look into his own envelope to carefully count the money as was his custom. Not until Rose, Mildred, Mary and he were all crowded together in the elevator on their way down did he open the envelope. A blue slip confronted him.

"I was getting tired anyhow - I needed a little vacation," Rose was saying, as if her discharge was a huge joke.

She looked up to see how Brayman had taken this bit of bravado. He was standing, still and white, the blue slip in his hand, stunned. His mouth was gaped in a cry of involuntary surprise.

Rose had to laugh.

"Let's go into the apple-peddling racket, Mr. Brayman," she suggested, "I'll be your little efficiency expert."

TWO

The rooming house where Rose lived was an old brownstone front on West Fifty-sixth Street. At one time it had boasted a handsome stoop with broad steps leading up to an entrance door, but, now, in accordance with the building laws for that zone, the stoop and the broad steps had been removed. One entered the house through a square, ugly door in what had been the basement and was now the first floor. In the grimy hallway stood a china umbrella holder with leprous red dragons in design on its dirty white sides, a three-legged table of varnished wood on which the lodgers' mail was laid out in thin, orderly heaps, and a coat tree on which a dusty derby hung perpetually. Mrs. Feinberg, the landlady, had forgotten long ago to whom it belonged. The derby was as much a familiar spirit of the house as the one-eyed, ash-grey tomcat who patrolled the corridors, or the ever-present smell of cooking.

Entering, Rose shut the front door behind her and looked on the table for her mail. There was a letter from her mother. She read it quickly, holding the letter up to the thin light from a curtained window beside the door. It contained a request to buy and send various sundries from New York department stores, a promise to pay for these, and ended, "we are all well." Rose tore the letter into four parts and threw the pieces into the umbrella stand. Her mother's promises to pay for the things Rose sent up to Athol, Massachusetts, where her family lived, were merely promises. Now that she was out of a job, Rose did not feel she could allow herself to be imposed upon. Previously she had grudgingly complied with her mother's requests, buying household utensils, cheap dresses and other things that her mother had seen advertised in New York papers, and sending them home with no hope that she would ever be repaid. This was by way of being what her mother called "a good daughter."

There was no great love or clan feeling between the members of the Mahoney family. Rose's father was second generation Boston-Irish. As a young man he had moved to Athol, opened a small shoe store and married one of the Polish girls from the mills. Rose, her brother, Tim, and three children who had died in infancy were the result of this union.

The little shoe store Mahoney owned could not compete with the chain stores and money had always been scarce. Rose had gone from grade school into a so-called business college and at sixteen had taken out her working papers and found herself a job as filing clerk in the office of a cotton mill. A year later a friend had coaxed her to hitch-hike to New York, where salaries were better and life more replete with motion picture theatres, boyfriends and chop suey restaurants. Rose had not been home since.

Climbing the two flights of stairs which brought her up to her own landing, Rose wondered if the depression had hit her father's business. It was the first time she had thought of him in a year. The last time had been when she had selected a tie - fifty-eight cents marked down from a dollar - for his Christmas present.

"Well the old man should worry about his business so long as Tim's got his job on the force," she said to herself. "They never fire politicians."

Her elder brother, Tim, was a member of the Athol police department. He had been voted Athol's handsomest cop in a competition sponsored by the local newspaper.

Rose searched through the litter in her pocket book for the room key, found it, and unlocked the door. She switched on the electric light, threw her handbag onto the bed and then knelt to light the gas burner which heated the room.

Rose paid eight dollars a week for her room. It was not a luxurious dwelling place, but it had its advantages. There were two large windows facing the street, and through these the sunlight poured generously in the early mornings. Rose liked to get dressed with the sunlight flooding in warm streams over her bare legs. The casements were deep, and old-fashioned inner shutters were folded against their sides. As there were no blinds, Rose had to push the shutters forward when she made herself ready for bed at night. The walls were covered with a flowered wallpaper, the design in pale grey on a paler background. The flower petals reminded Rose of a hound dog's floppy ears. A chair, a table, and a studio bed were the only furnishings, and a dusty oriental rug covered the black painted floor. The gas burner stood between the windows.

It was an old-fashioned place and had none of the smart, modern conveniences which Rose could have had for the same amount of money at the Y.W.C.A. or some women's hotel, but Rose liked it. She could not endure the regimented life of an institutional boarding place. Here she was free to do whatever she wished and to entertain anyone she pleased. Mrs. Feinberg never grumbled about male visitors. She had met Bill Taggart sneaking downstairs one Sunday morning and had not said a word. Such slight inconveniences as the gas heater did not greatly matter. Rose often said:

"I don't mind it. It's almost as cozy as a fireplace, and if I ever get tired of life all I have to do is close the window and turn on the gas."

The bathroom was just down the hall from Rose's room. Three people used it beside herself. One of these was a floorwalker in a department store who had lived in Mrs. Feinberg's house for fifteen years. The fatty wreck of a once-handsome man, he always gave Rose what he would have termed the glad eye when he met her in the hall. The other two who shared the bath with Rose were stenographers like herself, and had the same hours as she did. Consequently there was a rush to get into the bathroom first in the morning. But, even if one lost this race, it was not too bad. Mrs. Feinberg's handyman, whose name, Larsen, could be heard echoing up and down the corridors when anything went wrong, kept a hot fire under the heater, and there was always plenty of hot water.

Rose hung up her coat, kicked her shoes off into the back of the closet and put on a pair of cheap red and gold mules. Lighting a cigarette, she took towel and soap and went into the bathroom to wash her hands. This done, she returned to her room, hung up her towel and curled up on the edge of the bed to finish the cigarette.

She had a date with Bill Taggart that night, and she was glad. She wanted someone to talk to about losing her job. Among the girls in the office, the American code of lightheartedness had forced her to pretend it didn't matter. Not that she was worried. She had forty-three dollars in her Christmas Club account and that would carry her safely until she could get another job. It wasn't worry. It was the shock of losing a job in which she felt secure; the breaking up of friendships with the girls in the office; the nuisance of having to go out and find a new job and then work hard until she had convinced her new bosses she was a more than average stenographer. She felt sure that Bill would understand and sympathize with her.

Rose glanced at the alarm clock. It was six-thirty. She had an hour in which to eat and get ready before he came. It was dark outdoors and she could hear the wind whistle coldly as it sluiced through the narrow street. It was not a night in which she cared to go out to eat - too cozy here in slippers beside the gas burner.

Getting a nickel out of her pocketbook, Rose shuffled out into the hall where a pay telephone hung on the wall and dialed the number of the corner drugstore.

"Sam? This is Rose Mahoney at Mrs. Feinberg's. Will you send me up a tuna salad on rye and a container of coffee? Yeah. And a piece of Danish."

In a few minutes, a white-coated Negro boy came up with her order. She paid him and gave him an extra dime for himself. Then, putting a towel on the table in lieu of table linen, she spread out her purchases and began to eat.

When she had finished eating, she dusted the crumbs into the paper bag in which her sandwich had been wrapped and threw this bundle into the waste basket. With the end of her toothbrush she opened the cardboard container of coffee, and then retired to the bed, to drink it and smoke the accompanying cigarette in comfort. She was thoughtful.

Peddling apples? That's what Mary had said, but surely things weren't so bad as that. Not for persons like her. The depression was just for the bums. They were always having depressions. She'd get a job in no time. It was just something people were yelping about; it wasn't real.

She took another puff at the cigarette.

"Why, I've been thrown out of jobs before," she said aloud. "Better jobs than the Landsman & Miller job."

It cheered her, and presently, when she had finished her cigarette, Rose stood up, stretched luxuriously and took off her dress. In her pink slip she made a dash for the bathroom, washed, steamed her face with a washcloth wrung out of hot water and put a smeary mess of cold cream on her face. Then she made the return dash to her room and before her own mirror completed the beauty treatment with powder and rouge. She did up her hair quickly, her fingers fluttering agitatedly about her head, poking in a strand here, fluffing out a lock there.

From her closet Rose selected a red silk dress with a neat white piping at the neckline. It was a deep, rich red, and Mary, she remembered, had told her it would not be becoming to a blonde. But it was becoming. She slipped it over her head and pulled it down. It made her look bright and colorful, the red material soft against her white skin and a background for her blue eyes and her blonde hair. On the subway platform at Fifty-ninth Street was a poster advertising a hair rinse, and the blonde girl it depicted wore a dress of the same color. Looking into the mirror, Rose thought she saw some resemblance between herself and the poster.

"Gee," she said, "I'd like to get a job like that, posing for some artist. It must be a cinch."

On the table was a pulpwood magazine with a gaudy cover, displaying two lovers in close embrace. It was from this magazine Rose had taken her conception of a model's easy life. There was a story, "The Virtuous Model." In this story a beautiful young model, who refuses to pose in what the author constantly referred to as "the altogether," wins the hand of the noted artist for whom all her more wicked sisters had set their caps in vain.

If this were the formula to win fame and fortune in the studios, Rose knew she too could say "No" on practical occasions. And she could say "Yes," too, and had said it.

Rose was not a virgin. At sixteen, with more curiosity than passion, she had given herself to her high-school sweetheart, whose name she had long ago forgotten. She only remembered that he had curly red hair, that he used to bite his nails, and that he was more shy and awkward about the whole business than she was herself. It was only several years later, when she was going with Tony Ricci, that she found out lovemaking was almost as much pleasure as love stories and dirty jokes would have one believe. Since that first high-school sweetheart, Rose had always given herself to the current boyfriend. This was a matter of course, and equally as a matter of course was the pretense, among the other girls, that she was still virginal.

Although Bill Taggart, with whom she had been going about for the past year, left her fairly cold, Rose had calmly accepted the fact that this, too, was part of their relationship, and had given herself to him. Ever so often they stayed home, in her room, and made love. It was the least part of their relationship to her.

Rose took a final look at herself in the mirror, pulled her dress down about her trim hips, kicked her slippers into the closet with a practised gesture and then, standing in stocking feet, rummaged through the disorderly bottom of her closet for shoes. She found a pair of black calf oxfords with high heels and put them on. She had a small foot with a high instep and thin, nervous ankles. She was proud of her feet and her legs. During her vacation a boy had told her she had the prettiest legs on the beach. He was looking at her white rounded thighs when he said this. Rose had been pleased.

Ready, Rose sat down on the bed again and waited for Bill to come. She decided they would stay in that evening. She could tell him about losing her job and ask his advice on what she should do. Men always knew more about such things than women.

Hardly had she settled herself than there was a peculiar whistle from the other end of the room. She jumped to her feet. It was the old-fashioned speaking tube by the doorway.

"Hello!" she yelled into it.

Bill Taggart's voice came up the tube, thin and echoing.

"Hello, Kittens!"

"Come on up."

"Right."

She could hear his feet slapping the carpeted steps as he ran upstairs. He always ran upstairs. It was one of the things she liked about him. When she heard his feet on the landing, she opened the door.

He was flushed and panting from the run when he came into the room. He waited a moment to catch his breath before he closed the door behind him and took her in his arms. They kissed. His hardly caught breath was hot and ticklish around her lips.

"Hello, Kittens," he said, releasing her.

"Hello."

"What'll we do?"

"Let's just stay here. It's cold out isn't it?"

"Yeah. I saw the unemployed guys in the park as I came up. They were wrapping newspapers around their legs to keep warm."

"That's tough," Rose said.

"Yeah. But they're used to it."

"Some of them aren't."

"Sure they are. They're just bums. Decent people when they lose jobs have families to help them out. Those guys in the park are just bums."

He took off his grey soft hat and his grey overcoat and hung them up in Rose's closet. As he did this, Rose thought to herself: I'll wait before I tell him I've lost my job. The conversation about the unemployed had made her reluctant to speak about it.

Bill Taggart was tall, good-looking, with red-white cheeks and curling black hair. In the summer he tanned beautifully. On the beach Rose would look out of the corner of her eye to watch the other girls' admiring glances as they looked at him. He was always neat and well-dressed, and Rose had noticed that when they bought the early edition of the *Daily News* on their way back from the movies, he always turned first to the department on what the well-dressed man will wear.

Bill could afford to spend a great deal on his clothes. Although his salary as a clerk in the auditing department of the Burton Advertising Agency was nothing to brag about, Bill had few responsibilities. He lived with his mother, paid less than a nominal sum for his board, and what he did not spend on clothes he put in a savings bank. Rose was by no means an expensive sweetheart. She liked a good time, but she was as well satisfied with a fifty-cent seat in a motion picture house as an orchestra seat for the wittiest stage play in town. As a matter of fact, she preferred the movies. Their biggest evening together had been on her birthday, when Bill had taken her to see the *Vanities* and then on uptown to Connie's Inn, where they danced until morning. Usually motion pictures and trips to Roseland sufficed, so far as Rose was concerned. Once in a great while they had supper together at an Italian speakeasy where dinner and a bottle of wine could be had for a dollar. With two cocktails before dinner to make things merry, the bill at such times never came to more than five dollars and Bill was well repaid, for drinking made Rose amorous.

Bill was ambitious. He worked hard in the office, and at night studied a home correspondence course in accounting. He often told Rose what he would do when he made one hundred a week. He planned to buy a home on Long Island and a Chevrolet, and then, after he had obtained all these material proofs of success, he would get married to "some nice girl." That, as both he and Rose understood it, left her out, but it did not leave out the possibility of some other man thinking her "a nice girl," some man whose advances she could stave off, and whom she could trick into believing that she was still pure and innocent.

Bill finished hanging up his coat and hat and turned back into the room.

"How's my Kitten?" he asked, taking Rose into his arms again.

She kissed him.

"Fine."

"Sure you don't want to go out?"

She gave him a hug.

"Much rather stay here," she said meaningly.

He sat down on the edge of the bed, looked at her and then at the gas heater.

"That thing's hot," he complained. "Mind if I take off my jacket and vest?"

"Go ahead. I like to see you in your shirt sleeves. You've got nice shoulders."

He stood up again and took off his jacket and vest, hanging them carefully on one of her plush covered hangers, a purchase from the five-and-ten cent store.

Rose crossed the room and stood before him, running her hands over his shoulders.

"Umm!"

He put his arms about her and drew her down to the edge

31

of the bed. They sat this way a moment, kissing, and then he placed one hand under her knees and swung her legs over onto the bed.

"Wait a minute," she counselled. "You'll rumple this dress."

He helped her pull it over her head and then threw it across the back of the chair.

She settled back onto the pillow and Bill lay down alongside her and put his arms about her.

After a minute, fingering the hem of her slip between thumb and forefinger, he asked: "Nothing but this?"

She shook her head with a slow smile.

She was so warm, so warm, so exquisitely comfortable. It was as if she were suspended in nebulae of dreamy peace and languor. It was as if she were balanced between twin chasms of sweet sleep and sweeter wakefulness. Only the weight of Bill's tousled head on her shoulder kept her awake.

"Love me?" she asked in a breathy whisper.

"Uh huh."

"Happy?"

"Uh huh."

She turned her head to kiss his eyelids. He sat up with a start.

"What the hell time is it?"

"Look at the clock."

He craned his head around.

"Oh, I thought it was much later than that," he exclaimed, and then yawned. "Where're my cigarettes?"

"In your pants' pocket, I guess," she told him.

He swung his legs over the edge of the bed and groped on the floor for his trousers. They were lying in a crumpled heap.

"I should have hung these up."

Rose's voice had a slight edge when she answered:

"Well, why didn't you?"

He made no reply, continuing to look through his trousers for cigarettes and matches. He found them, lit a cigarette and stood up, pulling on his trousers. They had turned out the light and the gas heater cast a ruddy glow on him as he stood there, cigarette dangling from his lip, in trousers and sleeveless undershirt. Rose reached out and patted his arm.

"Why the hurry?" she asked.

"No hurry."

"Stay around awhile."

"I'm going to. I just want to get dressed." And then in explanation, "Suppose your landlady should come up?"

"She won't. She knows you're here. Nobody gets by her door without Mrs. Feinberg seeing them. That's why she has money in the bank."

"Say, she is a hatchet-face! I'd love to owe her my rent money."

"Don't worry; she wouldn't let you owe her anything. Rent in advance, that's her motto," Rose explained. "But she likes me. If I were hard put, I guess she'd let me coast along for a few weeks."

"No need to think of anything like that."

This was her opening.

"Maybe -"

"What do you mean?"

"Maybe she will have to let me coast along - I don't know. They let me out this afternoon down at Landsman & Miller."

"Gee! That's tough."

"Not so tough as it might be. I've got a little dough and it'll last until I can connect somewheres."

"That's good. How much have you got?"

"About forty-three dollars."

"Oh!"

"What's the matter? That'll last me at least three weeks if I'm careful."

"Yeah. Sure. But you won't get a job in three weeks."

"Aw, nerts! Things aren't that bad."

"They're pretty bad."

"Well, if I do happen to be out of work four weeks instead of three, I guess I can find someone to stake me for a week."

"Maybe," he said listlessly.

They were silent for a moment, and then Rose felt uncomfortable lying before him half-naked. She got up and put on a cotton coolie coat which she used for a negligee.

"You'd better get on home to your family," he advised. "It's going to be a tough winter all around."

"It'll be just as tough for my family. They couldn't do much for me."

"They can do more than any stranger will."

"You don't know my family."

He snubbed his cigarette in a pink ashtray with a little china dog perched on the rim. Rose had bought it because she thought it cute.

"You'd better get home," he repeated.

She shook her head.

"I'll stick around. I'm bound to connect," she said, and she felt sure she would. She knew it would be hard on her family if she were to return home. They had a hard enough time of it trying to get along without her. In her business school days she had almost bankrupted her father buying cigarettes.

"You'd better go home," he said again.

"No use. I tell you, I'll get a job - easy!"

"Not now."

Rose switched on the light. Somehow the whole air of

intimacy had fled since she brought up the subject of her employment. She felt as if he were almost a stranger. He sat quietly, looking at the little china dog on the ashtray. Finally he picked it up and kept passing it from one hand to the other. The cigarette and the ashes fell down on the floor.

"I've felt the depression too," he began hesitantly.

She looked puzzled.

"Well, that is," he went on, "not directly. My salary hasn't been cut or anything like that. But, you see, my mother -"

Rose remembered he had once told her his mother lived on the interest from his father's life insurance. That was when he was explaining to her what an advantage it was to carry life insurance.

"- my mother isn't too well off. A lot of her securities have depreciated in value since 1929. I have to help her out a lot, and I'm afraid I'll have even more to shoulder after the first of the year."

"That's too bad," Rose said.

"Yeah. This depression. It hits a guy. Now take me -"

"Yes?"

"Well, I was getting along well on my salary, saving a little now and then. Along comes the depression and I have to give most of my salary to my mother to keep the home fires burning. Why, we won't be able to go anywhere or do anything."

"That's all right with me. I'm no gold digger."

"Oh, I guess we can manage a movie every once in a while," he assured her.

She said nothing.

"But," he went on, "If you were to get in a jam, I wouldn't be able to help, no matter how much I might want to."

It was out, Rose saw it clearly now. He was afraid she might ask him for money. She looked at him. He was repulsive to her in that moment; his eyes still dull from lovemaking and his too handsome mouth set primly in righteous, self-satisfied lines.

"I haven't asked you for help," she said, her voice harsh.

"Oh, I know you haven't. You wouldn't. You're too good a sport for that. Now, some of these dames, they think just because you've had a little fun with them that they own you. You're not like that."

"No, I'm not. But -"

She could say no more. His sly cheapness irritated her.

"Get out!"

"What?"

"You heard me. Get out! Get your coat on and get out!"

"Why, Kittens -"

"Get the hell out!"

"But -"

"But! I'm sick and tired of you - so damn afraid I might ask you to lend me a dollar that you begin crawling and skunking like a - like a damned worm. Get out!"

"But, Kittens, I'd be glad to -"

"Get out."

She stood in the corner while he dressed, her coolie coat drawn close around her and her arms crossed over her breasts. He dressed hurriedly, flushing red under the hard scorn in her glance.

"But, Kittens -" he began as he put his hand on the doorknob.

"Get out! The hell with you!"

She turned and looked out through the shutters into the dark street. After a few moments she heard the door click as he closed it behind him. She kept her eyes on the street, blinking back the tears. The rat! Just because she had no job. Scared. The rat!

The alarm clock whirred weakly. She had forgotten to wind it the night before. Rose woke up. Stretching lazily, she turned over on her stomach and looked out of the window. It was a cold, electric day with a white light which made every detail of the building opposite stand out sharply. People, muffled up, their breaths frosty on the air, hurried along on their way to the subway. Idly, Rose looked to see if she could see one person who was not hurrying. Only one, a panhandler on the corner who shambled first to one prospect and then another while the traffic held a little knot of people at the corner curb. She watched him for five minutes but did not see him make one successful touch. Finally he drifted away. Again her eyes went to the hurrying workers.

The sight of them, on their way to workshops and offices while she lolled in bed with no thought of getting to the office before Brayman looked at his watch and discovered it was nine o'clock, put Rose in a holiday mood.

"Feels like a Sunday," she said as she scrambled out of bed and pulled the yellow coolie coat over her cheap, cotton print pajamas.

Mr. Earle, the floorwalker was just locking up his room as she stepped out into the hallway. His black overcoat was spotless and his white, starched linen shone in the dim light of the hallway.

"You'll be late this morning." he warned her.

"Not this morning," she answered as she closed the bathroom door behind her.

Back in her room again, Rose looked out the window. The crowds were still hurrying past.

"Just looking at them makes me tired," she said, stripping off her coolie coat and tumbling back into the warm disordered bed.

It was eleven o'clock when she got up again. She looked in the mirror. Her eyes were bright and sparkling and the muscles of her face were relaxed from the good rest she had enjoyed.

"No wonder these debutantes look so swell - with nothing to do but sleep all morning."

She bathed, dressed carefully, applied powder and lipstick and then sat down to wonder what in the world she was going to do. All her friends were working, and whatever she did she would have to do alone. She had no thought of looking for a job. Being out of work had always meant a short vacation, and, depression or no depression, she intended to have a few days rest before getting back into the grind. In the end she decided to go to Gray's and get a seat for a cut-rate matinee.

On her way out, she met Mrs. Feinberg, sorting the mail in the lower hall. Mrs. Feinberg was short, squat, and had absolutely no chin. Her lower lip ran down into her neck without a break. Her face was heavily made up, and over the make-up there was always a film of dirt, and dirt was lodged firmly and visibly in the creases of her thick neck. She always reminded Rose of a golliwog on a perfume bottle.

"Late this morning, Miss," she said amiably, but Rose saw the look in her eye was sharp.

"No, I'm not going to work this morning."

Mrs. Feinberg turned back to her mail.

"Good jobs are scarce," she said.

"Not for me," Rose said.

"You been fired?"

"No," Rose lied glibly. "My doctor ordered me to take a rest. I may run down to Atlantic City for a few days."

"*Nu!* You'll come back with roses in your cheeks," Mrs. Feinberg answered, all amiability again. People who went to Atlantic City had money to pay the rent.

Rose started for the door, and then paused to make assurance doubly sure.

"I'll pay you for next week now and get it off my chest," she said lightly, then rummaged through her handbag for money.

"Good. Money's hard to get these days. That Miss Pierce on your floor hasn't paid me in two weeks. I'll have her out if she ain't more careful."

"Yes. People should pay their rent," Rose agreed as she went through the door.

The sun had warmed the streets and it was pleasant outdoors. October brings rare days of electric snap and clearness to New York, and this was just such a day. Rose felt happy as she walked along in the sunshine to the corner drugstore for her breakfast.

On the corner she bought a newspaper and read the scandal and Winchell's column as she ate her Danish pastry and drank her orange juice and coffee.

"Taking Saturday morning off?" the soda clerk asked her.

"Nope! Just another victim of the depression," she answered gaily, and then took care to leave a dime tip.

At the drugstore entrance, on her way out, she paused, the newspaper still in her hand, and tried to make up her mind as to what she should do until matinee time. She could go back to her room and loaf, finish reading the paper, or she could take a walk through Central Park. Neither alternative appealed to her. She was used to companions, and being alone bored her. She decided to go to Jerome's, a speakeasy to which Bill Taggart had taken her several times, and have a drink. It might give her appetite for luncheon, and she might meet some of his friends there. She wanted to talk to someone.

She went down Broadway to Forty-fourth Street and turned West. Jerome's was near Eighth Avenue. To find it, one had to count the houses from the corner, as the street number, painted on the wooden door, was so badly worn that one could not read it from the sidewalk.

To enter Jerome's one had to step down into a sort of entry-way, push a bell and wait until one of the waiters opened the door and inspected you through a grille work. This inspection was more embarrassing than effective, as none of the four waiters in the place had a memory for faces. A short argument was always in order, and inevitably ended with the phrase, "But I've been here before," on the part of the prospective patron, and "Okay," on the part of the waiter.

Rose submitted herself to this inspection and after she had given the necessary password, "I've been here before," was admitted. Jerome's had a long bar running the entire length of the front room. On the opposite wall were little booths in which chairs and tables were set for the convenience of lady patrons. The initiated knew, however, that there was nothing convenient about these tables. In each cubicle was an electric buzzer by which the Bacchantes who frequented the place could summon the white-aproned Gambrinus. Unfortunately, the battery which served these buzzers had been dead a long while, and the only way one could get service was by going over to the bar. Rose disdained the tables and went directly to the bar.

The place was almost deserted. One bartender stood behind the shining brass beer spouts and a waiter was busied polishing glassware at the free-lunch counter. There were only four customers. Two men stood at one corner of the bar engaged in what seemed to Rose a furious argument. As a matter of fact they were two Cuban tap-dancers, quietly discussing the routine for a new vaudeville act. In a booth sat two girls with pony beers before them. One of them was nodding, half-asleep, and the other was quietly reading her paper. The hair of the drowsy girl was dyed a brassy red, and the other was a pronounced brunette with an olive complexion. They were both pretty and smartly dressed.

The bartender, flirting a damp cloth over the immaculate surface of the bar, looked up questioningly as Rose laid her handbag down before her on the mahogany.

"Let me have an Old-Fashioned."

She liked to suck the orange slice after she had drained the liquor.

Rose drank the Old-Fashioned and was thinking of ordering another when she heard a snore behind her. She turned to find that the red-haired girl had fallen asleep. The other girl, grinning in a friendly fashion, leaned over and shook her companion.

"Oh, let her sleep," Rose said, smiling back at the brunette.

"She's had a tough night," the girl explained, desisting in her efforts to waken her friend. "Hooked a regular sap from Syracuse. He got his money's worth in noise alone."

Rose puzzled over this, but the desire for companionship was strong.

"Have a drink with me?" she invited.

"Just a beer. Liquor before breakfast is bad on the bright eyes," the black-haired girl answered, getting up and strolling forward to stand at the bar with Rose.

Rose had another Old-Fashioned and paid for both the drinks.

"I haven't seen you around here before," the girl ventured, sipping her beer.

"I've never been here in the daytime before."

"Out of a job?"

"Yesterday."

"Too bad."

"Are you working?"

The other girl smiled.

"If you call it work."

"What do you mean?"

"Sue and me are hustling for a living," she explained to Rose without either shame or bravado. "We haven't had regular jobs for more than a year."

Rose was interested.

"I suppose hustling is hard work?"

"No, it's a cinch. Just one long party, if you want to look at it that way. I do. But Sue's from Boston. She makes a grandstand play. You know. Oh, the pity of it!"

"I see."

They brought their glasses up to their lips again. Rose took out a packet of cigarettes and extended them to the other girl.

"No thanks. I don't smoke."

Rose lit her own cigarette.

"What were you before - before the depression?" she asked.

"I was a reception clerk for a commercial photographer. Sue was a chorus girl. What were you?"

"I *am* a steno," Rose answered, stressing the present tense.

"You only think you are. You haven't looked for a job yet. Wait. They're not so easy to get."

"I'll get one."

"Maybe you will. I hope you do. If you don't -"

"I will," Rose insisted.

The black-haired girl only smiled and went on with what she was saying:

"- if you don't, look me up. I'm usually around here in the afternoons. Jerome gives us free drinks. Likes to have girls around. It boosts business. Men like to feel that there's a girl around to be *made*, even if they don't try to *make* her."

"What would you do for me?" Rose asked.

"Introduce you around. Hustling's like anything else, you've got to know how."

"I thought all you had to do was go out on the street and wink at men who look as if they have money."

The other girl laughed.

"Boy, if it were only that easy!"

"Well, isn't it?"

"Not these days. There's too much competition. It's a regular racket."

"How did you begin?"

The girl laughed again.

"I was so damn green," she said, "it's a laugh. Sue and I were living together. We'd been out of work six months - getting hungry. You'll find out what that's like."

"Not mc," Rose said with an obstinate shake of her head. These things happened to other people, not to oneself. Soldiers under fire feel the same way; they'll only get a "cushy" wound at worst.

"Well, anyhow, we had boyfriends - just like you have - but they weren't doing us much good. We decided we'd make what

Sue calls the 'great sacrifice.' I can't see it that way."

She broke off to laugh and take another drink of her beer.

"We did just what you thought you should do. We walked up and down Broadway all one Saturday night, right up until two in the morning. The only guy that gave us a tumble was a theatre usher who thought he was going to get something for nothing. He didn't even have coffee money."

"That next Sunday was a black day. We didn't have a thing to eat. We sat around crying. Monday morning Sue remembered a guy who'd been nice to her when she was on the road with one of the shows, a press agent, a married gent. We went around to see him, and Sue asked, 'How do you become a prostitute?' He didn't know, but he phoned a friend of his, and the friend told him how over the phone. He advised us to get a two-room apartment if we were going to be partners, and have a telephone put in, and then start 'phoning all our old boyfriends and asking them down. When they got down and got what they're all looking for, we put the bee on them. Loans, at first, and then real dough. It worked. It works better now. Both of us are on good call-house lists, and when we aren't working on our own, we can always pick up a job there. I'll give you the call-house number. It might come in handy. Jerry!"

The bartender ambled over.

"Let's have a pad and pencil and another drink. What'll you have?"

"Beer," Rose said. She wanted to make it light for her new friend.

When Jerry had brought their drinks and writing materials, the girl scribbled on the pad, then ripped off the sheet and handed it to Rose.

She looked down and read:

"MRS JUDITH TOMPKINS,

567 ¹/₂ RIVERSIDE DRIVE,
APT. 3C."

There was a telephone number scrawled under the address.

"Call Mrs. Tompkins any time you need dough, and tell her Connie Manning told you to 'phone. Tell her you're new at the racket and she'll have you up for a once-over. She needs good-looking girls."

"Thanks," Rose said, folding up the sheets of paper. "But I don't think I'll need this."

"Keep it. You might."

"Okay."

Rose glanced at her watch. She had just time to have luncheon and get a cut-rate ticket for the matinee.

"I'll have to run along. Thanks, and so-long."

"I'll be seeing you again, probably," the other girl said.

Rose had lunch at The Lobster, a restaurant patronized chiefly by stenographers from the theatrical district in search of a shore dinner. Then she went to Gray's and bought a ticket for the second balcony at a comedy. It was based on the comical feats of a high-pressure publicity man in Hollywood. Most of the humour went over her head, but she enjoyed it tremendously just the same. The furious pace of the comedy, the agility of the leading man and the almost constant laughter of the audience put her in splendid spirits.

It was dark when she got out of the theatre and Broadway was aglow with lights and teeming with the Saturday night crowd. The sidewalks were so thick it took her almost five minutes to walk a block. As she walked up-town, a man in a dashing pearl-grey fedora and carrying a cane sidled up to her and smiled. She smiled back involuntarily, without thinking, and then regretted it when he said:

"Won't you have supper with me, my dear?"

Rose had no scruples about being picked-up, but she didn't like this man. He talked in the grave, sonorous tones of a ham actor who has played society parts in stock, and his face was white with powder and blue at the jowls from close-shaving. She walked on without answering, and soon lost track of him in the crowd.

The incident set her to thinking of the girl she had met that morning. Of course, she would have no difficulty getting a job, but even if she couldn't get one, she certainly wouldn't become a hustler. Not that Rose's moral scruples were strongly set against such practices. She felt that it was all right for those who wanted to do so, but for herself she thought it too crude and unremunerative. She knew her tabloid newspapers; the wages of a love nest are a bullet in the pump.

At Forty-sixth Street and Broadway, Rose went into a Child's restaurant and had her supper. Then she had the evening to kill. She went to see a motion picture. It was dull and did not amuse her, but she sat through to the very end. To her mind, sitting there in a crowd was much better than being alone.

Tired, but a little dissatisfied with her first day of freedom, Rose went to bed and slept soundly. Church bells woke her in the morning. As she bathed, she could hear hymns from the radio loudspeaker next door. She accompanied the hymn singers by humming as she soaped herself.

Fully dressed, she went out and got her breakfast and bought a Sunday paper to read until it was time for her to go up to the Bronx. Mary Schmidt had asked her up to have Sunday dinner with her family. At twelve she took the rotogravure section, which she had saved for last because it was most interesting, and walked to the Subway. She took a Bronx express.

The Schmidts lived on Fox Avenue and it was a long, boring ride. Rose's only amusement during the trip was watching a young Negro dandy who boarded the train at One Hundred and Twenty-fifth Street. He had achieved a grey ensemble for his Sunday costume. A jaunty grey derby rode high on his head; a grey, form-fitting overcoat molded his figure; sharply-creased grey trousers went down from his overcoat to light grey shoes of glazed kid. The only note to spoil the color scheme was the orange colored copy of the *Graphic* which he was reading. Rose could hardly take her eyes off his grey shoes. They seemed to her among the funniest things she had ever seen.

The Schmidts, Rose discovered, were a small family. Mary's father, Otto, was a cigar-maker who worked in the window of a little store on Thirty-ninth Street. His wife, a big, fleshy woman, hardly said a word, but kept sighing constantly as she served the excellent dinner. There was another child beside Mary living in the house, a paralytic girl who seemed pathetically glad to have company.

Rose had not been there an hour before she realized why Mary was so timid. Mrs. Schmidt's constant sighing and groaning filled the atmosphere with an air of weary foreboding. It seemed certain they would all die tomorrow. Otto, Rose learned, made little money. There were few customers for handmade cigars, and even less now that a big tobacco company was warning smokers against spit on the end.

"Spit is a horrid word, heh?" he said to Mary. "No good cigar-maker spits on his cigar leaves - they wouldn't have enough spit. Look in my window some day. You will see. I have a little saucer of nice, fresh water. Spit is a horrid word, heh?"

Ruth, the crippled girl, was a constant drain on the family purse. Mrs. Schmidt had not yet given up hope of her cure, and the doctor bills were enormous. Although several reputable specialists had told Mrs. Schmidt long ago that Ruth would never be any better, and that any doctor who led her to believe she would was a quack, Mrs. Schmidt, for all her sighing, was optimistic enough in this instance to spend thousands of dollars in hopeless attempts to cure the cripple.

As a result, Mary's small salary was greatly needed. When Rose left that night, she no longer blamed Mary for her cautious regard of office rules. It would be tragic indeed if she lost her job.

Mary went downtown with Rose that evening and, by arrangement, they met two young men, Mary's friends, and went to a motion picture. Mary's friends were young Jewish law students, smart and argumentative. Rose was bored to death after the picture when they went to a chop suey restaurant and the boys began setting the social and economic ills of the world to rights. Rose's discharge gave them a jumping-off place for their conversation.

"Do you realize," one of them shouted, banging his fist on the table so that the little Chinese teacups rattled in their saucers, "it's only the working man who suffers in the depression? People whose money is working for them haven't suffered any loss. It's only those who have invested their labor that suffer.Take these figures -"

"You take them," said Rose.

The young student paid no attention to her.

"Do you realize that in 1920 - what with wage cuts, part-time jobs and millions of men unemployed - aggregate wages in the United States dropped off to the extent of $9,600,000,000? Do you realise that?" he shouted.

"Who cares?" said Rose.

"And, listen to this, in that same year, the investors of the country, people whose only connection with industry was their lousy money, made money; lots of it! Wait, wait!"

He went fumbling through his pockets and brought out a newspaper clipping.

"Listen: interest payments in the year 1929, a prosperous year, came up to a total of $7,500,000,000. But, in 1930, a bad year, they actually rose to a flat eight billion. See what that means?"

"Aw, nerts," Rose grumbled as she lifted a forkful of chicken chow-mein.

"That means," the young fellow went on, "that the reason you're out of a job is because there's no protection for a man who has only his labor invested in industry. But there is for a man who has his money properly invested - and, now, get me, I'm not talking about the stock market - but real investments. The wages of labor rise and fall, and go completely out sometimes, but the income of the investor is assured."

"That's so," the other young man agreed. "We ought to have unemployment insurance. Why, they don't let the machines in the factories rust when they're idle. They cover them up, they soak them in grease, they coddle them with cosmoline, but the human element - out with them, out into the snow and rain, let them rust and fall apart; it doesn't matter. There'll be plenty of human machines to take the places of those that fall apart from hunger and the dreariness of idle days, but you have to spend money for new machines. It's the rotten system, I tell you."

"Boloney!" Rose said. "Let's talk about something sad for a change. You guys are always thinking of things to eat."

But they would not be turned away from the enchantment of their own cleverness. Rose and Mary talked about dresses, while the two young men went on cursing and ranting against present social evils. Only one phrase startled the girls for a moment.

"Seven million jobless men tramping the streets. Seven million! Seven million!" one of the law students shouted.

"Jesus! That's a lot of men," Rose said.

"Terrible," Mary agreed.

At one o'clock, when Rose and Mary finally persuaded the boys to stop talking and go, the girls had to leave the tip for the Chinese waiter. The boys had only enough money to pay for the supper.

"Law clerks don't make any money - not until they're admitted to the bar," Mary explained apologetically to Rose. They were her friends.

"Sure. I know," Rose said. "But, those guys ought to be carnival spielers. They'd make lots of money. I never heard anyone talk so much except old Father Walters back home, and he's a priest."

The next morning Rose's problem of what to do was even more difficult than before. She had seen one play and two motion pictures in the last two days and she did not feel like going to the theatre again. In the morning she washed all her underwear and stockings and made some greatly needed repairs to her wardrobe. She was surprised at how few clothes she owned. There were only two dresses she could wear to work, two party frocks, an evening gown that was badly out of fashion, several hats, a Fall coat she was ready to discard, and a brown winter coat with beaver collar and cuffs, a last year's purchase which was going threadbare on the underside of the sleeves. She had plenty of stockings. She had a habit of forgetting to wash soiled stockings and then having to buy an extra pair to tide her over. She had bought enough extra pairs to last all winter. She had two and a half pairs of gloves. The half pair she had had for two years now, always hoping to find the mate somewhere, as she could not remember where she had lost it. Going over her things, she decided to buy another pair of shoes. Rose, like so many office workers, purchased a great many shoes and dresses. But they were cheap shoes and inexpensive dresses. They wore out quickly. She had never arrived at the point where quality and good materials guided her in her purchases. She purchased because of price and first appearance. As a result, her shoes never lasted more than a few weeks, and many of her dresses she had worn once or twice and then discarded.

She made up a bundle of her old shoes and worn-out dresses and brought them downstairs to Mrs. Feinberg.

"Mrs Feinberg," she said, "here's some of my old duds you might be able to give away."

"Thank you," Mrs. Feinberg said, smiling. "But I ain't going to give them away. I can get money for them. The ol' clothes man comes around on Wednesdays."

"That's fine," Rose said.

It had never occurred to her to sell her discarded garments, and she was not in the least put out to see Mrs. Feinberg taking such good advantage of her generosity.

"When do you go to Atlantic City?" Mrs. Feinberg wanted to know.

"I may not go," Rose said. "I'm enjoying a good rest right here."

"*Ach*, but you're such a lively one!" Mrs. Feinberg said admiringly. "So popular with the boys. *Nu*, I wish my Goldie was so popular as you are."

Rose had seen Mrs. Feinberg's daughter, Goldie. She was as homely as her mother, but thin and flat-breasted, and had copious amounts of gold in her crooked teeth. Her hair was always elaborately marcelled. Rose thought it no wonder that Goldie wasn't popular with the boys. She was downright ugly, and as silent and uncommunicative as her mother was talkative. But Rose had to be polite.

"Why, I'm sure Goldie is popular with the boys," she protested.

"Naw! She ain't. It's terrible. She's almost twenty-five, and no boyfriends. If we were on the East Side, I'd go to a *schadchen*. But we're too fancy for that now."

Rose had no idea of what a *schadchen* might be.

"You're so pretty - so popular," Mrs. Feinberg went on, throwing her hands, palms out, into the air in an admiring gesture.

Rose, pleased in spite of herself at this flattery, turned to go up the stairs.

"Thanks for the clothes - I'll get a couple of dollars for them," Mrs. Feinberg yelled up the stairs after her.

After luncheon, Rose finished darning torn stockings and ripped gloves and then spent half an hour manicuring her hands and putting a red glaze on her nails, the color carefully chosen to match her lipstick. It was the latest fad. She had read somewhere that debutantes in Florida did the same thing to their toenails. She would have to do that the next time Bill Taggart came up. But she had forgotten. He wasn't coming up anymore.

"The hell with him," she said as she caught the thought.

Around three o'clock Rose was bored to death. She yawned and stretched, walked around the room, sat down and tried to read, threw the magazine into the corner, and finally put on her hat and coat and went out for a walk. As she went along, looking into shop windows, she was trying to remember friends or acquaintances who might be out of a job. Her walk had taken her down Broadway, and as she came abreast of the Roseland Dance Palace, the electric display lights were turned on. Rose stopped short. Roseland reminded her of two girls she had met, hostesses in an uptown dance hall. They would be free in the daytime. She would go and see them.

Stopping at a corner cigar-store, she searched through the telephone directory for the right number and 'phoned.

"Come on up!"

The two girls, whom she had met at a party with Bill, lived on Seventy-eighth Street near the Park. She took a bus up Riverside Drive and then walked across town.

The address was a fine old house with a marble foyer. The marble had been unwashed for many a day, but the place still retained an atmosphere of elegance, despite its conversion into a cheap apartment house. The names of her two friends were hand-printed on a slip of paper beneath their bell: Grace La Salle and Yvonne Adoree. Rose had a feeling these were not the names by which her friends had been christened. As she rang the bell, she looked at the other names listed: Gypsy B. Love, Leone Adele Jordan, Lorraine LaVerne.

"Phonies," she said to herself.

In response to her ringing, the latch of the front door began to click repeatedly, a signal for her to enter. Climbing the stairs, Rose looked up; Grace's frowsy blonde head was hanging over the third floor railing.

"Hello!"

"How're you?"

"Swell," Grace answered her.

"Go tear yourself to pieces," Rose said.

They both laughed. Rose reached the third floor landing.

"Why aren't you working?" Grace asked.

"Fired."

"Come on in."

Two other girls were in the apartment, talking together. Yvonne Adoree, a girl with brown hair and eyes and a swarthy complexion which ill-suited her pug nose and wide-spread mouth, looked up as they came in.

"Hello, Rose," she said.

"How're you?"

"Fine," Yvonne answered, all unsuspectingly.

"Go tear yourself to pieces!"

Yvonne rolled on the bed with laughter. It was the funniest thing she had heard in days. Positively killing! As Rose took off her hat, she looked into the mirror and saw the third girl watching her with wise, curious eyes. Rose wondered who she might be. The girl was a natural blonde, and her hair was unkempt and fell in strings about a sallow face with thick, sensuous lips. There was an almost unnatural pallor on her cheeks, and Rose could see that she wore no make-up. She sat smoking, dressed in a green silk slip that was ripped under one armpit.

"Rose has just lost her job," Grace was explaining.

"She needn't worry," the pale blonde answered in a matter-of-fact voice. "She's pretty."

"Thanks," Rose said, grinning, as she turned back into the room.

"Oh, excuse me," Yvonne twittered. "You don't know each other. Rose Mahoney. Barbie."

"Glad to know you," Rose said, extending her hand.

They shook hands. Rose noticed that Barbie's hand was long, well-kept, but strong. It looked like a capable hand, a hand that might have done a lot of work, and yet it was limp and unhealthy in her grasp. But Rose did not find this repulsive. On the contrary, she found herself strangely drawn to Barbie. She went and sat down beside her on the couch.

Rose did not like the apartment which Grace and Yvonne shared. It was horribly dirty. There was a living room and a large alcove, which served as a bedroom. The furniture was cheap, gaudy and most of the upholstered pieces were badly stained. There was a white dresser in one corner. Its top had been scarred with cigarettes, so that the burns made a pattern around the edge. There were signed pictures of boys on the dresser top, a glass ashtray full of cigarette butts, a hairbrush and hairpins, a saucer with some small change in it and a half empty gin bottle. The windows were shut tight and the steam heat was on full blast. The room was full of cigarette smoke.

The girls were talking about boyfriends. Rose noticed that Barbie had little to say while this went on.

"What's happened to Bill Taggart?" Yvonne asked Rose.

"I just gave him the gate."

"What for? He was a nice looking guy."

"He crawled - thought I might ask him for money - when I lost my job," Rose explained. "It disgusted me."

These girls, Rose knew, were not like the girls with whom she worked in offices. Here there was no need for pretense about one's personal life. They took it for granted that one slept with one's boyfriends. She felt more free with them.

"How's taxi-dancing standing up in the depression?" she asked Grace.

"Fine. We still do a lot of plain and fancy belly-rubbing out on the floor. I haven't noticed any fewer customers than usual."

"Are they taking on any girls?" Rose asked.

"No. The old regulars would make it pretty hard in our place for any new girl. The boss knows it. He isn't hiring anyone."

"But you could get me in," Rose ventured.

Grace laughed.

"Say, I'll pay you to keep out of that dance hall. I'm not making a hell of a lot of money, but I'd be making less if you were dancing at the Melador. The boys would just go for your looks."

"Wouldn't the boss give me a job just for that reason?"

"Not on your life. He's wise. Some guy would come in some night when you were tired, talk your ear off and set you up in a nice apartment, and the boss would have to get another girl. He's no fool. He picks them right, but he doesn't pick them pretty - he knows better."

"No chance, then?"

"Not in the dancehall racket," Yvonne answered.

Barbie touched Rose's arm.

"Are you hard-up?" she asked.

"No, I haven't even started looking for a job. I'm a pretty good steno - I'll connect. I was just asking out of curiosity - more or less."

"I see," Barbie said. "But you might not find a job. What then?"

Rose shrugged.

"I guess I can get along."

"Ever been hungry?"

"Sure."

"How hungry?"

"Hungry enough to eat a bear," Rose said, laughing.

"Ever been hungry enough to kill a bear?" Barbie asked.

"No, I guess not. I've never gone more than a day without a good, solid meal. I was hungry when I tried to diet and get thin."

Barbie laughed.

"Then you don't know what I'm talking about. I'm talking about being hungry. God!"

"Say," Rose asked, "you're not hungry now?"

"No. But I have been. You haven't. I hope to Jesus you never are."

"Amen," Rose said with a grin.

"Don't go hungry," Barbie advised. "It's not worth it. I can put you in a way of making a little money. Not too hard work, either, and no whoring -"

She glanced at Grace and Yvonne. They laughed, short, forced laughter.

"What kind of work?" Rose asked.

Barbie again exchanged glances with Grace and Yvonne. None of them answered. Rose repeated her question.

"What kind of work?"

"No use bothering about that," Barbie answered curtly. "Not now at any rate. Wait until you're hungry, then come and see me. Come before then, if you want to, but just for a visit. My name's in the book."

"What's your last name?" Rose asked.

"Just Barbie - I'm listed that way. I've had a couple of last names, and I've been called a lot of hard names, too, but my first name will do for anything short of a police blotter."

"All right, Barbie," Rose said.

A few minutes later, after a swig from the gin bottle on the dresser, Barbie prepared to leave. Rose was surprised to see she had nothing on but the green, torn slip, and that over this she merely put an old, ragged cape before going out. She had no hat, no gloves and no handbag.

When she had gone, Rose turned curiously to Grace and Yvonne.

"Who's she?"

"Oh, Barbie's all right. She's regular. I'd rather have her for a friend than a lot of rich people I know," Yvonne told her.

"What does she do for a living?"

Again Yvonne and Grace exchanged cryptic but meaning glances.

"Nothing much," Grace answered evasively.

"But you do what she told you: look her up if things get bad. She'll help you out in one way or another," Yvonne advised.

Rose saw that they did not want to answer questions about Barbie, and asked no more. But, whatever mysterious business Barbie followed, Rose felt sure she could trust her. Grace corroborated this feeling.

"Barbie's regular. I know a young gent on a newspaper who's always broke. I met him at Barbie's. He drinks up his pay in the middle of the week and then has to borrow money until pay day. One day I was with Barbie. She's just told me she only had fifty cents for the next day's food, and no more money in sight, when we met this gink. He told Barbie he was bust and hadn't had any lunch. Barbie actually made him take that fifty cents."

"And she didn't eat the next day?" Rose asked.

"I don't know - maybe not. I know I didn't give her anything."

"I guess she is a pretty good egg," Rose decided.

Yvonne and Grace had to be at the dance hall by seven o'clock. At six, Rose went with them to a delicatessen store on the next block for supper. The two hostesses had to rush through their meal and get away so as not to be late. Rose ate her supper leisurely, and then walked across town to Riverside Drive for a bus. She smoked as she walked along the street. The side streets were dark and she knew no-one in the neighborhood.

This was her third day out of work and already she had two openings - if you could call them such. Not so bad. The thought amused her. The girl in the speakeasy had recommended prostitution and Barbie had offered some sort of work, and whatever it was, Rose knew it must be immoral. She guessed that from the covert glances the other girls had exchanged.

"Boy, I *am* the *it* girl," she said aloud. "And have I sex appeal!"

She laughed as she walked along in the darkness. It seemed funny. Tomorrow she'd go out and get herself a real job.

"And this time Rose's going to be private secretary and get seventy-five a week," she said to herself, and laughed again.

FOUR

"Full of pep this morning!" the soda clerk said, handing Rose her breakfast check. "That's the way I like to see 'em."

"That's right, Big Boy. I'm going to knock them dead. Watch my smoke!"

"I'm watchin' and I'm inhalin' it - it smells good to me."

The soda dispenser came from Georgia and had curly hair. Rose always passed the time of day with him in wise-cracking badinage.

"You're looking real brisk this morning," the cashier remarked as he handed her change from the dollar bill she had passed over to cover her check.

"I'm feeling good," Rose said, and smiled.

The cashier, who was also a registered pharmacist, but found little opportunity to practise his profession in this store, smiled so vigorously in answer that his toupee crept up half an inch on his glistening head.

Rose stepped out into the hard sunshine. She felt full of life. She sang under her breath as she walked to the subway.

" - don't take it serious,

Life's too mysterious -"

The subway platform was crowded. Rose shoved and elbowed her way through the crowds with joyous abandon. She was feeling good, and she knew she looked well. She had on her best dress and her newest shoes and her face was a masterpiece of make-up. The dress was a dark blue silk frock she had taken in until it fitted her figure with glove-like tightness. The shoes were black, with shiny rhinestone buckles. She had on her brown coat and a brown felt hat with a narrow, upturned brim and a little red feather jauntily riding in back. Most women would have thought her too flashily dressed for business, but Rose knew the tactics of job-hunting. In all probability, she would have to sell her services to a male executive, and only women are critical of overdress. Men see what they see, and think no more about it.

Rose was on her way to Kleinert's Placement Bureau. It was the employment agency from which she had been sent to the Landsman & Miller Pneumatic Tool Co. She had always remembered Mr. Kleinert. He was so big and jovial and well-dressed. A flashy Jewish gentleman with a big cigar tilted between his thick lips, he seemed constantly in good humor, laughing and joking with the girls who called at his office. Rose looked forward with anticipation to seeing him again. She knew he would kid her about losing her job, and she would have fun kidding back.

At Fourteenth Street, Rose left the subway and walked to Kleinert's office. It was on the second floor, and Rose knew it was quicker to walk. She was still humming as she started to climb the stairs.

"Life is just a bowl of cherries -"

Another girl was coming down the stairs, a well-dressed girl. Her face was white and she looked faint. As they came abreast of each other on the stairs, the other girl put out her hand and took Rose's elbow, stopping her.

"Are you going to Kleinert's?" she asked.

"Yep!" Rose answered, wondering why she asked.

"Don't go. It's horrible," the other girl said quickly, intently. "Don't!"

"Holy Mike! Why not? I'm going up to get a job."

The girl tightened her grip on Rose's elbow.

"Listen," she said.

Rose listened. From the second floor came a faint sound of sobbing.

"What's that?" she asked.

"They're crying," the girl told her. "They just sit there and cry. It's awful. Don't go. He can't do anything for you anyhow. You've still got decent clothes. You don't look hungry. Don't go."

She was a little hysterical. Rose put her arm about the girl's shoulders.

"Hey! Quiet down. Don't fuss. What *is* the matter?"

The pale girl took a deep breath and tried to get a grip on herself.

"Sorry," she said. "It's just because it's so horrible in there. I don't need a job bad. I live with my folks in Brooklyn, and I've only been out of work three weeks. My clothes are still good. I'm not going to look for work anymore. There isn't any work to be had, and when you go into the agencies and see all the girls sitting around - in rags some of them - and crying - it just busts you all up. I'm not going to look for a job anymore. I can just feel their eyes on my clothes - and their stockings all runs. Don't go in. You won't get a job. There aren't any. And just seeing them will take the heart out of you."

Rose patted the other girl's arm gently.

"Don't worry about me. I'm hard-boiled. And I need the work. I'll give 'em a laugh to cheer them up."

She gave the pale girl's arm another pat and went on up the stairs. As she walked along the corridor toward Kleinert's door, the sound of sobbing grew louder. It made her jumpy.

Rose threw open the door and walked in briskly. The place was crowded. All the chairs in the reception room were taken and one or two girls were leaning against the wall. At the water cooler a girl was drinking thirstily, cup after cup of water. Rose looked at her. There was a smudge of dust on the girl's felt hat, she wore no stockings and there was no powder or rouge on her face. Her face was pale and her eyes were staring. Rose was to learn later this was the common look of the unemployed girl in hard circumstances. No stockings, because there was no money to buy them. No make-up, because that was too quickly exhausted and when one had a quarter one would rather eat than spend it on one's face. Other clothes lasted longer, and a careful girl could make a fairly decent appearance with the exception of stockingless legs and pale face.

Many of the girls were crying openly. All of them looked up as Rose came in, and she could feel their eyes, hungry and envious, fastened on her clean clothes and smart make-up. One girl broke into louder sobs at the sight of her. Rose felt uncomfortable, but stiffened her will to appear unconcerned.

Looking around for a chair, and not finding one, she crossed the room and leaned against the partition which divided the place into waiting room and interviewing office. She remembered Kleinert's as it had been in 1929: one or two girls sitting quietly, waiting, calm and self-possessed; a smart reception clerk, passing out blank forms and chatting with friends; the click of a typewriter in the inner office. Now there was no reception clerk and she could not hear the typewriter. The only sound was the low sobbing of the two or three girls who were crying and, from the inner office, Kleinert's voice as he talked to an applicant.

Hardly had Rose settled herself against the partition than the door opened and Kleinert ushered out a tall girl with the same pale face, devoid of make-up, which Rose had seen on the girl at the water cooler. Kleinert seemed thinner. His clothes looked rumpled. There was a worried frown between his eyes and circles beneath them. He was not smiling.

As they came through the doorway, the tall girl gripped his sleeve in thin, demanding fingers.

"But, Mr.Kleinert," Rose heard her plead, "can't you even lend me two bits? I'm hungry."

Kleinert sighed wearily.

"Sweetheart," he said, "if I lent two bits to every girl that asked me, I'd be hungry myself. I'm not eating too well as it is."

Rose heard this, but she was still game. She turned so that Kleinert might see her.

"Hello, big boy," she said brightly, "how're you feeling?"

"Not so good," he said wearily.

That stole the point of her little joke, but Rose went right on.

"Well," she said loudly and briskly, "go tear yourself to pieces."

She waited for a laugh. No-one seemed to have heard her.

"What do you want?" Kleinert asked.

Rose looked at him. He didn't seem to remember her.

"Don't you know me?" she asked

"Don't waste my time. Of course I don't know you. When were you here last?"

"Two years ago."

He laughed bitterly.

"Nineteen twenty-nine. And you expect me to remember

you? Say, since then I've seen millions of girls, millions of them, and I don't remember any of them unless they drop dead in this office. I can't do anything for you."

He said, "Next," and started to turn back into his office, but Rose hooked her arm through his and made him wait.

"Listen - you remember me - I'm Rose Mahoney - the girl you used to kid with. You sent me up to Landsman & Miller. Don't you remember?"

"No."

"Well it doesn't matter. What are my chances of getting a good secretarial job?"

"No chance. I won't even register you. I've four thousand, five hundred girls on my stenographic list now, and I've only placed two girls in three weeks. You haven't a chance. Better stay home if you've got a home and help mother save the pennies. You'll be more use than tramping the streets for a job."

"I haven't any home to go to," Rose said, thinking this might touch him.

"None of them have," he said. "But I can't help it - I'm a placement bureau, not a home for girls."

"Say, I'd go to a home for girls if you were in charge. What a place that would be!" Rose said, forcing a grin.

"Yeah," Kleinert answered dully, but he was flattered nevertheless.

"At least register me- that's a Sweetie!" Rose coaxed.

"All right! But don't hang around here when you want to get warm. Go to Grand Central! It's more comfortable there. I'm sick and tired of hearing girls crying and crying."

The registration was accomplished in a few minutes. A little, thin, hunch-backed girl, who seemed to have taken the place of the brisk, good-looking stenographer of former years, dug through a file and found Rose Mahoney's former card. On this she added the information that Rose had been two years at Landsman & Miller, that she had been discharged because of retrenchment, and that she was now available for all secretarial and office work.

"What salary?" she asked Rose.

"I'd like forty-five a week."

"You were only getting twenty-five."

"Make it twenty-five then, I should worry about a few bucks."

"I'll make the salary anything you can get," the girl told her. "You won't get a job anyhow."

As Kleinert saw her to the door, a habit with him from the old days when he gave service in the manner of his kind, Rose asked him:

"What's become of your old steno?"

"She left. Married a boy to get away from here, and told me to give her job to this kid who seemed to need it worst of all. On account of her back, you know."

"Try and get me a job, Mr. Kleinert."

"I can't even promise that," he said.

Rose went through the reception room. The girls were still there, and two or three of them were still crying. Again she felt their eyes on her clothes, on her make-up.

"Good God!" she said as she stepped out into the street.

The brief experience had shocked her deeply. It was her first real contact with the depression.

"Good God! I didn't know things were like that."

For the first time she was frightened. She walked to Union Square and paused there to count the money in her handbag. She had six dollars left from her last pay envelope. And in the bank there was forty-three dollars in her Christmas Club account. She had planned to get a new coat with the money. But not now. She would need that money.

"Have your shoes shined for luck," an old man said to her. He was on his knees and already pushing his box forward to her feet.

"For luck," she repeated, and put her foot on the rest. She gave him a dime tip for further luck. She needed luck more than she needed the dime - lots of luck if she were to get a job with all those girls out of work.

The brightness of her freshly shined shoes in the sun lifted her spirits a little. She decided to walk back to her room and think things over. She remembered an old saw:

"When you're going *up* take Fifth Avenue; when you're coming *down*, take Sixth."

She was going *up*.

Fifth Avenue was bright and sunny. The plate glass windows sent shivery facets of light back into the street, and behind the windows were noble displays: rich fur coats, expensive silks, crystal perfume bottles resting on pillows of satin and velvet. Rose forgot herself as she walked along, looking from one window into the next. At Altman's she stopped and looked for a long time at a wooden model dressed in a green skiing suit. She could imagine herself in such an outfit. It was a shade of green particularly becoming to her.

In the street, thousands of expensive automobiles were gliding by, the thickly-treaded tires making a humming sound on the asphalt. Rose's attention was held by two pretty young women in a yellow roadster with a long, gleaming bonnet of polished metal, a Fiat with a custom-made body. Behind it a Rolls-Royce purred along, a footman and chauffeur on the front seat and an old lady the solitary occupant of the tonneau. A smart, suburban matron, driving her own sedan, and with a little fox-terrier beside her, came next. Her neckpiece was of red fox, a rich, glowing red that caught Rose's eye.

Looking into the shop windows and at the gleaming parade of motors on the Avenue, Rose found it hard to recall the crying girls in Kleinert's office. It was like something she had thought about and put from her mind. In the face of all the luxury around her, how could there be people crying just because they had no jobs? There must be something wrong with them; it must be their fault not to have enough in a world so full of things. She would have no trouble finding work.

Her confidence came back by degrees, and she felt happy, swinging along the Avenue at a good, brisk gait. At Forty-seventh Street, seeing ahead of her the yellow dust floating across the roadway from the Radio City excavation, Rose decided to turn West. She crossed Fifth Avenue and started down the side street.

On the corner was an apple vendor, shivering despite the two thicknesses of sweater and the threadbare overcoat he wore. He stood a little to one side of his crude stand of packing boxes. On this was a pathetic display: four red, gleaming apples, an orange and a chipped saucer with a dime and two nickels in it. Rose passed him quickly. She did not want to be reminded of the depression.

A few paces away from Fifth Avenue, Rose stopped to look into Brentano's big show window. Her eye was attracted by a drawing for a magazine cover. Looking at it, she was suddenly conscious of someone at her elbow. She glanced out the corner of her eye. It was a seedy-looking man of about thirty, shoulders drawn together against the cold, who stood there without an overcoat, white-faced and weak.

"Miss, I'm hungry."

It was not for coffee or carfare that he was asking, the old trade-formulae of the panhandlers, but for food.

"Miss, I'm hungry."

Rose dug quickly into her handbag and gave him a quarter.

"Thanks -"

"Good luck."

Rose walked on. Her spirits had taken a sharp drop. It was easy to remember Kleinert's now.

FIVE

Grey, driving sheets of rain lashed against the window. It was only three o'clock, but already so dark that Rose had lit the electric lights. She sat in the little straight-backed chair and held her slippered feet toward the gas heater for warmth. In her lap was her pocket book, and, using this for support, Rose was writing on the back of an old laundry slip. Pencilled on the paper were two columns of small figures, both adding up to a two-figure total, and also a list of addresses. Her plucked eyebrows were drawn close in a frown. The money had gone faster than she had thought it would, and so far, in spite of diligent efforts, there was no job in sight.

She had discovered that employers were no longer using the old standby, "We'll keep you in mind." "Nothing doing," "We don't need any help," "We've cut our staff," and "Don't you know there's a depression?" had succeeded it as stock expressions with which to ward off the applicant.

"Two weeks out of work and only sixteen dollars left," Rose said aloud, and the words echoed for a second in the close confines of her room. It frightened her, and she sat still, holding her breath like a little girl. The rain whipped on the pane with hard splashes and the gas flame sputtered a moment.

Rose jumped out of her chair and the pocket book and her slip of paper fell to the floor.

"I'll go nuts if I sit around here by myself," she said.

Crossing the room, Rose threw open the window and looked out. A few people were hurrying by, umbrellas raised against the rain, and the street lamps sent long, tortured beams of yellow light across the wet, black asphalt. From the loudspeaker in the radio store down the block she could hear the unctuous and amplified thunder of an announcer's voice:

"Schwartz passes to Garvey - Garvey slips in the mud and a Cornell man is on him. Too bad! Boy, oh boy! That's the sloppiest field I've seen this season. Here we go again - the ball is on -"

Rose shut the window. It was Thanksgiving Day and she had had her Thanksgiving turkey in a chainstore restaurant, a meagre, overcooked portion on the seventy-five cent luncheon. Counting her money during dinner, she had decided not to go to a motion picture. The dreadful, boring afternoon in her room had been the price of her economy. Alone, and with no-one to talk to, and nothing but the newspaper to read, Rose had begun to do a little serious thinking about her problem. She had counted her money, and then she had budgeted the remaining money and discovered she could make it last only a week more. She had to have a job.

A weary round of visits to employment agencies and employers had convinced her she could not hope for office work. Nor were shop girls and factory hands in demand. There remained to her only two other forms of legitimate employment: domestic service and house-to house selling.

In common with all other girls of her particular class and upbringing, Rose detested housework, knew little about it and felt that it was degrading. She had thought, however, she could get a job as a maid if all else failed, but this hope had been wrecked by a conversation with another unemployed girl who had tried housework. She had discovered, Rose learned, that a girl used to office employment is not fit for any but the lightest kind of housework. She herself, she informed Rose, had been forced to give it up after two weeks through sheer physical exhaustion, and her job, as parlor-maid, had not been too arduous.

Selling was something else again. Rose felt that she would be a success at selling. A salesman had once told her that the chief requisite was "personality," and Rose credited herself with an inordinate amount of this peculiar charm. So she had spent the afternoon poring over the advertisements for saleswomen. There were many of them. The great American game of selling had not lost its popularity even in the economic crisis.

Rose selected two of the advertisements as the most likely. They were the two ending with the tag-line, "no experience necessary." She cut them out and determined to apply bright and early the following morning.

This resolution, and the breath of fresh, rain-washed air that had come through the opened window heartened her. When Rose was in good spirits, she had to spend money. Away went the resolution to stay home. That evening found her weeping at a motion picture. It was the best "cry" she had enjoyed in some time. The picture, featuring a pug-nosed child star, was tailor-made to jerk tears from the ducts of the sentimental. Rose wept copiously at the little boy's unreasonable love for an old racehorse and his equally unreasonable, but more tragic, affection for his father, an old broken-down prizefighter.

Her eyes were red and inflamed with crying when she got out of the theatre. Yet it had never occurred to her that she herself was in a tragic situation, and that a tear or two of self-pity might be excusable. She just did not feel that way about herself, no matter how miserable her plight.

In the morning, Rose had a cup of coffee at the corner pharmacy, and hurried off to the most promising of the two addresses she had cut from the newspaper.

The office, above an automobile showroom on Broadway, was magnificent. Heavy carpets and mahogany furniture impressed her with the wealth and power of the organization. Rose had no difficulty in getting to see the sales manager, whose name as the gold-lettering on his door informed her, was Trent. Mr. Trent, a short, stubby man with an engaging smile and nervous, affable mannerisms, seemed overjoyed to see her.

"Have you ever sold before, Miss Mahoney?" he asked politely when she was seated beside his desk.

"No, Mr. Trent."

"What previous business experience have you had?"

"I was a secretary," she answered. Lying during a job-hunt was perfectly legitimate to her mind.

"Why, that's fine," Mr. Trent told her. "We need more business people in selling. Most salesmen don't know beans about office procedure."

He stroked his chin.

"Do you like people?" he asked.

"What?"

"Do you like people - meeting new people and talking things over with them?"

"Sure. I guess so."

"Fine! Fine! That's the essential thing in this game."

Rose felt flattered.

"You're an American?" was Trent's next question.

"Yes."

"Splendid! Just the background for this sort of work. And it's work you'll enjoy if you're a patriotic American."

"What is it that I have to sell?"

"Rich's *History of America in the Great War* in twelve volumes, bound in full morocco with fourteen carat gold lettering. The price is two hundred dollars. No truly American family can afford to be without it. They sell like hot potatoes in Dublin on a January morning."

He leaned forward in his chair and pointed to a smartly-dressed woman standing in the outer office.

"See that lady in the grey fur coat?" he asked.

Rose craned forward to look.

"Well, that lady makes anywhere from one to three hundred dollars a week selling our history. She's one of our best saleswomen."

Rose felt a thrill of pleasure on hearing this. Considering her lack of experience, she'd make less, of course, but even so she'd probably make at least fifty the first week and seventy-five thereafter. That would end her personal depression right away. She could do a lot with seventy-five a week.

"The book sells for two hundred dollars a set, payable on the installment plan, through an independent finance company, and the salesman gets fifty per cent. It's one of the best selling propositions in America. When they see these books, they buy - complete, authentic, entertaining, a great aid to the school child - wonderful value!"

Rose's blue eyes went wide with excitement. Why hadn't she thought of selling before? Seventy-five dollars a week!

"Now, let's see," Trent said, glancing at his wristwatch. "Dr. O.H. Spears, our instructor in salesmanship - he gives courses to all our salesmen - is speaking now. I'd like to have you drop in a minute and listen-in on his course. Then we'll sign you up, and I'll give you your portfolio, order blank, book of references and a set of the history. Step into the other room with me for a moment and we'll listen to Dr. Spears. You'll enjoy his course. It'll make a crackerjack saleswoman of you, Miss Mahoney."

He led the way through the general office to a smaller room. In this room was a speaker's rostrum and three rows of chairs with sidearms on which one could steady a pad for writing notes. Dr. Spears occupied the rostrum and his pupils sat in the chairs, scribbling furiously to copy down his golden words of sales wisdom.

Dr. Spears, a tall, stout man with the clipped, staccato intonation of a circus barker, had large white teeth and tried to dress and look like the late President Roosevelt.

Rose and Trent remained in the back of the room and listened to part of the lecture.

"Now, ladies and gentlemen, the approach! It's important. You'll find it completely outlined in the book of instructions. But just a word or two to fix it in your mind. When you ring the bell, stand in such a way that the door, swinging open, will hide you for a moment. Then, when the lady of the house has opened the door, take a step forward and get your feet over the threshold. That's important! She can't slam the door when you do that. If the woman doesn't ask you, ask yourself in. Sit down before you begin your sales-talk. It's harder to move you out when you're in a chair. The woman can't yank you to your feet, you know -"

Mr. Trent touched Rose's arm.

"You can listen to all this tomorrow. I just wanted to give you a line on what the company'll do for you. Let's go."

He led the way back to his office, called his secretary and asked her to bring in a complete salesman's outfit.

With the help of an office boy, she brought it in. It consisted of an elaborate leather portfolio, heavy with brass, two loose-leaf leather books filled with printed pages and photostat copies of letters from government officials, generals and notables, all recommending the history, an order book with an automatic pencil attached, and the ten, cheaply bound volumes of the history.

"Here's the outfit," Trent said, running his hand admiringly over the smooth leather of the portfolio. "Now let's get you signed up for it, and give you a chance at some real money. This is the best proposition you've seen, isn't it, Miss Mahoney?"

It certainly was. How foolish she had been to spend the last two weeks in a hopeless search for a mere stenographer's job when such a position awaited her for the asking. And Mr. Trent was so nice and so polite. She agreed with him heartily. It was, without question, the best proposition she had ever heard.

Trent pulled open the top drawer of his desk and drew out a printed form.

"Read this through," he ordered kindly, "and then put your John Hancock on the dotted line."

He waited patiently while Rose waded through the legal twaddle of the contract without understanding one half of it, and then extended his fountain pen. Rose signed her name.

"Fine!" Trent applauded. "Now only one more formality."

He drew a small sheet of printed matter from his desk drawer and extended it to Rose.

"We have to ask you to buy your own sample set," he explained. "This is the order blank. Two hundred dollars."

For a moment Rose was aghast. Perhaps she hadn't understood him.

"You want me to give you two hundred dollars for this?" she asked, touching the books.

"That's the purchase price," Trent said blandly. "The fifty per cent salesman's commission is retained by us to cover the cost of your sales outfit."

"I haven't the two hundred dollars."

"Oh!"

Mr. Trent's bland, backslapping courtesy evaporated as quickly as wax on a hot iron. Three minutes later Rose was on her way out.

"The hell with it!" she said. "The dirty gyp artists!"

Nothing daunted, Rose went on to the second address on her list, the Silver Magic Novelty Company. She found this to be a small office in an old building. There was only one person in the place when she came in, a stout, thick-set Jew, tilted back in his battered chair reading a Yiddish daily and munching on a hot pastromi sandwich. He looked at her over the edge of his newspaper, but made no move to get to his feet.

"I came to get this job you advertise," Rose informed him, holding up the clipping for him to see.

He took another bite at his sandwich, and with a full mouth and a greasy chin began to speak:

"I am Mr. Farbstein. What can I do for you?"

"I came in response to this ad," Rose told him again.

"Fine! Fine! Wait till I finish here, then I show you the demonstration."

He lifted the newspaper again and began to eat and read, paying no attention at all to Rose. She stood there, embarrassed and not knowing what to do with herself. After about two minutes of mental and physical mastication, Mr. Farbstein put down his paper and struggled to his feet.

"Come. I show you," he said, leading the way into a little back room, empty except for shelves and a cast iron sink.

Working quickly, his pudgy hands flying from one object to another, Farbstein filled a pan with clear water, took down a little grey metal disc from a pile on the shelf, put it into the pan, and then brought out a teaspoon and dipped it into a jar of some white powder.

"Baking soda," he explained, dumping the spoonful into the water.

He dipped into another jar and dumped a teaspoon of white crystals into the water.

"Salt."

Rose looked on in amazement.

Farbstein opened a box and took out a handful of silverware, knives, forks and spoons, all grey and tarnished.

"Dirty!" he said, throwing these into the water.

Then, rolling up the cuff of his right shirtsleeve, he dipped his hand into the clear water and arranged the silver in such a way that all the pieces touched the piece of grey metal at the bottom of the pan.

"Look!"

Rose looked. Before her eyes - as if by magic - the tarnished silver was growing bright and clean.

Farbstein drew out a piece and showed it to her. It was miraculously clean and shining.

"Say!" Rose ejaculated. "This is grand!"

"You help your mother polish silver?" Farbstein asked.

"No. But I've watched her. This beats polishing and saves elbow grease. What do you sell these for?"

"I sell them for almost nothing. One Silver Magic Bar I sell for a dollar and a half. Dirt cheap. Look at all the work it saves. They go like nobody's business. I can't keep them in stock."

"Can I sell them for you?" Rose asked. They looked like a good thing to her. She felt sure she could sell them. Almost any housewife would be glad to pay a dollar and a half to be saved the drudgery of polishing silver.

"Sure. Sure. I sell them to you for twenty-five cents each and you sell them for a dollar and a half. How's that?"

"Swell. I'll take twenty of them," Rose said, taking a five dollar bill from her handbag and laying it on the corner of the cast iron sink.

Farbstein pocketed the money and took down twenty of the little metal plates. They were wrapped in cheap red paper, and on this paper were printed the directions, the firm name and the retail price. Rose found that she could carry all twenty under one arm with ease.

"This is going to be a great graft," Rose thought as she went toward the subway. She planned to start work immediately, and, as she walked along, figured out the best place to sell the Silver Magic Wonder Bars. Not the Bronx. A lot of people were out of work there, and what silver they had was in hock. Not Harlem. The Boogies spent their dough on a good time and could not afford to waste gin money on silver. Not Park Avenue. The owners of silver didn't have to clean it on that street. That's what maids and butlers were paid to do. Not the Village. They used five-and-ten cent store silver and threw it away when it got too rusty. The best place, she decided, would be Washington Heights. The people were good, solid, well-to-do apartment dwellers, proud of their fine things and their canny house-keeping. She boarded an up-town express and got off at One Hundred and Thirty-seventh Street, then walked north a few blocks and turned toward Riverside Drive. On the side street, a yellow-brick apartment house with an awning over the sidewalk appealed to her as the logical place for the first strike. She turned in the doorway and found herself in a marble hall at the back of which were two elevator doors. Corridors led off to right and left. Rose took the left corridor.

The first apartment, 1A, was inhabited by Mrs. Francis Xavier Tierney, she learned from the card stuck behind the bell. But she didn't see Mrs. Tierney. In response to her ring, the door opened a fraction of an inch, a rough, female voice shouted, "Go away," and the door slammed shut again.

"The nerve of some people's brats!" Rose said loudly and turned to Apartment 1B. It belonged to Mrs. Sigmund Weil.

Rose rang the bell and a buxom, black-haired Jewish matron came to the door, smiling.

"I'd like to show you a new house-cleaning device, Mrs. Weil," Rose said. "It'll only take a minute to demonstrate and it will save you a day's work in a year's time."

Rose had composed and memorized this little speech on her way uptown.

Mrs. Weil held the door open for her to enter and then led her along a narrow hallway to the kitchen.

"All right, Miss," she said, still smiling, and put her hands on her broad hips to stand and watch.

Rose unwrapped one of her metal disks, asked for water, dishpan, salt and baking soda and made her preparations.

"Have you any dirty silver?" she asked when she was all ready.

"Sure," Mrs. Weil told her and, opening a cabinet drawer, drew out a handful of tarnished spoons.

Rose put them into the water, arranged them, and then beckoned Mrs. Weil to come up and watch.

"Oh, it cleans like magic!" Mrs.Weil exclaimed, clasping her hands together delightedly.

"The Silver Magic Wonder Bar," Rose said pertly, pleased at the sensation she had created.

Mrs. Weil drew out a spoon, examined its shining surface and asked:

"How much?"

"A dollar and fifty cents and well worth it," Rose told her.

"This Wonder Bar never wears out. It'll last a lifetime."

Mrs.Weil turned halfway around and shouted through the door:

"Irving! Irving! Bring me my pocket book."

Rose laid a Silver Magic Bar on the table and waited for her money. Presently, a thin boy of about thirteen, with shell-rimmed goggles low on his nose, came shambling into the kitchen, a school book in one hand, his thumb between the leaves to hold his place, and his mother's heavy, black handbag in the other.

"Just look, Irving, and see how this cleans the silver," his mother said, pointing to the dishpan.

Irving gave her the handbag and went over to the sink. He glanced into the pan.

"Electrolysis," he said.

"What?" Rose asked.

"Electrolysis - that's what cleans the silver," Irving explained. "It's a chemical reaction. I studied it last year in school."

"Well, it works, and I think it's well worth the money," Rose said pleasantly, unconcerned.

"What money?" the boy wanted to know.

"The dollar fifty for the Wonder Bar," his mother explained.

"A dollar fifty for that little chunk of aluminium? Why, it isn't worth ten cents!"

"It's worth its weight in gold - think of all the work it's going to save," Rose argued.

"But any old piece of aluminium will do the same thing," Irving said.

"You're crazy!" Rose said, angry.

"Watch."

He plucked out the Wonder Bar, grabbed a saucer lid of aluminium and put it in the bottom of the dishpan. His mother handed him a tarnished fork. The same reaction was visible; the fork turned bright and clean.

"See?"

Rose could hardly believe her eyes.

"Okay, big boy, you win," she said, putting the remaining Wonder Bars under her arm.

"I'm sorry," said the affable Mrs. Weil, "but why should I pay for something I've already got?"

"You're right," Rose told her.

In the hallway, Rose sighed as she crossed over to Apartment 1C.

"I was a sucker, now I've got to find other suckers to hang this on," she said to herself.

A pleasant, thin-faced woman with light hair just turning grey lived in 1C. Rose spoke her little sales piece.

"No need to demonstrate, my dear," the woman said, "just tell me what it does."

Rose described the process as best she could. The lady smiled.

"But, my dear," she said, "when I was a little girl in Brattleboro, Vermont, we used to do that, using a piece of aluminium instead of your Wonder Bar. It's all right for flat silver, but it ruins hollow wear."

"No sale," Rose said jauntily, turning away.

The thin-faced woman closed the door behind her. On the street again, Rose let her eye run up and down the block in search of a garbage can. They all had been taken away. She threw the twenty Wonder Bars into the gutter.

"Taken! And, how! Five bucks shot to hell! I'd sue that Farbstein kike, but he's probably paying Max Steuer a retainer," Rose said to herself as she started back to the subway.

"You out of a job too? How come Miss Wise?"

Fanny Wise looked straight ahead of her at the sunbeams which came in long streams through the enormous windows of Grand Central Station. They were golden, misty, alive with floating dust particles. She looked at the long shafts of sunlight and swallowed nervously. Rose's question was hard to answer.

"Gee, I thought you had a job for life at Landsman & Miller," Rose went on.

"So did I. That's the worst of it. I have some money saved up. It ought to last until I can get another position."

"But why did they fire you? I should think you'd be the last to go."

"I was getting too much money for a secretary. Mr. Flynn had kept raising my salary, and when they started to cut I imagine they decided he could do with a less expensive girl," Fanny explained.

The two girls had met on the upper level of the station and stood talking. Their old enmity had disappeared in the face of mutual joblessness. Rose even felt angry at the injustice of

Fanny's dismissal. She wondered a little herself at this friendly feeling for her one-time enemy.

"Have you been around the employment agencies?" Rose asked.

Fanny grinned hopelessly.

"I've been everywhere."

"But you saved a lot of money, didn't you?"

Fanny laughed.

"I wish I hadn't. My bank closed. I had three thousand dollars. It all went."

"Gee, that's tough - but you'll land," Rose said.

"I don't think so. I've been everywhere. I'm too old."

"Too old?"

"Thirty."

"But what's that got to do with it?"

"Thirty is old nowadays. They don't want to hire a stenographer that old, and they don't need girls like myself in an executive capacity. They figure a stenographer who hasn't made anything of herself before she's thirty can't be much good. I was *somebody* at Landsman & Miller. But, when they ask what my job was, all I can say is 'secretary.' That sets me down as a steno in their minds and they don't want stenographers my age. They'd rather have them young and snippy looking."

"I hadn't thought of that," Rose said.

"Oh, I can tell you some funny stories," Fanny volunteered. "I went to one office where the big, fat yokel in charge made the girls march around the room in file while he picked out three Broadway blondes. A regular beauty contest, with the dyed blondes winning the jobs."

"I'm a blonde," Rose reminded her, smiling.

"Oh, I'm sorry -"

"Don't worry about it. I'm a blonde, but I'm not sensitive

about it," Rose told her.

Fanny laughed.

"We weren't very good friends at Landsman & Miller. My fault, I'm afraid."

"Oh, I know. You thought I was a tart - and I am a little tart. And I thought you were just a sour-ball with a yen to get on in the world. Things are different when you're out of a job - they look different."

She put out her hand and Fanny took it. They smiled at each other.

"This is funny - meeting you and becoming friends."

"Where were you going?" Fanny asked.

"To the washroom - scrubbing myself up for the next call. There's some guy in the Graybar Building who wants a filing clerk."

"I was going to the washroom too. My feet are tired. I thought I'd sit down there for a minute and smoke a cigarette."

"Let's go together."

They went in and sat down on a wicker settee in the restroom. On another settee a girl was stretched out, her face ghastly pale and her eyes half closed. She looked worn out.

"One of the jobless - one of us," Fanny said, nodding her head toward the girl.

"No stockings - no make-up. You get so you can spot them after a while," Rose answered. "I don't know what I'll do when my stockings, lipstick and powder give out."

"But what are you doing?" Fanny asked.

"Honest, I don't know what to do. I've only got a dollar and fifty cents left and my next week's room rent is due tomorrow. But Mrs. Feinberg, my landlady, likes me, and I'm sure she'll let me hang up a week or two until I can find something. What are you doing?"

"You're not so bad off," Fanny said. "You've only yourself to worry about. I've got my father and it's not the rent I'm worrying about so much. Our landlord's a nice fellow. He won't bother me at all. We've lived in the house fifteen years. It's food and things like that that are going to wreck me. My father is a total loss - he'll just whine when things go bad. When I left L. & M. I only had my week's salary. It won't last much longer."

"We both have to get jobs! Right away."

"But how?"

"I don't know," Rose admitted.

"And there's so many girls out of work. You remember Mildred Purdy?"

"Sure. What happened to her?"

"She was fired with me a week after you left. I saw her a couple of times in various offices. She'll never get a job."

"That's tough about her - she can't take care of herself. She wasn't as wild as all the other girls thought she was - just a big mouth. But she'll go fast once she gets started. I hate to see it. She's not a bad kid at heart," Rose told her.

Fanny shuddered.

"I'm afraid a lot of us will go bad if this keeps up," Fanny said.

Rose laughed.

"Lose our honor, huh?"

"No. I wasn't thinking of that alone. That doesn't always seem so dreadful. I was thinking of things we might have to do to earn a living - things that'll make us go rotten inside. Prostitution for a girl like Mildred, a rotten marriage for me, and God-knows-what for you."

"How do you mean - a rotten marriage for you?" Rose asked.

"There's a man, the son of one of my father's old cronies,

who wants to marry me. I don't like him, but I may have to marry him; he has a little business, a stationery store, and it makes money."

"But, I thought you liked Mr. Flynn? That's what everyone in the office used to think."

"I did. I still like him. But I see now that doesn't mean anything."

"And you don't like the fellow that wants to marry you?"

"No. I detest him. But if I can't get a job -"

"What's the matter with him?"

"Nothing really. Just uncultured - a different sort of man than I was used to meeting in the office."

"Cheer up, there's always the breadline!" Rose said in order to change a conversation which she saw was painful to her companion.

"Yes," Fanny said, shrugging her shoulders. "That's a great consolation. If we get hungry there's always a breadline to go to. I was noticing the list of places in the evening paper the other night; dozens of places that will give you food and a place to sleep. But I couldn't do it - I'd feel like a backward scholar. Maybe it's pride - I didn't think I had any left."

"Well, I'm not proud. I'll do anything," Rose told her. "But breadlines and free employment agencies and Y.W.C.A. canteens and municipal flophouses are out of my line. They don't want me around. I'm not one of the deserving poor; I can't get that grateful look on my homely map. I'm the kind of dame that wants silk stockings, powder, rouge and a shot of gin instead of good nourishing soup. Bread and soup just don't seem enough to me. The rich old hags that run those shows don't want my kind around. For the first time in years they've got a chance to be nice to the poor, and they want poor people that look like poor people."

They both laughed.

"I suppose they do some good," Fanny said.

"I suppose so - but not for girls like you and me. One visit to some charity organization and we're so sunk for the rest of the week we can't even look for a job. I tried to register for a job at the Municipal Employment Bureau. I waited four hours in line with a lot of ninnies and then they shut the door just as I got there. 'No more today,' the cop told me. I'd wasted the best part of the day hanging around that dump. No more charity for little Rosie. It comes too high."

Rose powdered her nose and tucked up some loose strands of blonde hair. She jumped up quickly.

"Can't sit around all day. I've got to get along and see about that file clerk's job."

Fanny got up and pulled her skirt straight around her wide hips. She sighed as she put her weight on her feet again.

"Sore dogs?" Rose asked.

"Awful."

"Yeah. I've had them. Shop girls get used to standing on their feet they tell me. I was talking to one girl the other day and she said it takes about ten years before you get used to it."

At the entrance to the Graybar Building, they said their goodbyes.

"I'm in the 'phonebook," Fanny said, "even though they may take the 'phone out tomorrow. You can get my address there. Look me up sometime."

"I'll look you up in a few days and we'll go job-hunting together," Rose said. "We might have luck going together."

"We might."

"So long, I'll be seeing you," Rose said, turning away with an airy wave of her hand.

"She isn't half bad," she said to herself. "It did her good to lose her job." It seemed to Rose that Fanny was almost a different girl from the officious harridan she had known at the office.

Kleinert had given Rose a tip that the Amour Perfume Company wanted a filing clerk. Looking on the huge directory board she discovered that their offices were on the fourteenth floor and took an express elevator up. Opening the door, Rose found herself in a reception room unlike any she had seen before. It was a large, airy room, with two enormous windows overlooking the New York skyline. The floor was covered with a rose-beige carpet that let one's feet sink gently at every step. The furniture, even the desk at which the reception clerk sat, was empire, and the walls were hung with light grey silk. It looked more like a fashionable boudoir than the entrance to a business office. The only evidence of commercial purpose was a crystal shelf on which elaborate perfume bottles were arranged in such a way that the sun from the long windows poured down upon them, making them glow with jewel-like colors. Rose noticed the reception clerk was a tall girl with beautiful red hair.

This young lady looked up as Rose came in and said in an ultra-refined voice:

"What may I do for you?"

"Mr. Kleinert told me you needed a file girl up here."

"Just one moment, if you please."

She rose and went, with swan-like grace, into the other room.

Rose could hear the low buzz of her explanation, and then a high-pitched voice, which she judged to be a woman's answering:

"I will see the young lady, Suzanne."

Suzanne stepped out and beckoned to Rose, and she passed through the doorway into a small office, decorated in an orange shade that was almost a glowing red. There were three desks in the office and a large set of files, all finished in dull black enamel. A dandified little man got up from the center desk as she came in. He looked at Rose and made a little clicking noise with his lips to indicate disappointment.

"You will never do," he said in the voice Rose had thought was a woman's. "You don't fit into my color scheme at all. Suzanne should have known better than to send a blonde into this office."

Rose's mouth gaped open in surprise. Then she looked at the two stenographers, busy at the other desks and realized what he meant. They were both olive-skinned brunettes, and their particular type of beauty was well-suited to the orange walls and draperies of the room.

"A blonde!" the little fellow exclaimed disgustedly, and looked at Rose as if she should have known better than to bring her bleached hair into his orange room.

Rose had to grin. It was really funny. Now she could cap Fanny's beauty parade story with this experience. She turned to go.

"I believe in harmony for the worker," the little man explained by way of an apology. "You would be an aesthetic discord in this office."

"Sure," Rose agreed and walked out.

Passing through the reception room, Rose saw with what care the red-haired girl had been chosen to fit in with her grey background. A Chinese vase near her desk was the same shade as her hair.

Rose was still chuckling with amusement when she reached the street level and started across the Grand Central to the subway.

It was dark when she got to Fifty-sixth Street and Rose turned into the doorway of Mrs. Feinberg's house with a sigh.

She was tired, and planned to take a hot bath and lie down on the bed for a few minutes before going out for her supper.

As she started along the hallway to her room, she heard a sound of sobbing. It came from her room. She unlocked and threw open the door. Mildred Purdy was sitting there, twisting a handkerchief in her gawky fingers and crying.

"What in the hell brings you here?" Rose asked.

"I had no place to go. They threw me out of my room. Please let me stay, Rose. I haven't anywhere to go."

Rose saw that Mildred's battered suitcase was on the bed.

"That's okay. You can stay here as long as I do," she said. "But how did you get in?"

"I told the landlady I was a friend of yours and asked her if I couldn't wait for you in your room. She said all right, but that she'd have to lock me in so I couldn't swipe anything. That's why the door was locked."

"What did they kick you out of your place for?" Rose asked, slipping out of her coat and throwing it onto the bed. "Didn't you pay your rent?"

"It's paid up until the day after tomorrow, but my landlady threw me out because I let Frank stay overnight yesterday."

Rose sat down on the edge of the bed, leaned forward and patted Mildred's knee.

"Well, that's nothing to cry about. Take a brace."

"But I haven't any money and Frank socked me on the nose, and the landlady wouldn't give me back the two days' rent she owed me and said she'd call the police if I made trouble and -"

Mildred burst into another series of sobs.

Rose could not make head nor tail of what she had said. She pulled down a washcloth and a towel.

"Here, wash your face and I'll take you down and get you something to eat," she said, throwing the towel into Mildred's lap.

SEVEN

Mildred looked up brightly as Rose opened the door and threw her handbag onto the bed with a weary gesture.

"Oh hello! Did you get a job?"

"I got nerts!" Rose said, disgusted.

She slumped down onto the edge of the bed and kicked off her shoes. Rose was tired. She had shared her narrow bed with Mildred the night before and, as a result of Mildred's tossing and turning, she had slept badly. Then, all day long, she had rushed furiously from place to place in desperate search of a job. She was down to her last dollar and this was the day her room rent was due.

"Then we'll have to leave!" Mildred exclaimed. "Where will I go?"

Rose pursed her lips and stared in amazement at her guest.

"Calm down," she said finally. "Things aren't as bad as that. I've been here more than a year. The landlady likes me. She'll let me hang up a week's rent. I'll run down and see her in a few minutes. What did you do all day?"

"I just stayed here - I couldn't bear to go out and look for a job after what I've been through."

"You know, Mildred," Rose said, "I don't think you can take it. I've heard you yelling about what you've been through ever since I came in last night. What have you been through?"

Mildred began to cry, the tears running in large drops down her cheeks.

"Aw, I'm sorry," said Rose. "I didn't mean anything. But I'd like to know what happened to put you in a state like this."

"It was so terrible."

"What was terrible?"

"Everything."

Rose lit a cigarette, and blew out the match before asking again:

"What?"

"I just can't tell you."

"Okay. I don't want to hear secrets."

Rose turned over on the bed and lay on her belly so that she could reach into the closet. She got out her slippers and put them on.

"Want to come in and talk to me while I wash up?" she asked Mildred.

Mildred, frizzy hair in wild disorder, followed her disconsolately into the bathroom, turned down the toilet cover and sat down on it to wait while Rose washed and refreshed her make-up.

Then, without further urging on Rose's part, she began to tell the story of her troubles.

"I owed all my salary when they fired me," she said, "I had to hock the ring I bought last year. That carried me along until a couple of days ago. Then I asked Frank for some money and he got nasty and fresh."

Rose looked at her friend in the mirror as she filled the

washbasin with warm water.

"What do you mean?"

"Oh, he said he couldn't give me any money unless I did what he wanted me to do."

"Sleep with him?"

"Can you imagine?"

"What did you expect?"

"I always made him stop when he got fresh before."

"Go on," Rose prompted. "What happened?"

Mildred began to cry again.

"It was terrible, and he wouldn't give me any money anyhow because he had to go to Philadelphia to see his wife. She had another baby. Then he hit me when I began to cry. He said I was no good. And Mrs. Landor came up in the morning and told me to get out and called me names and wouldn't give me the money back for the last two days. Oh, it was terrible!"

"Yeah!"

"And I thought Frank was so nice - he always took me out and spent money on me."

"Those small-time wise-guys are all like that; they're just waiting to get you in a jam before they put the proposition to you. What did you expect? Did you think he'd keep you just because you have a nice smile?"

"But he was so nice -"

"Sure," Rose said and brought the washcloth up, dripping, between her cupped hands, and sluiced water on her face.

Back in the room again, washed and made-up, with her shoes on once more, Rose started for the door and then hesitated.

"I think it would be a good idea," she said, "to eat before I go and see Mrs. Feinberg. Got any money, Mildred?"

"Four bits."

"It'll do. Let's go and eat."

They had sandwiches and coffee in the drugstore, and each girl paid her own check; then they walked back to the rooming house. In the entry-way, Rose took her key from her handbag and gave it to Mildred.

"Here. Go on up and wait for me. I'm going in back and see Mrs. Feinberg."

She knocked on the wall near Mrs. Feinberg's open door.

"Come in, Miss Mahoney."

Mrs. Feinberg, with horn-rimmed glasses a size too large perched on the bridge of her nose, looked up from the game of solitaire she was playing.

"How're you, Mrs. Feinberg?"

"Fine, fine! And you, Miss Mahoney?"

"Not so good."

"You should have gone to Atlantic City like the doctor told you."

"It isn't that. It's that I haven't any money to pay my rent for the coming week. I wish you'd let me slide a week. I'll pay two weeks' rent next week."

Mrs. Feinberg looked down at the cards as if she were deeply engrossed in her game. Then, suddenly, she threw down the deck in her hand and stood up. Her chinless face was working with fury.

"No!"

"But, Mrs. Feinberg. I've been here more than a year and I've always paid promptly before. It's just that I won't be able to pay until next week."

"No. Some girls are all right to trust. Not you. You've had men in your room. If I let you stay you'll give my house a bad name."

"But, I've made no secret of it," Rose protested, taken aback. "You knew before that I had men visiting me. It was all on the up-and-up."

"No. You'll have to get out. I can't afford a bad name for my house. Now you got another girl with you. Soon the police come and my house has a bad name. No! No!"

"But I can't leave just like this. You'll have to give me time to find another place," Rose said, trying hard to keep calm.

"I rent my rooms from week to week. When I say 'go,' you got to go."

"All right, and the hell with you!" Rose said. "It isn't men coming up that worries you. There hasn't been a man in my room for the past three weeks. It's the money you're afraid of losing. I hope my room stays unrented all winter!"

Mrs. Feinberg smiled a smile of triumph.

"*Nu!* You wish me bad luck? Well, I'll tell you. A nice, young man, a college man, came this afternoon. I rent him the room. Maybe sometime he sees my Goldie and they go out together, who knows, maybe he marries her. I rent your room to him tomorrow."

"Okay! I'll get out tomorrow morning," Rose said, and started away.

"Tonight you get out! Tonight! If you don't go, I call a policeman."

Rose went on out of the room and up the stairs as if she had not heard this last order, but she knew that she would have to get out that night.

"We can stay?" Mildred asked eagerly when Rose came into the room.

"No. We'll have to get out right away. The old bitch turned nasty. She was sweet as sugar when I had money. '*Nu!* Why don't they put you in the movies? With your looks -' " Rose said, mocking Mrs. Feinberg. "But it's 'out' when I ask her to let me hook up six bucks."

"But where will I go?"

Mildred was panicky, clasping and unclasping her big, soft-looking hands. Her fright steadied Rose.

"Wait a minute," she said. "Let little Rosie figure it out for you. We're both in the same boat."

Rose took out a pack of cigarettes, passed one to Mildred and took one herself. She walked around the room, the cigarette hanging from her lip, and made a mental list of her belongings.

"Here, get off the bed, Mildred. I want my suitcase."

She dragged a cheap imitation leather suitcase from under the bed, opened it and began to throw in her things, helter-skelter. She had few possessions. Besides her few dresses, underwear, shoes and other articles of clothing, Rose had a cheap ring or two, and some five-and-ten cent store bangles. She owned no books, no *objets d'art* except the little ashtray with the China dog on its rim, and no pictures except some snapshots of her family and two photographs of boys she had known.

She threw the boys' photographs away.

When the suitcase was filled, Rose dragged down a little cardboard hatbox with a rose lithographed in deep pink on its shining black side and into this she packed a nightgown, the yellow coolie coat, a pair of slippers and some toilet articles.

"I'll check the bag at Grand Central," she said to Mildred. "It's too heavy to tote around. I've got all I need in this box."

"What'll I do?" Mildred asked.

"You'd better strap up your bag," Rose advised.

When she had finished packing, Rose put on her hat and overcoat and picked up her handbag.

"I'm going out and make a 'phone call in the hall," she said.

"Wait a minute," Mildred asked, struggling into her overcoat.

"Don't worry, I'm not going to leave you. I'm just 'phoning to get a place to sleep."

She called the apartment where Grace and Yvonne lived. One of them might be home even though this was the time for them to be at work in the dance hall. There was no answer to her ring, and she got the nickel back and called information. She asked for Fanny Wise's number and had the operator call it for her. Fanny herself answered the 'phone.

Briefly, Rose described her plight.

"Come on up," Fanny said. "You can sleep with me, if you don't mind having my father in the same room."

"No," Rose said. "I think I can get a place to sleep. It's Mildred I'm worrying about. She's here. I wonder if you could put her up? Just two nights. I promise to get her off your hands by then."

"I'd much rather it was you," Fanny said.

Rose laughed.

"I don't blame you, but I can get along. I'm afraid she can't."

"All right," Fanny said, "send her up."

Rose went back into the room. Mildred was still sitting on the bed.

"Hey, snap out of it. We've got to get out of here, or old lady Feinberg will be raising hell. I don't want to get in a row."

Mildred got slowly to her feet.

"Pack up your suitcase," Rose said. "I'm all ready, and I've got a place for you to go."

Mildred brightened immediately.

"Gee! Have you? Where?"

"You'll never guess. With Fanny Wise."

"No?"

"No kidding!"

"Gee, that's sweet of her."

Rose bent down and shook her finger before Mildred's nose.

"But you listen. You get out of there in two days or I'll come up and yank you out. She's none too well off. See?"

"I'll get out tomorrow," Mildred promised.

"I'll make sure you do. You meet me with your bag in Grand Central at five o'clock tomorrow night."

Carrying their heavy suitcases, the two girls made their way down the stairs to the first floor. Setting her burdens down on the floor by the entrance, Rose took her room key and threw it through Mrs. Feinberg's open door. It fell, clattering, on the floor.

Bringing her cupped hand to her mouth, Rose made a jeering, explosive noise.

"That for you, Mrs.Feinberg!" she called out, and picking up her bags again, went through the door and let it slam heavily behind her.

EIGHT

Rose came out of Grand Central. She had seen Mildred safely to the subway and had checked her bag. Now, the hatbox hanging from her arm and eighty-four cents in her handbag, she stood on the curb. Commuters on their way home swept past her into the station. There were many young girls in the crowd, laughing and rosy with the cold. Rose stood and tried to figure out her problem. Grace and Yvonne would not be back from the dance hall until long past midnight, and she was dead tired. She would like to lie down and rest her feet. A dreary wait in a ladies' room was not a cheering prospect.

Turning on her heel, she went back into the station. She had seen a booth of the Traveler's Aid Society. They might be able to tell her where to go for a place to sleep.

A blonde young lady in an expensive fur coat, the attendant, looked up from her *Saturday Evening Post* when Rose came to a halt before the booth.

"What can I do for you?" she asked with a professionally kind smile.

"I'd like a place to sleep," Rose said. "I thought you might be able to tell me where to go."

"A hotel?"

"No, I haven't any money. A charity place," Rose said with an effort of will.

"Where do you come from?"

"My landlady just put me out - uptown, Fifty-sixth Street."

"Oh. But this is the Traveler's Aid Society. We can only help strangers and transients."

"Do you know where I could go?" Rose persisted.

"Certainly. I'll tell you."

She consulted a printed slip.

"Go," she said looking up, "to the Central Bureau at 62 Spring Street and they will refer you to the proper agency."

Rose had an idea what she might expect: half a dozen blank forms to fill out and sign, directions how to reach some free lodging place, a trip by subway, more blank forms, a grudging admittance, the foul- smelling bath for herself, and the steam room for her clothes, and, finally, a bed in the horror of the general dormitory. She had heard other girls talking about such places.

"I have a little money," she told the representative of the Traveler's Aid Society, "less than a dollar. Maybe there's some place I could get a room for about fifty cents."

"I'll see," the girl said and bent again to the printed slip. She looked up with the set smile Rose had noticed before.

"The Y.W.C.A. has rooms for as little as fifty cents a night, and free rooms for destitute girls. Perhaps you'd like to try down there. It's only a short walk down Lexington Avenue."

"Thanks. That'd be fine," Rose said, relieved. "I'll go down and take the fifty-cent room if they have one left. I'm tickled I don't have to accept a free room."

"What about tomorrow night? Haven't you any relatives or

friends?"

"I have friends. But I'll have a job by tomorrow night. Your luck has to break sometime you know."

"I hope it does break for you."

"Thanks."

Rose walked across the station to Lexington Avenue, and then, because her feet were so tired, she took the trolley down to the Y.W.C.A. building.

The lobby of the Y.W.C.A. was crowded with clean, well-fed, well-dressed young women of a more sedate type than herself. She made her way toward the desk. A bespectacled little woman with hard, dry features, her hair done up in a stern bun at the back of her neck, looked up at her inquiringly.

Rose could feel the animosity in this woman's eyes. She was not the type which this woman official wanted to have at the Y.W.C.A. She did not look like a girl who would take an active part in the Y activities - more like the sort that would cause trouble by staying out until all hours of the night. She much preferred the type of girl whom she described as "serious," and whom Rose would have described as a "pill" or a "wet sap."

Seeing this antagonism in the woman's eyes, Rose was perversely impelled to appear even more reckless and devil-may-care than usual.

"Could you fix me up with a room for the night for four bits?" she asked boldly.

"We do have rooms," the woman at the desk answered in a soft tone which she felt Rose would take as a rebuke, "and we even have some we rent for as little as fifty cents a night if the applicant is out of work - or for nothing if she is destitute. Are you out of work?"

"I wouldn't come around to the Y if I weren't," Rose said candidly.

The desk clerk frowned. This seemed impudence on the part of one who came as a suppliant. She was sorry the rule of the institution forbade her to turn the girl away, and thankful at the same time that there were rules to help her in an exigency of this sort. Plainly, the girl was not one that merited the aid of the Y.W.C.A.

Bending down behind the counter, the desk clerk drew out a printed form and took a pencil from where she had stuck it in her bun. She poised the pencil over the paper.

"What is your name?"

Rose told her.

"Christian?"

"Mahoney," Rose repeated.

"Occupation?"

"Stenographer."

"Place of business?"

"I'm out of a job."

"Quite so. You did tell me that. Former residence?"

Rose told her.

"Reason for leaving?"

"I couldn't pay the rent in advance."

"Can you give your former landlord or landlady as a reference?"

"Sure. Mrs. Feinberg is her name," Rose answered, hoping the landlady would give the true reason for her leaving. She was sorry now that she had given her "the bird," as she termed it, on departure. That had been stupid.

The desk clerk went on with her questioning. Rose answered each time as best she could. The answers seemed to satisfy the woman. Then suddenly she looked up and held Rose's eye for a second. She had the air of one about to achieve a triumph. She asked:

"What is your pastor's name?"

"My pastor? I haven't been to mass since I came to New York. Father Walters was my pastor in Athol."

"We usually expect the girls who live here to have a letter from a clergyman attesting to their moral character."

"I know. But I don't go to church any more. I don't think Father Walters would even remember me."

"But we would like to have a letter from him. The very character of this institution demands a high moral tone of all its members."

"But what would Father Walters - a priest - know about my morals, anyway?"

"It's a matter of form. But I'm afraid we couldn't let you have a room unless you had such a certificate of good character."

"All right," Rose said. "I'll write to Father Walters tonight and sleep in the park until he answers my letter and tells you I'm a good girl."

"We don't expect you to do that. I'll phone the Central Bureau and have them assign you to some girls' shelter or free lodging house."

Rose grinned.

"If I went to the Central Bureau, when would I get a bed?"

"That all depends - some time tonight."

Rose's grin widened.

"That's a hell of a lot of comfort," she said loudly.

A girl in the lobby knocked her elbow against a vase full of flowers and upset it. A dozen pairs of startled eyes turned to Rose.

"So long," she said, made a sketchy gesture of farewell and walked across the lobby toward the street door.

"The hell with charity!" she said to herself. "There may be some who find comfort in it, but I'll be damned if I do. I'd rather have sore dogs and sleep on a park bench than listen to any more righteous old hags like that dame."

She felt at the same time indignant and well-pleased. "The hell with them," she repeated as she started north on Lexington Avenue. There was a sharp wind blowing, pouncing at her from around street corners and pushing chill claws through the thin defense of her worn clothing. She was half-frozen by the time she regained the warmth and protection of Grand Central Station.

She looked at the clock on the information booth. She had pawned her wristwatch days before. It was only a few minutes after eight. It would be three hours before Grace and Yvonne would get back from work. She sauntered into the waiting room and found a seat near the entrance to the ladies' room. A rumpled tabloid was on the seat beside her and she picked it up, turning, almost automatically, to the want-ad section. As she did so, it occurred to her she had never looked in this particular tabloid for help-wanted advertisements before.

The jobs offered, she discovered, were unlike those in other papers. There were no secretarial or domestic positions listed. But there were dozens of advertisements in large type describing places where a girl could "earn as she learned" such mysterious arts as manicuring, pedicuring, massage and tea-room management. None of these appealed to Rose. She knew there was some catch in the smoothly-worded advertisements. Following these came a list of more legitimate want-ads: masseuse wanted; dance hostess wanted; models wanted. Rose had heard from Grace about the hopelessness of trying to get work as a taxi-dancer; she knew nothing about massage, but she felt her trim figure and pretty face would allow her to qualify as a model. She went carefully through these advertisements. One of them struck her as very promising. She cut it out with a hairpin and made up her mind to call at that address in the morning. It read:

"MODEL: Art photographer requires pretty girl, blonde, size sixteen. Easy work. Seventy-five cents an hour."

Not a munificent salary, to be sure, but Rose felt it would help out and that this sort of work would allow her to search for a better job during the hours when her services were not required before the camera. At least, if she could get two hours work a day, she would be sure of a place to sleep and food enough to keep her alive until she got a more desirable position.

She tucked the torn-out pieces of paper into her handbag and relaxed, leaning her head against the hard wooden back of the bench. It was too warm in the station and she had on her overcoat. The heat made her sleepy. Her eyelids grew heavy, drooped down, and Rose dozed off.

She was awakened by someone shaking her shoulder and a man's voice asking:

"What train, Miss? What train?"

"What? Huh? What?"

"Your train - your train! What train are you making?"

It was a station policeman in a blue uniform. But Rose did not notice the silver buttons. She saw only the blue uniform. He was a "cop" as far as she could make out.

"I'm not making any train. I'm just resting here."

"Scram! This is a waiting room for ticket holders. Get on out - you can't sleep here. Go to a flophouse."

"Aw, go to hell!" Rose said wearily, getting to her feet.

"Scram!" the special policeman shouted after her.

He had a brother haunting the breadlines in Pittsburgh. From his small salary he had just sent him enough money to pay his fare to New York, and the special was curtailing his own Christmas spending in order to take care of his brother when he arrived. But he had his orders: "Keep the place clear of dead-beats."

Rose looked at the clock on her way out of the station. She still had two hours to kill. Crossing to Broadway, she strolled uptown, looking at the crowds. In the main, people seemed happy, brisk, animated by the cold wind. Only now and then did Rose catch sight of a pale, rougeless face and stockingless legs, or the drooping shoulders and bearded face of a male derelict.

She remembered having heard someone say, "It takes only three days without money to make a bum of a man in New York. Lose the crease in your pants and let a beard grow on your face and you're only fit to get a job at manual labor."

She went up past Columbus Circle. Her feet hurt her and her clothing seemed to be no protection against the icy cold. A little past the Circle, the lights of a theatre marquee cast a warm, bright light on the pavement. Rose looked at the list of admission prices by the cashier's window. For fifteen cents she could occupy a top balcony seat. She could kill time there, keep warm and rest her feet. It would be fifteen cents well-spent.

There was an outside entrance to the top balcony. Rose had to climb innumerable flights of stairs to reach her seat. Settling herself with a sigh, she rested her hatbox on the empty seat beside her. She was almost too tired to watch the picture. The figures on the screen were blurred and their actions disjointed by her fatigue. She sat through the feature picture, a comedy and a newsreel and made up her mind to stay until the theatre closed. Then she would be sure not to come to Grace's and Yvonne's flat before they came home.

The second showing of the feature picture was boring. She looked around her. The seat she occupied at the back of the auditorium was near the projection booth and light streaming out of the half-opened door lit up the back of the balcony and the rear aisle. Two usherettes, trim in their tightly-fitting uniforms, were gossiping. She watched them idly as one girl nudged the other, indicating the stairway with a nod of her head. A sailor, his little white cap perched over one ear, his hands buried deep in the breast pockets of his watch jacket, was climbing the last step.

Rose watched the two girls and tried to overhear what they were saying. She caught the word, "mine," and then watched one of the girls, a little, thin creature with carroty red hair, as she strolled up to the sailor, flashing her light before her.

"This way, please," she ordered, and began to lead the way to the extreme left of the theatre, her light flashing on and off as she walked across the back of the auditorium. The sailor, rolling his shoulders, followed her.

The light went off as the girl reached the dark corner where the last aisle and the back of the auditorium formed an angle. Rose tried to peer into the darkness and see what was going on. It was too dark. She could imagine, however, and it amused her. That was one way of making an extra dollar. She remembered how the girls in the mill at Athol used to call prostitution "working overtime".

She turned back to the screen and watched the picture for a little while. Then two whispering voices in heated argument came to her ears. The little usherette and the sailor were standing in back of her.

"Two bucks?" she heard the sailor ask. "You're nuts! I could have done it in a bed for that."

"Not with me, big boy!"

"All right. Here's a dollar."

"Make it two."

"Take it. You're lucky to get that much. You ain't got no overhead working here in a theatre like this."

There was a little silence. Evidently the girl had accepted the dollar. Then the man's voice:

"Ain't you going to show me to a seat? It's dark as hell."

"You want service for your dollar, huh?"

"I ain't had any yet," the sailor said.

Rose could hear him chuckling in appreciation of his own humor. She felt sorry for the little girl.

The usherette guided the sailor to a seat three rows ahead of Rose and then came back up the stairs, flashing her light on and off officiously. Its beam rested for a moment on Rose. The usherette halted.

"How long have you been here, Miss?" she asked.

Rose was as good as anyone else on whom to vent the disappointment at her small fee from the sailor.

"A couple of hours, I guess. What's it to you?"

"Listen, you've been here three hours. Your admission don't entitle you to sleep here."

"I'm staying here until the theatre closes."

"Yeah?"

"Yeah! And what are you going to do about it?"

"Call the assistant manager, that's what. You're going out on your tail," she threatened.

Rose let her patter hurriedly away to fetch the assistant manager. She had paid her fifteen cents and felt she could stay until the theatre closed.

The usherette came back with a stout, bald man. He seemed kindly enough.

"Listen, lady, the girl says you've been here five hours. We can't let you do that, you know. You've been snoring and disturbing the other patrons."

Rose laughed. The usherette was inventive enough.

"What time is it?" she asked the assistant manager.

"It's eleven-thirty."

"Time I ought to be going anyway. Thanks for coming up and telling me the time."

The man walked off, shrugging his shoulders, as Rose got up, lifted her hatbox and prepared to leave. The usherette stood over her, flashing her light on and off with every intention of irritating Rose as much as possible.

Rose walked past her, then stopped, turned and said:

"Perhaps I ought to tell your assistant manager what you do up here when sailors come in, huh?"

"What?"

"You heard me. The gob gave you a dollar too much, if you ask me."

She went down the steps and out of the theatre. It was quieter now. Broadway was dimmer. Streams of taxi cabs fought their way uptown, and only a few empty taxis came down. People were on their way home.

Rose walked up to Seventy-eighth Street and began looking for the house number of the place where Grace and Yvonne lived. She noticed that this street, supposedly residential, was lined on either side with parked cars.

Her heart beat a little more rapidly as she waited, holding her breath, for a response to her ring at Grace's door. They might be out on an all night party! After a moment or so Grace opened the door and put a tousled head out.

"Oh, hello, Rose," she said, slipping out into the hallway and closing the door behind her.

Rose wondered at this, but said:

"I've just been thrown out of my room. I wonder if you and Yvonne could let me stay in your place tonight?"

"Sure," Grace answered without a moment's hesitation. "Stay as long as you want. But wait a little while before you come in.

I'm giving a dancing lesson."

"Oh, I see! How long do you want me to wait?"

"Give the sucker an hour. He's in the fur business and he promises to give me a fur coat sometime."

Rose put her hatbox by the door.

"I'll leave this here," she said.

"Sure, I'll take it in with me. And say - how're you fixed for dough?"

She shrugged.

"I mean, you've got enough to eat, huh?"

"I guess so."

Grace pulled up her skirt and rummaged into the top of her stocking. She pulled out a dollar bill.

"Mad money," she explained. "Get yourself a feed."

Rose shook her head.

"Thanks," she said. "I've got enough. I'll get a cup of coffee and a sandwich while I'm waiting for your boyfriend to get out."

"Oke!" Grace said, putting the dollar back. "I'd let you in right now, only this guy's particular as hell. I even had to chase Yvonne out. I'd like to get that fur coat. Run along now, I've got to get back. He's probably biting his fingernails to pieces. You know how these guys are?"

Rose smiled and nodded her agreement as Grace went back into her room and closed the door.

She was tired now and did not feel like going out. She walked down one flight and then sat down on the stairs, leaning her back against the balustrade. It was not too comfortable here, but it was warm. She lit a cigarette.

A girl in a red coat with a saucy red beret on her head, her lips made up to exactly the same shade as her costume, came up the stairs, a young man in tow. They both stared at Rose as they passed and when they reached the landing above her, she could hear them laughing.

"Must be drunk," the young man ventured.

"Say, I never seen her here before."

"Maybe a dead-beat, huh?"

"Should I call a janitor?"

"Might be an idea."

Rose waited until she heard an apartment door slam on the fourth floor, then she got to her feet and started down the stairs. If the girl in the red coat and hat did call the janitor, and Rose was forced to make explanations, it might put Grace in an awkward situation.

It was colder now outside and the wind was driving great, scudding masses of cloud across the sky. Rose wrapped her coat tightly around her middle as she went down the street. Remembering the delicatessen store with a back room in which she, Grace and Yvonne had once eaten supper, she headed in that direction.

Walking through the delicatessen store, Rose made her way to the room in back where porcelain-topped tables and iron chairs were arranged for the convenience of patrons. A sleepy-eyed waiter rose as she came in and held back a chair for her.

"A cup of coffee and a hamburger sandwich with a slice of onion," Rose ordered.

The waiter shambled off through a scarred swinging door, into a kitchen from which there came strong odors of sawdust and cooking. Rose sipped at the glass of cold water he had left before her and looked around the restaurant. Only two tables were occupied. Three taxi drivers sat at one table, counting their money as they sipped hot coffee from heavy cups and discussed their night's experiences. At another table were a young couple, the boy very badly drunk and the girl very sober and very solicitous. At intervals she kept saying:

"But, darling, this coffee'll do you good!"

Wordless grumbles were his only answers.

One of the taxi drivers was complaining bitterly. He had knocked down a woman at an intersection and had been forced to take her to the hospital. The resultant loss of time had made his receipts slimmer than usual. He seemed utterly unconcerned about his victim, and not unduly excited about the accident, taking it as just another part of the day's work.

The waiter brought her sandwich and coffee. Rose ate and drank listlessly. She was not hungry. She had come only because she wanted a place to sit where it wasn't cold. The cigarette she smoked as she drank the second cup was much more pleasing to her than the sandwich she had eaten. The tobacco smoke soothed and comforted nerves rubbed raw by fatigue.

The warmth and the drowsy hum of conversation from the knot of taxi men made her sleepy. She yawned, nodded, caught herself dozing, and then gave up the fight and let her head sink down onto her arms on the table. She slept.

A slap on the shoulder woke her. A busboy was standing in front of her, grinning, a big, slovenly fellow with blonde hair falling into his eyes. His two front teeth were missing, and when he spoke, their absence gave an uneasy sibilance to his speech.

"Closing," he said.

Rose looked about her sleepily. The taxi drivers and the couple were gone. Half the lights were out and all the chairs but the one she sat on were piled up on top of the tables. There was a strong smell of soap and dirty water. The busboy had been mopping the floor. Again his water-reddened hand touched her shoulder.

"Closing!"

Rose got to her feet.

"All right, what's the damage?"

"A quarter."

She put the money on the table, tucked her handbag under her arm and wrapped her coat tightly about her hips. The busboy watched her as she made these preparations for departure. His eyes went up and down her figure. He put the tip of his tongue through the wide gap in his teeth and delicately allowed it to touch his lips.

"Out of a job?" he asked.

"Yeah."

His interest increased.

"Broke, huh?"

"I paid you, didn't I?"

"Yeah. I was wondering - maybe you'd like to have a place to flop?"

"Well?"

"I was just wondering. I could let you sleep in back - we got a nice pile of potato bags - if you'd be nice to Hymie and me."

Rose looked at his red hands and at an angry red pimple which glowed in the midst of a yeast-pale cheek. She shuddered.

"Hymie's the dishwasher," the busboy volunteered.

Rose pushed him angrily aside with her elbow and went out.

"Little Rosie was propositioned," she said to herself as she pulled her coat tighter in the doorway, "and what a proposition! The busboy and the dishwasher. If mother could only see me now!"

She laughed aloud and a man coming up the street looked at her and then crossed the sidewalk so as to pass close to her.

"Hello, honey!" he ventured.

Rose hurried on. Just as she was to turn the corner into Seventy-eighth Street, a big, yellow touring car sidled in toward the curb and coasted along beside her for a few paces. Two young men in raccoon skin coats sat on the front seat. They inspected her boldly and then, seemingly satisfied, brought the car to a stop some paces ahead of her. The one nearest the sidewalk jumped out and blocked her path.

"Too cold for little, wee girls to be running around without no clothes on," he said, a silly grin on his face.

Rose laughed. She couldn't resist the temptation to ask:

"Haven't you ever seen them without clothes on, baby?"

"When they haven't got 'em on, I'm too busy to look," he said.

Rose laughed, her breath frosty on the cold air.

"Hop in and we'll take you home."

Rose shook her head.

"I've heard that before."

"Just two nice boys - sure we'll take you home, if you live alone. Where do you live?"

"I just don't!"

"Aw, the poor little girl with no bed of her own," the boy at the wheel chimed in, starting to climb out in order to add his sales talk to that of his companion.

Rose started away, but the first boy took hold of her arm.

"Don't walk out on us - we drove all the way down from New Haven to find a girl like you."

"Run along, sonny-boy, I've got places to go."

"Sure. We'll all go."

Rose looked at the two boys again. They were nice looking young fellows. Then she looked past them at the car. It was an expensive car and it looked expensive. She had made, she deemed, enough protest.

"What's your name?" she asked. "The right one."

"Never give away my right name - it's Joe Blair. And this is

Alec."

"Alec what?"

"Pierce," the boy who had been driving told her.

"I'm Rose Mahoney."

"Oh, a little Jewish girl."

"Let's go. Climb in Rosie, we're going to do the town."

In happier circumstances, considering that the boys were attractive and seemed wealthy, Rose would have allowed them to "pick her up," and thought nothing more about it. But now, she unconsciously tried to plan some way in which she could use for her own ends their desire for companionship.

"Where are you going?" she asked.

"We don't know. Pick your spots," Joe Blair said.

"To look on the juice when it is red in the black dives of Harlem," the boy who had introduced himself as Pierce told her.

Rose thought of her feet. They hurt badly. To dance on them, tired as she was, would be painful pleasure.

She shook her head.

"I wouldn't want to do that."

"Well, climb in anyhow. We'll talk about where we're going when we're on our way."

"No."

"Well, what do you want to do?" Pierce asked her.

"Nothing much," Rose said, her mind still trying to find some way in which she could make these friendly and obviously wealthy boys useful to her.

"Where were you going when you stopped us?" Joe Blair asked.

"Stopped you? - you bum!"

"Have it your own way. Be modest and say that we stopped you then, but tell me where you were going."

"I'm going to stay with a girlfriend overnight."

"Oh!"

"Girlfriend! Is she as pretty as you are?"

"She's pretty."

"Let's go!" Pierce said, starting to climb into the car.

Joe took Rose's elbow.

"Now, wait a minute, boys. She may not want you up in her place."

"'Phone her."

"It's just around the corner," Rose said.

"We'll go around and you can run up and ask her if she's set for a big time," Pierce advised.

"All right."

Rose climbed in next to Pierce and Joe got in beside her. It felt warm and comfortable there between the two bulky, fur-coated boys. She let her tired back relax against the deep, leather cushion of the seat.

Pierce put the car into gear and nosed out into the traffic. They rode to the end of the block.

"Turn here," Rose said.

He swung the car around the corner and put on speed.

"Slow up - it's just a little further."

He slowed down.

"Here."

The car slid to a stop before Grace's apartment house.

Joe climbed out and helped Rose to climb down.

"Hey," he said, "you're not ditching us, are you?"

"I'll come right down again."

He looked quizzically at her.

"Sure?"

"Oh, here," Rose said impatiently, shoving her handbag at him. "I'll leave this with you. There's nothing in it anyhow, but

I like the bag."

"I'm sorry," Joe said, " I didn't mean to doubt your word. Here! Take it back. I don't want to do that."

Rose grinned.

"That's a sweet!"

She turned, ran into the house, and climbed the stairs quickly.

Grace's door was ajar. She went in. The room was thick with cigarette smoke, airless and hot as a greenhouse on a July day. Grace, in pink cotton pajamas and bare feet, was sitting in an armchair, reading a morning tabloid.

"Frozen?" she asked Rose. "I'm sorry I couldn't take you right in, but you'll learn how it is after a while. The customer is always right until he pays up."

"Did you get your fur coat?" Rose asked, smiling.

Grace made a gesture of disgust.

"The damn fool. He's been rushed, trying to get out coats for the Christmas trade. He was so tired he just sat around. I can't get fur coats just talking to guys. I tried to love him up a bit, but he was too damn tired. Now I've got a headache."

Rose knew what she meant.

"I've got your aspirin for you," she said.

"There's some in the bureau, but it's no good for what I mean."

"I didn't mean that kind of aspirin. I just met two cute boys. Fur coats! A great big car! Nice looking! Want to go on a party?"

"Sounds good, but I'm too lazy to get dressed. Tell them to come on up. Yvonne just 'phoned to say she was staying down at Sophie's. You don't know Sophie Lozo. She's a hell-raiser. They got potted at Barbie's."

"I'll run down and tell the boys to come up." Rose said.

She was in no mood for a party, and yet, although she had no understanding of this, the sight of the boys' fur coats, their big car, their well-fed and expensive air, made her want to share, no matter how briefly, the richness of their life.

Swinging open the front door, she called out:

"Grace says to come in. She doesn't want to get dressed!"

"Whoops, my dear!"

They made a rush for the doorway, laughing and making stupid jokes. Going up the stairs, Rose had to warn them to be more quiet.

"So this is little Gracie! Look what Santa brought you!" Alec Pierce said, coming into the apartment.

He threw open his fur coat and showed her two whiskey bottles protruding from his jacket pockets.

Grace came forward, a cigarette in her hand, looked at the bottles, and then turned Alec about as if she were inspecting merchandise.

"You'll do," she said.

"Wait a minute. I've got to see if you'll do or not," Alec told her. Laughing he threw his arms around her, then kissed her.

When he released her he said:

"You'll do!"

Joe turned to Rose.

"I'd better try a sample."

She held him off at arm's length.

"Better not until I've had a drink."

They all laughed at this.

Joe took a patented corkscrew from his pocket and uncorked the two bottles.

"Drink it straight? Or will you have a ginger ale with it? I'll send out for some."

"This isn't a hotel, buddy," Grace told him. "You'll have to go out for it if you want it."

"The hell with it," said Rose.

Grace brought a glass from the bathroom and set it on the table without the formality of washing white streaks of soap and toothpaste from its sides. Rose found two wine glasses of cheap red glass on the bureau and a broken tumbler.

"Try our Southern hospitality," said Joe, filling the varied array of glasses.

Alec lifted his tumbler.

"Here's to the girl's chemises -"

"Aw, nerts! Get a new one!"

"Down the hatch!"

"Now for a little gut warmer!"

"Haven't you any music here? No radio? No victrola?"

"This isn't the Ritz," Grace informed him. "But I can borrow a victrola from next door if you want me to."

"Sure. We need music. What's wine and women without song."

Grace went out to borrow her neighbor's phonograph and some records, while Joe refilled the glasses.

He and Alec had another drink before Grace came back with a battered portable phonograph and a dozen popular records. Setting it on the table, she wound it and put on a record. With increasing acceleration, the phonograph ground out,"Tonight or Never".

The words of the title recurred again and again in the song, sung by a brassy voice that forced the high notes in a ridiculous fashion.

Joe nudged Rose.

"Tonight or never," he hummed, "them's my sentiments, baby."

"Tonight or never is when I catch up on sleep," Rose informed him. "I'm tired."

"Aw, quit crabbing. This is a party."

Alec, excited by the kiss with which he had greeted Grace, was awkwardly fumbling for another opening to caress her. His demand for music had been the only approach he knew. It was part of his "line." He had discovered, simply enough, that it is easier to kiss a girl when she is already in your arms, dancing, than to lead up to the caress in more subtle ways. He did not realize that even the subterfuge of dancing was unnecessary with Grace.

They danced to the music, cheek to cheek, pausing in the corners of the room to kiss each other.

"Dance?" Joe asked, turning to Rose.

She shook her head.

"I've been job-hunting. My feet hurt me."

Joe watched Alec and Grace dancing together. They made him envious. He wanted to dance with Rose and kiss her whenever they turned in the corners of the room. Then he might feel as if he were getting somewhere; one couldn't get anywhere just sitting like this.

"Have another drink," he urged.

"Not for me. Drink if you want to. I'm so tired, I'm groggy already."

Alec was whispering to Grace as they danced, and she was laughing, a self-conscious, exciting laugh. Finally, she took him by the hand and led him into the little alcove which served as the apartment's bedroom. An open arch connected this chamber with the living room and there was no door between the two rooms. Grace and Alec secured privacy by the simple, but none too effective, method of turning out the lights in the bedroom alcove.

Joe turned off the phonograph. It seemed rather senseless

to have it blaring away in the midst of a silent room. It was just his luck to pick a dead one. Then he lit a cigarette and strolled across the room to where Rose sat in an armchair, her legs sprawled out before her from weariness. She had not realized she was so tired or she would not have asked the boys up. But it was just as well she had. Grace was enjoying herself, and Rose knew it would raise her in her friend's esteem to have brought two good-looking young men to the place where, usually, only such men as haunted the cheap dance halls of the upper east side could be found.

"Have another drink," Joe suggested again, hoping in some way to break through the barrier of Rose's weariness.

She shook her head.

Sitting down on the arm of her chair, Joe passed his hand across her shoulders. She tolerated this. He did it again. Emboldened by this slight success, he bent down and tried to kiss her mouth. She pushed him away.

"Cut it out."

"Aw, say - be a good sport. Look at Grace and Alec. They're getting along fine. What's the matter with me - am I a step-child?"

"I'm not in a mood for fooling around."

Rose looked across the brightly lit room into the dim alcove. She reasoned that Grace and Alec would probably stay there the rest of the night.

"I'm going to bed," she announced, getting up out of the chair.

In the corner of the living room was a studio couch covered with a badly-stained velvet cover. She knew that under the cover there were blankets, sheets and pillows. It was where Yvonne slept when she was home.

Rose stripped off the velvet cover and turned back the

blankets. The sheets were none too clean and the flat, soggy pillow was smeared with lipstick, but Rose was too tired to be overcritical.

"Hey, what about me?" Joe asked. "Are you just going to leave me sitting here?"

"Suit yourself," Rose said, opening her little hatbox and taking out nightgown, slippers, toothbrush and the yellow coolie coat.

She brought these into the bathroom and got undressed there, brushed her teeth and combed out her hair. She could hear Joe chuckling as she did this and wondered what could be amusing him so much.

When she went back to the living room, she found the source of his amusement. He had undressed quickly and slipped into bed. Now he was sitting up in the middle of the bed, the covers drawn up around his naked chest, and laughing as if he would never stop.

"That may be funny to you," Rose told him, "but to me it's just a pain in the neck. Get out of that bed, big boy."

"Say, this took strategy! I'm not going to call a retreat when the battle's half won."

"Scram out of it. I'm tired. I want to sleep."

He moved over a little way and turned back the covers, indicating the place at his side with a sweeping and lordly gesture.

"Nothing doing," said Rose. "Get out."

"Not on your life. I'm tired, too. I want to sleep here. You - you suit yourself," he answered and rolled with merriment.

Rose grinned. It was funny.

"All right," she said. "You're foxy. But I can't sleep unless I sleep next to the wall. You'll have to hop out and let me on that side of the bed."

"Okay," he responded, leaping out.

Rose wrapped the coolie coat tightly about her and started to get into bed.

"Aren't you taking that thing off?"

"No. I always sleep in this," she answered, laughing.

"Hey!" he protested.

"Pipe down! I always sleep this way."

She got into bed, went as far over as possible, rolled into a tight ball with her back to the wall and her knees and elbows touching, and said:

"Good night, Joe. Pleasant dreams."

"Hey!"

She stifled a laugh and closed her eyes.

Joe stood for a moment, looking down at her, and then climbed into bed beside her.

"Aren't you even going to kiss me goodnight?" he asked.

Rose kept silent.

He pulled the covers up and then reached out to turn off the light.

"What about that goodnight kiss?" he asked again.

She pretended to be asleep, and actually she was already drowsing off.

Several times in her half-sleep, she sensed Joe's hands making tentative overtures. She ignored them. Only once did she murmur sleepily:

"Handy-Andy, keep your hands to yourself."

It was morning when she woke up.

Alec, in undershirt and trousers, was wandering about the apartment, looking for a match to light his cigarette. Joe was dressing, lacing his shoes. Water was running in the bathroom, and from this Rose judged that Grace was taking a bath.

She yawned and stretched, then slid out of bed.

"Hello, big boy!" she said to Joe, groping for her slippers under the couch. "Are you sore?"

He laughed.

"No. It's the first time I ever slept with a girl all night when nothing happened. Self control - that's me in person!"

Alec looked over from the table where he still rummaged for matches.

"Don't kid the troops," he said.

"I'll swear to it," Rose said. "He behaved himself like a perfect little gentleman - because I made him behave."

Alec and Joe laughed at this.

"Say, that's a yarn to tell when we get back to school!" Alec chortled.

"You're darn tootin'. Anybody can make a dame; it takes a hero to exercise self-control."

It was Rose's turn to laugh.

"Self control?" she asked, and had to laugh again.

Grace came out of the bathroom, her blonde hair wet at the ends and her face glazed with heat. A little puff of steam from the bathwater followed her into the overheated living room. Behind her Rose could see the bathroom was foggy.

"That damn janitor never gets the water hot enough," she complained. It was her constant plaint. She kept the room at a temperature of eighty degrees, all the windows tightly shut, and even stuffed paper into the keyhole to keep out the air. Yet the room and the bathwater were never hot enough to suit her.

She went behind the tall dresser in her little bedroom alcove until she had put on panties and a slip, then came out to finish her dressing in the living room.

Rose, with her clothes over her arm, went into the bathroom. She took a bath, put up her hair and then dressed quickly. They were all ready to go out when she emerged.

"Hurry up, Rose," Grace said, "we're hungry."

While Rose put on her hat and coat, the other three had a drink of whiskey. Joe offered her a drink, but she refused it.

As they were going out, Rose picked up her little hatbox.

"Where are you going with that thing?" Grace asked. "Leave it here. You can stay until you get a place of your own. Yvonne won't mind, and I'm glad to have you."

"Thanks," said Rose and put down the hatbox.

"Now for some food," Joe said. "I'm starved."

"Let's go to Childs. I like their breakfasts," Grace suggested.

As they reached the sidewalk, and started walking to Alec's car, he said:

"Gosh, I forgot all about the car. I hope I haven't got a ticket."

"You can park here all night if you want," Grace told him. "The girls in the block give the cop a little something so he won't trouble the boys when they park all night. That's just an extra service."

The two boys looked at each other. They had not been aware of Grace's semi-professional status. Behind the backs of the girls, Alec pointed to his pocket and shrugged to signal Joe he did not have money enough to pay Grace. Joe merely shrugged in answer.

Grace, turning around at this moment and catching the exchange, whispered to Alec:

"Never mind. Breakfast will be enough. I can afford to treat myself to a nice boy once in awhile."

NINE

"So long, see you again sometime, little bedmate," Joe Blair said, shaking Rose's hand as he climbed back into the car.

"Well, I had a good sleep anyway," Rose answered. "So long!"

Joe lifted his hat, Alec put the gear in low, and the big yellow car edged into the traffic and was off. Rose watched it go along for a block and then lost sight of it. They had had a pleasant breakfast together, then Grace had gone back to her room and the boys had driven Rose down to Forty-eighth Street and Broadway, the corner nearest the address given in the advertisement for a photographer's model.

She started walking across Forty-eighth Street, looking up at the house numbers. In the middle of the block she found the number she was looking for. The photographer's studio was evidently on the second floor, but a display case was fastened to the wall next to the door, and in it were saccharine studies of vaudeville actresses, a glossy print of two male jugglers in tights and leopard skins, and a long, panorama print showing the massed freaks of a side-show before a huge poster advertising their circus. Rose studied this display for an instant and was about to turn in when a taxi drew up to the curb and a man and a bear, both the same height, and of much the same build, got out and waddled across the sidewalk and into the building. Rose watched the two as they climbed the stairs and disappeared through a door which she supposed led into the photographer's.

"Me and the trained bear," she said to herself as she climbed the stairs.

She had been right. The bear and his owner had come to have their pictures taken. Both were waddling about in the waiting room. Again she was struck by the resemblance between beast and master, and had to put her hand to her mouth to hide a smile. The bear trainer mistook her gesture for one of fright.

"Don't be uneasy Ma'am. George's a great lover of the fair sex," he assured her.

George, as if wishing to prove this assertion, shifted his ponderous weight from one flat paw to another as he inspected the samples of feminine pulchritude hung up on the walls of the waiting room.

"Oh, I'm not afraid," Rose said, and patted the leather muzzle enclosing George's snout.

A gawky boy of about eighteen with a pale, pimply face and long, slender legs, which seemed even longer because his trousers were cut so high that they almost reached the armpit, came into the waiting room.

"Rex and George!" he called out.

"Bye Ma'am. Say goodbye to the lady, George," the human partner of the act said as he followed the gawky boy into the studio.

"What'll you have, darling?" the pimply-faced young man asked Rose, popping out into the waiting room again.

"Anything but you darling," Rose answered with sweet politeness.

"Say, you must be a cash customer!" the young fellow exclaimed.

"No, I came to get a job."

"Oh," he said, and walked a little to one side in order to get a better view of her.

"Well?" she asked, her voice edged with irony.

"Well, I guess we'll hire you," he answered.

"Are you the boss?"

"I'm the boss's assistant, and don't get fresh. My name's Elmer, and don't kid me about it, or I'll see that you lose your job. That's just a warning."

"Okay!"

Elmer lit a cigarette and opened the door into the studio.

"We got you for bangles and soft-toe slippers. Go right in when Rex and George come out. The boss is at the camera," he instructed her just before going through the door and closing it behind him.

Rose grinned happily.

"Boy!" she said, and then again, "boy!"

She snapped her fingers.

"A job at last! If he only gives me an hour's work a day - that'll be something."

She was overjoyed and paced up and down the waiting room, smiling to herself.

In about fifteen minutes, George, followed by Rex, came out of the studio. George came out on all fours, but reared up politely to give Rose a chance to pat his muzzle again. Rex, with equal politeness, doffed his wide-brimmed black hat as he passed her.

Rose sidled through the half-open door into the studio. The

place was burning bright with the purple-blue neon lights that the photographer used in his work. It was a larger room and filled with all sorts of odds and ends, everything from a polar bear rug, representative of the north, to a stuffed shark and an artificial palm, representing the south. Between these poles of junk were all varieties of props and costumes, littered about the room in mad disorder. There was a heavy rug on the floor and Rose noticed as she walked that at every step a cloud of dust rose from it and floated about her feet, fairy-like in the purple-blue light.

Camera and apparatus stood in the middle of this studio, but there was no sign of the photographer. Rose sat down on a Roman chair without a back to wait for him. Presently a little side door opened and a thin, nervous man, partially bald, and with eyes of so light a blue that they seemed blind, came into the room.

She stood up, but he paid no attention to her, fussing with his camera.

"Are you the boss?" she finally had to ask.

"I guess so. Why?"

"I'm your new model."

"Oh, yeah - that's right. Elmer told me he'd hired you. Said you were a looker."

He looked at her for a moment. Rose was beginning to get nervous when he added:

"And he's right, you are a looker. I'll have plenty of work for you."

"Gee, that's fine. I've been out of work a long while."

"You'll find a pair of tights and some bangles behind that screen. I got to take a couple of poses for a costume ad. Then you can change afterwards for the soft-toe picture."

It was all meaningless to Rose, but she went behind the

screen and looked at the things on a straight-backed chair which Elmer had evidently set out. It was a circus costume - tights and gaudy bangles. Peeking through the hinged crack of the screen to be certain that the photographer was not looking, she undressed. Then, hurriedly, she put on the tights and the bangles. At a little mirror nailed to one side of the screen she tidied her hair. She reached for her handbag to get powder and rouge when suddenly, behind her, she heard someone say:

"Never mind the make-up. We don't use it here. The boss likes the hard lines he can get from a greasy map. Wipe it all off. There's a towel next to the mirror."

It was Elmer. She turned around to look at him. He was lounging in a doorway she had failed to notice and evidently had been there all the while she was undressing. As long as he did not seem embarrassed, Rose saw no reason why she should be ashamed.

"The hell with it," she said to herself. "Let him look - he's seeing something."

She was proud of her trim hips and straight shoulders, broad for a woman, which gave character and an appearance of determination to her figure.

Ready, she walked from behind the screen and stood before the photographer.

"All right?" she asked.

He studied her.

"Shift that rose around a little to the front of your left hip," he said critically.

She did so.

"All right?"

"Good. Now climb up on top of that barrel."

There was a sugar barrel a few feet in front of the camera. Rose hoisted herself upon it, and stood erect.

"Ever seen a circus?"

"When I was a kid."

"Remember the equestrian artistes?"

"No."

"The girl horseback riders."

"Oh, yes. Sure."

"Take a pose like you was on the back of a horse. Hands up - touch the fingers together - gracefully - that's it. Now, the feet - one a little ahead of the other - toe to heel. Chin up! Smile. Big Smile! Hold it!"

He dodged around in back of his camera and looked through the plate, his head completely covered by the usual black cloth.

"Hold her - hold her, steady," he admonished Rose. Then, scuttling from under the black cloth, he called Elmer and asked him to take a look.

Elmer did so with a bored air and then straightened up and said negligently:

"It's okay, Sam. I'd shoot it just like she is, if I was you."

"Right."

Sam, as Elmer had called his employer, shot that picture and many more. Then Rose changed into a ballet costume and put on soft-toe dancing slippers. Sam posed her in a toe-dancing position, allowing her to support herself by holding onto a rope which Elmer had suspended from the ceiling.

All this consumed about three hours. Rose kept saying to herself joyfully over and over again as she went from one tiring pose to another:

"Seventy-five cents an hour. Three hours. Two dollars and two bits. Five-and-ten-cent-store powder. Pair of fifty cent stockings. A good filling dinner at a German bakery restaurant. And enough for breakfast in the morning."

It was almost a song of triumph in her heart. Yet a month

VAL LEWTON

before she would have thrown away two dollars on a worthless trifle without a thought. Now two dollars and twenty-five cents was all the difference between despair and exalted joy.

"All right," Sam said when he had finished taking the last picture, a close-up of her feet in the slippers. "That'll be all for today. Elmer will give you your money."

"Thanks."

She started to go in back of the screen again, but Elmer came forward and whispered in Sam's ear.

"Wait a minute Miss," Sam called out.

She turned around.

"Yeah?"

"Want to make a little more jack?"

"Gee!"

"You're a good looker. I'd like to take a couple of intimate poses of you for my own collection."

"What do you mean?"

"Oh, you know - semi-nudes and maybe a modest nude or two. Art photos, you know."

Rose considered this.

"No rough stuff?" she asked.

"Say, I'm married."

"How much?"

"I'll triple the rate for that kind of work. Two dollars and a quarter for an hour. And I'll keep you working for about two hours."

Four-fifty more. Six seventy-five in all. She could get a room of her own with that. No need to rely on Grace's generosity.

"Okay."

"You'll find a bathrobe behind the screen. When you're ready, go into the back room. I'll be waiting for you."

Rose cautioned him again.

"No rough stuff."

"Don't worry. I'm an artist. I don't look at women that way."

Elmer smirked as his boss said this. Rose noticed this grimace, but paid no attention. He looked like an evil-minded youth anyhow.

She took off the ballet costume behind the screen, found the bathrobe, a pink, quilted affair, very badly soiled, put it on, and strolled into the back room.

It was another room equipped with neon lights. There was a couch against one wall and a camera in the center of the room. Sam was focussing the camera on the couch. A young man whom she had not seen before, very white-faced in the vivid sharpness of the gas-electric lights, stood in one corner. He had on an old bathrobe and slippers.

Rose wondered what he was doing here, but remembered that Sam had assured her there was to be no "rough stuff." She stood waiting while Sam fussed with his equipment. The young man, when she looked at him, avoided her eyes. It was embarrassing to stand there facing him, both of them with bathrobes drawn about themselves.

"Now she's ready," Sam said. He was talking about his big camera.

"What do you want me to do?" Rose asked.

"Just a second, I'll tell you. Don't be in a hurry. First I want to tell you that George here," he pointed to the young man, "is a hell of a nice guy. I want you to get that through your nut first. He's an actor and ain't got no dough. You're on stage too, ain't you?"

"I was a steno." Rose said.

"Well, you don't need any experience for what you're going to do," Sam said kindly.

Rose wondered even more about what was required of her.

Elmer, bursting in, aglow with enthusiasm, explained matters to her by shouting:

"Say, Sam, I've got the most marvelous idea. A wow! Let's make a stag picture with the Siamese twins!"

Rose looked at Sam. It was all clear to her now.

"You dirty rat," she said. "Give me my money. I'm going home."

An ambulance stood across the street from the long queue of girls waiting to register for jobs at the municipal registration bureau. Its motor was idling. Puffs of smoke and gasoline fumes shot from its exhaust into the frosty air. The girls filed slowly along, entering the registration building by ones and twos, advancing only a few inches at a time. Their breaths were white and smoky in the cold. On the corner, a Salvation Army Santa Claus stood beside his tripod, ringing his bell at irregular intervals. His white whiskers had a fleck of black grease near the end.

Rose stood in line behind a stout girl who was panting with mingled asthma and excitement. In back of her was a thin, tall young woman with heavy rings under her eyes. The thin girl was silent, but the fat girl voluble, chattering constantly.

"I've been out of work six months. I'm a good typist. I won the prize for shorthand at my school. I've had three years' experience in brokerage firms. I just can't get a job. My money is almost gone. It's awful."

"Yeah," said Rose.

"Yeah. It's just awful. I haven't a thing to wear."

The girl had on a fur overcoat and her hat, although cheap, was brand new and in the latest mode. Rose looked at her and then down at her own worn coat. Rose's hat was an autumnal model, a modified Empress Eugenie, and already out of style. The seams of her gloves were ragged from much mending. With the money she had earned at the photographer's, Rose had bought a new pair of stockings, some powder and a cheap lipstick. She looked smart to masculine eyes, because she was brightly coloured, but to a woman's eyes she was poorly dressed.

"You're not so badly off," Rose said to the stout girl. "Your clothes are still good."

"Oh, but I'm down to my last hundred dollars."

Rose turned away in disgust. The thin girl behind her whispered:

"I haven't eaten for two days. I'm just looking at that ambulance and hoping to God it's not me that takes a flop and has to be crated to a hospital. I don't want to go to Bellevue - it's bad there."

Rose dug into her handbag and brought out a quarter. It was half the money she had left.

"Get yourself something to eat," she whispered, handing it over.

The thin girl took the money, said nothing, although her eyes spoke gratitude, and left the line.

The stout girl who was down to her last hundred had seen the transaction between Rose and the other girl.

"Isn't it awful," she remarked.

"Aw, hooey," said Rose.

A young interne sitting in the back of the waiting ambulance was joking with one of the girls in the line, a pert lass with dyed red hair. Rose amused herself by listening to them as they bantered back and forth.

She was dead tired. The line moved only inch by inch. She went forward, shuffling, with the rest, her feet aching, and her legs strained from long standing. The most she could hope for was to have her name registered as one of those seeking employment. It seemed hopeless, but she waited. It would be foolish, she reasoned, to step out of the line after she had waited so long.

Finally she reached the doorway.

"What kind of work?" a policeman asked her.

"Clerical."

"The door on the left."

She went into a long room, across the middle of which a counter had been erected by placing boards on carpenters' trestles. Behind this counter there sat a dozen clerks, registering the applicants.

Rose leaned against the wall until one of the clerks motioned her forward. The clerk was a pleasant, middle-aged woman who smiled sweetly at Rose.

Rose told her in detail her business experience, gave the name of her most recent employer and the other required information.

"Have you a 'phone, Miss Mahoney?" the woman asked.

"No, I'm staying with a friend. You could call me there."

She gave the woman Grace's telephone number and address.

"Just a moment," the woman said, and Rose waited while the other went through a pile of papers. The clerk found a typewritten list, saying as she did so:

"We've had several unfortunate incidents with girls from your neighbourhood, Miss Mahoney. I'll just have to look up your address and see if you live in respectable quarters."

She continued to search for a moment or so and then

straightened up and spoke to Rose again:

"I'm afraid, Miss Mahoney, that we won't be able to register you here. Your friend's address is one of those on our list of houses where immoral women live."

"But I told you it was my friend's apartment."

"I know and I'm sorry. It's unfortunate. Even your friend may be a good girl, but you must understand that many of the positions offered are from charitable persons who want to be certain they are not employing women of bad character. Of course, I can see you're a nice girl. But orders are orders."

The woman seemed so sincerely sorry for her that Rose could not be angry. She merely asked:

"What can I do about it?"

"If you have money enough, I'd advise you to move and come down tomorrow and register. I'll give you a pass to save you the trouble of waiting in line. Or, if you can't move, go and see Mrs. McCarthy; she'll try to straighten things out for you. That's Mrs. McCarthy at the desk."

Rose looked around. There was a crowd of girls at Mrs. McCarthy's desk.

"Thanks," she said. "But I can't move and I'm too tired to wait around Mrs. McCarthy's desk for heaven knows how long."

The woman clerk seemed to understand.

"I don't blame you. It is hard. I know what it is to be out of work. They only gave me this job because I was so broke. I used to be a buyer in a department store in the South."

"Well, thanks," Rose said, turning away.

"Good luck to you, Miss Mahoney."

The twilight that passes for deep night in the brightly lit streets of New York was settling down over the city. Rose walked to the subway and took a train for Grand Central Station. She had made an appointment with Mildred to meet at the information booth, for she wanted to be sure that Mildred did not impose herself upon Fanny for too long a stay.

Mildred, her suitcase at her feet, was waiting when she got there.

"Now what am I going to do?" she asked as soon as she saw Rose.

"I'm taking you up to Grace's apartment. You don't know her, but I think you two might get along well. Both of us will stay there tonight. We can sleep on the floor if they haven't any other place to put us."

"Haven't they got any beds to put us in?"

Rose was too tired to answer.

"Come on," she said.

Mildred, groaning and complaining about the weight of her suitcase, followed her to the subway.

"Put in your own nickel, Mildred," Rose said to her as she passed through the turnstile.

She knew that Mildred had some old change, and she did not want to lay out any money for her. Mildred was the sort that would let one do that indefinitely, and Rose had no intention of letting the other girl sponge on her.

Grace and Yvonne were just about to start for the dance hall when Rose arrived with Mildred in tow.

"Make yourself at home," Yvonne said.

"We'll be back at twelve. You can do anything you want while we're gone. There's some gin back of the bureau if you want a drink," Grace said from the doorway, then waved her hand and closed the door behind her.

"Thanks," Rose shouted after her.

She took off her things, put on her slippers and the coolie coat and made herself comfortable. Mildred wandered about the apartment looking at the boys' photos on the dresser and the various pictures on the wall.

"What's their racket?" she asked Rose.

"They're taxi-dancers."

"Yeah, I knew that, but don't they do anything else?"

"That's their business."

"Well, I was just sort of wondering."

"When you've got dough enough to get out of here and have an apartment of your own, then you can wonder all you want to, but as long as they're putting us up, Mildred, I'd keep my trap shut and my eyes and ears where they belong if I were you."

Mildred shrugged.

Rose read a confession magazine and Mildred walked about restlessly, looking out of the window every once in a while, until Grace and Yvonne returned.

"Hello," Grace said, grinning broadly as she entered the apartment. "We've brought company."

Yvonne followed her in, and then, their faces expressionless, two Filipinos came into the apartment. They were dressed with cheap elegance, their clever-cut suits fitting them as closely as the proverbial paper fits the wall.

Grace introduced them to Rose and Mildred. Rose did not catch their last names. She grasped only that one was Henry something or other and the second one Jim something else. Both Filipinos nodded gravely in acknowledgement of the introductions, and smiled blandly. They seemed quite used to associating with white girls.

Rose, who had no prejudices, wondered what in the world would attract Grace and Yvonne to men of their complexion. Short and so grotesquely ugly that they had a certain beauty of their own, they would never have appealed to her. On looking at Mildred, she was surprised to note how much animation there was in her countenance. She was getting a great "bang" from being on a party with the little yellow men. Dimly, Rose remembered that Mildred had once told her she had danced with a Negro when she was drunk. But, aside from bewilderment at Grace's and Yvonne's choice, Rose was not in any way put out by the Filipinos. To her mind it was one's own business whom one chose as friend or lover.

"Come on in the bathroom and help me mix drinks," Yvonne said to Rose, holding up a paper bag full of ginger ale bottles and another bag, wet on the bottom, which held ice.

Rose followed her into the bathroom. Yvonne shut the door after she had put her purchases on the sink. She made a face.

"I hate these damn Filipinos, but Grace likes to have them come up. They're generous as hell, you know. They save all their dough and then spend it on a big spree with the girls. We're rich for a month after these yellow boys come into town. But me, I got to get drunk before I can have anything to do with them. Grace don't seem to mind."

Rose, who had found a bottle opener in the medicine chest, pried off the tin top of a ginger ale bottle.

"I suppose Mildred and I had better take a little walk while you entertain."

"Naw! What for? They don't mind. Stick around. You can read the morning paper. I brought one back with me."

"I think we better take a walk. You know Mildred is -"

"Say," Yvonne protested, "your friend Mildred is just aching for a chance at one of those boys. Did she make bedroom eyes at them when they came in? It damn near floored me."

Yvonne shook out her thick, bobbed hair with her hands.

"I've got a head on me tonight. We were out on a bender with Barbie yesterday. I damn near passed out dancing tonight."

She broke off and was silent for half a second, holding in her hands the piece of ice she had brought. The she put it down in the sink and went on:

"You know, I've got an idea. Your pal Mildred seems to like these Filipinos. She can take my place tonight and make herself a bit of change. She don't look as if she'd be too good for that."

"I don't know," Rose said. "That's up to her. All I know about her is that she was a good girl until just a few days ago and then the guy practically forced her."

"They always do," Yvonne said, a little smile of unbelief on her full lips.

They busied themselves washing glasses, cracking ice, and mixing highballs. Neither spoke. Rose was debating in her mind whether she should save Mildred from Yvonne's projected plan, or whether she should let nature take its course. After all, it was none of her business. She made up her mind that Mildred could do as she pleased. She would have trouble enough looking after herself in the coming months, without trying to wet-nurse Mildred. The other girl was as old as Rose, and she saw no reason why Mildred could not take care of herself.

From behind the laundry hamper Yvonne pulled out a lacquered tin tray. Rose arranged the drinks on it and carried them into the living room.

Grace and the Filipino who had been introduced as Jim were sitting on the bed, their arms around each other, while Mildred and Henry sat on the couch in the living room, laughing and talking in animated conversation. Mildred seemed to be having a good time. Yvonne nudged Rose and nodded her head toward the couple. Rose shrugged her shoulders. It was none of her business.

Yvonne took the tray from Rose and passed the drinks. Rose noticed that the Filipinos drank sparingly and refused a second drink. Grace and Mildred eagerly accepted a second then a third. Mildred asked for more, but Yvonne held up an empty bottle to show her it was all gone.

As they drank, the girls talked, but the two Filipinos remained almost silent, only joining in the conversation with an occasional "yes" or "no", but always smiling their wide, ready smiles as if everything that was said and done was intensely gratifying.

After she had downed her third drink, Grace wrapped her arms about her boy's neck and pulled him down onto the pillow with her. They remained there, arms locked about each other, kissing for a few moments, and then Grace, without more ado, reached out and pulled the light cord, plunging the bedroom alcove into darkness.

"I suppose we ought to have a door there," Yvonne whispered to Rose and then grinned.

Rose, who had been rinsing out the glasses they had used, sat down in the armchair and Yvonne handed her the second section of a morning paper.

"Here, read this," she said and, leaning back in her chair, began to scan the first part of the newspaper.

Rose also read, but she could not help but glance every now and then in the direction of the couch where Mildred sat with Henry. Mildred sat on the very edge of the couch, her back and neck upright. They were talking in whispers and every once in awhile Mildred laughed a high, shrill laugh. Several times Rose saw Henry try to pass his arms about her, but each time Mildred forced him to stop. This had not escaped Yvonne. She got up.

"Want another drink, Mildred?" she asked.

"I thought there wasn't any more."

"Rosie and I'll go down to the corner and get a bottle. I feel like a little air. I've had a headache all day long, and it's too hot in here."

"I'll go with you," Mildred said, starting to get up.

"Sit down. You can talk to Henry until we get back," Yvonne

said. "Come on, Rosie."

She and Rose put on their hats and coats and went out. Rose noticed as they went downstairs that Yvonne had left her handbag behind.

"You've forgotten your pocket book," she said.

"Naw. We're not going to do anything but walk around the block. I'm just giving Henry a chance to work his points. There's another bottle of liquor in the bathroom. That was just a stall."

They walked around the block twice. It was a fine, starry night, cold, but crisp and invigorating.

"Nice out here," Rose ventured.

"Yeah. I always like it on a night like this - I like it just after work, when you step out of the dance hall into this air. It's grand! Like a shot of liquor."

"Lord, I don't see how you can live with Grace if you like fresh air," Rose said, laughing.

"Oh, it's not so bad. We've all got our little faults. Grace and I were brought up together. When we was kids in Bridgeport our old ladies used to send us out to get wood off the street, boxes and things like that. I remember how we used to go around, two little Hunkie kids, dragging a go-cart full of wood. We've been friends ever since."

"I didn't know you were a Hunkie?" Rose said.

"Don't let my French name fool you - it ain't mine. My folks are Bohemians."

They walked along and Yvonne began first to hum and then to sing a Bohemian song. It was gay and catchy and suited well the clear night and sparkling stars.

"I like that," Rose said. "It's pretty."

Yvonne stopped abruptly.

"Don't kid me. You don't even understand the words. You can't like Hunkie songs unless you're a Hunkie."

Under a street lamp, Yvonne halted and, taking Rose by the arm, brought her to a stop so that they faced each other.

"Want some advice?" she asked, a little self-consciously, her voice husky with embarrassment.

"It's cheap," said Rose.

"It's cheap enough," Yvonne agreed. "And that's just my advice to you. Don't be cheap."

"I don't get you."

"Stay away from Grace and me. We're no good. If you have to be no good, don't stick around us. Go to Barbie. She's not any better than we are - worse perhaps - but there's something about her that makes her seem better than we are. Go to her if you've got to be rotten and dirty. She'll teach you to be rotten and dirty in a way that other people will respect. I don't know what it is - but you'll see what I mean."

"Aw, go on, Yvonne," Rose protested. "You and Grace aren't rotten and dirty. What the hell - just because you aren't amateurs any more. Say - that's nothing."

"It's a lot," Yvonne answered, and began to walk again.

Rose caught up with her.

"I don't understand about Barbie. What does she do?"

"Nothing much," Yvonne said. "She's just a good egg, that's all. And, no matter what she does, it seems to leave her clean - you know what I mean."

"No. I don't."

"I guess I can't explain. That's the way we Hunkies are. It's just something I feel about her; she's so damn brave and full of guts. That's what makes her fine. She wouldn't sleep with Filipinos just because her pal wants her to. If she did, it would be because she wanted to, and for no other reason; not for money, not for a friend, not because she was scared, but because she wanted to sleep with a Filipino. I'm not that way. I'm too yellow

VAL LEWTON

and soft, but you could be, Rose, and you should be."

"Boloney!"

"Okay!"

They both laughed and Rose hooked her arm through Yvonne's as they walked back to the house.

The lights were out when they went into the apartment.

"Let's you and I go into the bathroom until the boys go," Yvonne suggested.

In the darkness of the two rooms, Rose could hear rustlings, whisperings and soft sighs, as she and Yvonne groped their way across to the bathroom door.

With the door shut behind them, Yvonne lit the light and sat on the edge of the bathtub. Rose perched herself on top of the laundry hamper and braced her feet against the toilet seat. Sitting this way, smoking, and taking an occasional sip from a highball which they passed back and forth, the two girls waited until the lights went on in the other rooms.

"I guess the boys are going. Let's go out and say goodnight," Yvonne suggested.

She strolled out and Rose followed her. Jim was at the door saying goodbye to Grace. Rose saw a bill pass from one hand to the other. Henry was putting on his dapper, snap-brim hat before the mirror, adjusting it as carefully as a woman fixes her hat before going out to keep an important engagement. Mildred was lying on the bed, face down, her head buried in the pillow. She did not stir until the two young Filipinos had left the apartment.

Then she jumped up, all smiles and chatter, holding a twenty dollar bill in her hand.

"Gee, Yvonne," she said, "I didn't mean to take him away from you. I just couldn't help myself - he was so nice. You shouldn't have left us alone."

"Oh, that's okay," Yvonne said, patting her arm. "I was so damn tired I was glad you liked him. Didn't I say that, Rosie?"

Rose acknowledged that this was a true fact.

"Gee, those Filipino boys are nice guys," Mildred said. "And look what he gave me. Twenty bucks!"

"Yeah," Grace informed her, "that's what the Filipino boys have to pay. They're just lousy unless they can fork over that much."

"You mean to say they always give the girls that much?"

"They got to."

Mildred looked astounded. She gazed down at the bill in her hand.

"Say!" she exclaimed. "I didn't realize a guy would pay that much money for so little fun - only a few minutes."

Grace and Yvonne rolled with laughter. This was funny. Rose smiled. Mildred was such a dumbbell.

"I'm dead tired," Yvonne said. "Let's go to bed. Rosie and I'll sleep on the couch and you two can sleep together in the bed."

They undressed. Then, all but Grace, they washed and brushed their teeth. Grace dispensed with such niceties of life. She was sound asleep when they came out of the bathroom.

Rose and Yvonne went to bed together on the couch, and Mildred sat down to finish a cigarette and talk to them before she turned in.

"That's an easy way to make a living," she said pensively.

"Some people think it is," Yvonne said.

"Well, don't you?"

"No, I don't think it's easy. It's hard."

"Why?"

"You'll find out. Don't you think we'd give up the dance hall and just do that if it were so easy? I tell you it's hard. You get punched around a lot and there's no money in it except with the

Filipino boys and they don't want just ordinary girls. They pick them out of the dance halls because they want to know they're getting the best. That's the way they figure it. If other men will pay to dance with the girls, they'll pay a lot more to love them. Get it?"

"Yeah. Couldn't I get a job at the dance hall?"

"There aren't any. We've too many now. Half the girls sit out almost every dance."

They were all thoughtful for a moment or so, Mildred smoking her cigarette with a preoccupied air. Then she said:

"How do you get into the other racket?"

"Stick around here. You'll get into it fast enough."

"Why don't you send her to Barbie?" Rose asked.

"That's not Barbie's racket. She's not pretty enough for what Barbie wants," Yvonne said bluntly.

Rose tried to soften the blow.

"She's got the nicest natural blonde hair I've ever seen."

"All the Polacks have that," Yvonne said and turned over to go to sleep. "Put out the light Mildred."

Mildred, pouting, put out the light and shuffled across the room to the alcove.

Rose, lying awake for a few moments, said to herself.

"This is no place for little Rosie. I've got to find some way out. I'm not the type for Filipino boys and twenty-dollar bills. It's too damn hot and dirty here. The hell with it! I'll have to find a place where they open the windows once in awhile."

She breathed in through her nostrils, trying to smell the air. It was hot and heavy with cigarette smoke and dust and face powder.

"The hell with it."

 ELEVEN

"You two are getting to be old regulars down here."

Kleinert, a cheap cigar in the corner of his mouth, stood looking down at Rose and Fanny Wise. They sat on the bench in his waiting room, the first girls in that day. At Rose's feet lay her little cardboard hatbox, the corners worn grey and ragged.

"Got to have someplace to go," Rose told him.

"I wish to God I had something for you," he said. "I guess both of you are pretty hard up."

Rose grinned.

"That's putting it mildly," Fanny told him.

He started toward the door of his office and then paused, turning around to face them again.

"Where are you living?" he asked, nodding at Rose.

"I was staying at a girlfriend's apartment, but the parties got too rough for me, so I picked out my own teddies from the general shuffle and made my graceful exit."

"You ain't got a place, eh?"

"That's right."

He nodded at Fanny.

"And you?"

"You want another hard-luck story? I should think you'd be tired of hearing them," Fanny said.

"I don't want to hear it; I want to help you."

Fanny nodded.

"I've just checked my bag at Grand Central. My father and I lived in the same apartment for fifteen years, but when we couldn't pay the rent for two months, they threw us out. I took my father yesterday to the home for old people on Welfare Island. I haven't got a place to go."

Kleinert sucked on his cigar for a moment.

"I've got a place for you girls to go."

Fanny moved forward eagerly. Rose sat still, a quizzical look in her eye.

"Listen," he began. "I know an apartment you can share with another girl until things get better. It isn't much of an apartment and the things in it are pretty bad, but you'll have a roof over your head. That's something these days."

"What's the catch?" Rose asked.

"No catch to it. This girl lives in my brother's apartment house. He owns a couple of apartments downtown. Her husband moved out on her about six months ago and left her with a little kid to take care of. She's been trying to find a job and can't. She used to be in a magazine office as a secretary to the editor. It's tough for her. She has to drag the kid around when she goes looking for a job. My brother is a kind-hearted slob and he lets her stay on, rent-free. I got an idea maybe you two could bunk in with her and take turns minding the baby while she looks for a job. How does it sound?"

Rose and Fanny looked at each other. Then Rose got up from the bench and threw her arms about Kleinert's thick neck. She kissed him on the cheek. There were tears of gratitude in her eyes when she said:

"Your brother isn't the only kind-hearted slob in the Kleinert family."

Fanny said:

"It's darn kind of you Mr. Kleinert."

"Good God, girls, don't begin crying. I'm just human, that's all. And I like you two. You're good kids. You don't make trouble around here like some of these dames do, yelling and carrying-on. Come on into the office and I'll give you the address. You can go right down now. There's no jobs today anyhow."

"That'll be great," Rose said.

An hour later, having walked to save carfare, they rang the doorbell of a little red-brick house in Perry Street. It was near the river and Italian children swarmed through the street, yelling and shouting as they played. A red-faced old woman with streaming grey hair and a breath redolent of whiskey and pipe tobacco opened the door.

"We'd like to see Mrs. Julia Bradley."

"Second floor - door to the right."

They went up and knocked. As they waited they could hear inside the patter of a child's feet running and the rumble of a wheeled toy being pulled across the floor.

"Like kids?" Rose asked Fanny.

"I don't know. I've never been around them."

"I'm crazy about them. I hope it's cute."

The door opened and a slim young woman with brown hair and an open, honest-looking face, let them into the apartment.

"If you've come to collect a bill -" she began.

Rose shook her head.

"No. Mr.Kleinert, the brother of your landlord, told us to come down and see if we couldn't make some arrangement with you to help mind the baby in exchange for a place to stay. We're both out of work."

Julia Bradley looked at them closely for a moment.

"Let me hear some more about it," she said.

Fanny explained to her that they could each take turns minding the baby during the day, leaving two girls free to look for a job while the other one stayed home. In this way each of them would have a rest from job-hunting every two days.

"That would be fine," Julia agreed. "I haven't any beds here except my own. The baby sleeps with me. But maybe we could get a large mattress and put it on the floor, or a couple of army cots."

"We'll manage somehow," Rose assured her.

"And what about your food? Have you any money at all?" Julia asked.

"A few cents. Not enough for two days' grub," Rose said. "But something's got to break. It always does."

"I know a place where you can get a good meal in return for an hour's work," Julia told them. "That's where the baby and I go to eat in the mornings, and in the evening we just don't eat. It's not so bad. Neither of us has lost any weight and the baby seems to thrive pretty well."

"Say, that sounds good," Fanny said.

But Rose had become suspicious from her experiences.

"What kind of work do they ask you to do for this grub?" she asked.

Julia smiled understandingly. She had evidently been through similar experiences. She was an attractive young woman.

"It's really charity," she said. "But they let you hemstitch towels for an hour before you eat in order to take the curse off the free meal. And it keeps the tramps away."

"I can't hemstitch," Fanny said in dismay.

"Oh, we can teach you how tonight," Rose said. "They taught

us to do it in public school up in Athol."

Julia moved into the back room.

"Come on and sit down and take your things off. You'd better meet Tommy and look around, as long as you're going to live here."

Rose looked around. There was no evidence of Tommy except a toy in the middle of the floor, a little red soldier on a wheeled platform. There was little furniture in the room and it looked bare. There were no rugs and no drapes at the windows. But it was clean and light, and a window was partially open - quite different from Grace's dirty, airless apartment with cigarette ashes, stubs and burnt matches strewn about everywhere.

"Tommy!" Julia called.

A door at the other end of the room opened cautiously and a little yellow head came into sight and then a pair of large blue eyes. Reassured by what he saw, Tommy came out into the open. He was a chubby child a little less than two years old, dressed neatly in a much-laundered blue romper.

"Say 'Hello,' Tommy, to the nice ladies," his mother urged.

Tommy dispensed with such formalities. Running across the floor, he embraced Fanny's knees, hugging them tightly, and looking up at her with a friendly smile.

Fanny, unused to children, was embarrassed and pleased at the same time.

She bent down and awkwardly patted his head with little, light pats, as if she was afraid he might break apart.

"You're a nice kid," she said.

Rose and Julia looked at each other and grinned.

Rose squatted down on her heels and opened her arms.

"Come here, Tommy. Come and see Aunt Rosie."

The little boy pattered over to her and she embraced him.

"How big is the baby?" she asked.

He gave the conventional response. Fanny was struck with wonder.

"Gee, he's smart," she said.

Rose and Julia had to laugh at this and the baby joined in with them.

"He can laugh, too!"

Tommy looked up at her. Now it was his turn to wonder.

"Tommy laugh," he told her.

"I haven't been around kids much, Tommy. But I guess I'll learn soon enough," Fanny told him.

Rose picked Tommy up in her arms. Julia opened the little door through which Tommy had come. It led into a tiny bathroom with a toilet and a washstand, but no tub.

"That's all there is," Julia explained. "Just this one room and a bathroom without a bath."

"It looks like home already," Rose told her.

She liked Julia and she could see that Fanny did, too. They would get along well. She was certain of that.

"We used to have a two-room apartment upstairs with a real bath when my husband was here, but since he's left, I've moved down here. Mr. Kleinert has been terribly good to me. On the first of the month when he comes to collect the rent from the other tenants he always brings down some groceries for me. Last time he brought a steak. I cooked it on that little gas ring on the window sill. It tasted so good. He and his wife have a little boy just a year older than Tommy. She sends his outgrown clothes for my little boy to wear."

Rose admired the calm, matter-of-fact way in which she had spoken of her husband's leaving her.

"These hooks on the back of the door are all I have by way of a closet. But hang your things up and make yourself at home."

Both girls took off their wraps and hung them up. Rose

stretched, grinned and picked Tommy up and hugged him.

"It's good to have a place to stay."

"It's like a safe harbor," Fanny added.

For the next month, the three girls lived together, taking turns to look for work and mind the baby. Rose and Fanny grew very attached to the little boy. He was a merry youngster and seemed well-satisfied with his few toys and his scanty meals. As a matter of fact, he had never known better. He was a "depression" child, born in 1929 just before the crash in Wall Street heralded the coming of lean years.

They learned in time that Julia's husband, a commercial artist, had been badly hit by the slump, and had not courage enough to face his responsibilities during bad times. He had left Julia a note, saying he could not stand to see his wife and child go hungry.

"He couldn't stand seeing us, but he doesn't mind knowing what we do," Julia used to say with a laugh.

It was a poor living that the three girls and the baby had in the Perry Street apartment, but not an unhappy one. They kept busy. During the day they looked for jobs, sewed for their dinners at the charity place on Bleecker Street, and spent the evenings reading the next morning's newspaper, a vital necessity to the job-hunter, and in making constant repairs to their wardrobe.

Stockings and cosmetics were their chief worry. Dresses could be washed, ironed and cleaned; felt hats could be steamed out over a tea kettle; shoe blacking was equally good on shoes and on shiny seams. But stockings and face powder had to be bought, and no matter how cheaply they could buy them - even at the five-and -ten-cent store - they always lacked cash.

Several times Rose, Fanny and Julia got temporary jobs. Once Rose worked for three whole days as a substitute for a reception clerk ill with influenza. Another time, Fanny worked as a shop girl for a few days. Julia was the most fortunate of all. She had a position of forty dollars for a whole week on the staff of one of the rowdy humour magazines which sprang up just before Christmas time - sprang up and then died away. The one for which Julia worked was the first to cease its rapid-fire of smut and wisecracks, but the week's salary worked wonders for her. She was able to buy a cheap coat to replace the thin spring coat she had been wearing and a warm sweater suit for Tommy. Not sure when she would get money again, Julia took the precaution to buy her baby a few toys for Christmas, although it was still a month away. She did not want him to miss his first real Christmas.

Although their meals were scanty, poor and irregular and the fact that there was no bathtub worked a real hardship on them, the three girls' morale was excellent. If any one of them complained, they had a set joke with which to squelch the girl who had found fault with things as they were.

"Apply at the central relief bureau," they would rattle off jokingly, "and be directed to the proper agency."

Organized charity had not worked very well so far as they were concerned. They preferred to rely upon themselves. It was better that way.

Their social life was restricted. They did not feel like going out. Once, when she had some money left from the temporary job as reception clerk, Rose treated herself to a cheap seat at a motion picture theatre. She felt guilty for several days afterwards.

Julia had no callers. The people with whom she had been friendly would have been glad to come and see her, but she steadfastly refused to allow former friends to witness her poverty. Rose went up to see Grace and Yvonne on occasion. Once she called on Mildred, who had taken a room in the same building as the dance hall hostesses, but found her busy entertaining a swarthy Turkish cigarette manufacturer who was promising her the moon and all the glories he could imagine if she would be kind. Rose left in time for her to be kind before the Turk grew too impatient. The cheap luxury in which she had found Mildred disgusted her, and she could forsee the girl's coming plight. For Mildred, never truly a pretty girl, was growing fat and ugly from idleness and dissipation. No matter how foolishly they lived, dancing kept Grace and Yvonne in good bodily condition. But Mildred was just letting herself go soft without a thought for the near future.

"She's got a steady boyfriend - a punk who is beginning to borrow money from her," Yvonne had informed Rose.

That, although Rose did not know it, meant the beginning of the end for Mildred. Yvonne knew it, but did not care. She had taken a dislike to the girl.

Beyond these infrequent visits to the apartment of the taxi-dancers, Rose had no social life.

Fanny, strangely enough, was the one who entertained most often. The stationer she had described to Rose as a claimant for her hand in marriage was almost a constant visitor. Although an insignificant little fellow with a black thread of moustache above thin lips, a hooked nose and a bald head, the girls welcomed him enthusiastically. He never came empty-handed. He always brought something to eat or drink or a toy for the baby. He was a kind person and utterly devoted to Fanny, whom he thought to be far above him - so intellectual and cultured!

Inevitably, his persistent courtship had a fitting end. One evening Rose came back to the apartment where Fanny had been minding the baby that day, and found her friend crying softly.

"Apply to the central agency -" Rose began.

But Fanny shook her head.

"It isn't that. It's because I'm leaving."

She held up her hand. A little band of white gold winked in the light.

"I've just married Yussel," she said.

Yussel was not the stationer's real name. His name was Gordon Berkowitz, but Fanny had nicknamed him "Yussel" because it seemed to suit him better.

"When?"

"We took Tommy downtown to the Municipal Building and got married this afternoon. Yussel is coming down tonight to take me home. He's got a flat over the stationery store."

"Gee! Best wishes. But I'm going to miss you something terrible."

"You and Julia have just got to come up and eat with us - often - as often as you can. I wouldn't have married him if it -"

She broke off and began to cry. Rose put her arms about Fanny's shoulders and comforted her.

"He's a sweet fellow - so damn kind," she said.

"I know - but I had such high hopes. I wanted to be somebody, to do things. And now, an apartment over a stationery store, and later an apartment in the Bronx! Thank God I've learned to like kids being around Tommy."

Fanny left that night. Rose and Julia had a good cry after they had wished the newly-married couple happiness and success. They felt, rather than realised, what a tragic disillusionment marriage was to Fanny.

Without her, the two girls had to take turn and turn about, one day looking for a job, the next day looking after Tommy. Life grew monotonous. Job-hunting can be as monotonous as a job, and an hundredfold more heartbreaking than the most heartbreaking of tasks.

Once, passing by the boarded-in excavations of Radio City, Rose saw a group of jobless men peering through the high boards at the men at work inside. It was not idle curiosity that held them there. Their faces showed hunger and greed, and it was not the greediness of men who watch other men eat or drink. They were hungry for things to do.

Rose peeked through a crack in the boards. Men were swarming all over the depth and breadth of the huge hole in the ground. Some were shoveling, others carrying boards, some nailing them into place, while others drove tractors and manipulated steam shovels. The street vibrated with the roar of motors and echoed with the shouts of men at work. For the first time, Rose was conscious of the joy that there is in work. In the hungry faces of the men who stood outside looking in, she could see the need of this joy, and she could remember what pleasure she had taken herself in turning out letter-perfect copy and perfect carbons. She had never realized that this had been so keen a pleasure.

She tried desperately hard to get a job that afternoon, fairly running from one place to another, always with the same result - nothing. Job-hunting had become a gamble with the odds a thousand to one against the hunter. Yet one kept trying, because to cease meant an immediate plunge into the ranks of the outcasts, the loafers, the bums, the prostitutes. One could approach that borderline safely only so long as one kept looking for a job. The moment the job-hunt stopped, that moment did one's feet slip on the verge of the abyss.

Rose saw all about her the people who had fallen. One evening, hungry from the long afternoon spent in the open air, going from place to place, Rose passed a Salvation Army soup line for men and women. The smell of the hot soup was so good she could not resist the temptation to get into line for a bowl.

It seemed easy enough. She took her place behind a slatternly old woman reeking of liquor and cheap perfume, obviously a former street-walker, grown too old to practise her profession. A seedy-looking man in a torn overcoat fell in behind Rose. The line went forward slowly. Rose felt the man behind her push against her. She thought it an accident, and did not even trouble to turn around. A moment later he did it again, and then she felt his hand on her waist.

"Lay off!" she said, pushing him away.

Hardly had she turned around than he rubbed his knee against the back of her knee. She whirled and slapped him.

"Lay off! You heard me."

The man laughed.

"Say, kid, I've been panhandling all day. Been lucky too. Want to come to my room?" he said pulling a roll of money from his pocket and singling out a five dollar bill to dangle before her eyes.

Rose gave him a shove and stepped out of line.

"You bum!" she said. "Why don't you buy grub instead of trying to buy women?"

She walked away, hunger forgotten in the warmth of her anger.

That night she had to count sheep before she could sleep. It was hard to fall asleep on an empty stomach. Nor was the bed over-comfortable, a second-hand army cot with no mattress. The sheets had not been washed in three weeks. They could not afford to send them out, and had no space to wash them in the tiny apartment. A rolled-up skirt served as her pillow and, for want of blankets, Rose spread thick layers of old newspapers over the top sheet to keep her warm. These, and the clothes she took off at night, were her only coverings.

"Damn that panhandling bum," she muttered drowsily as she dropped off to sleep.

TWELVE

Julia was minding the baby, and Rose, having spent all morning on the job-hunt, decided to call it a day and visit Grace and Yvonne. She got to their apartment just as they were coming out.

"Come with us," Yvonne said. "We're going down to see Barbie."

"All right."

Barbie lived on Sixth Avenue between Forty-fourth Street and Forty-fifth. They took the elevated down to Forty-second Street and walked back. It was an old, dirty building with narrow stairs that led past the entrance to a hardware store on the first floor and a Japanese restaurant on the second, then up again into a narrow hallway separated from the stairwell by a carved railing. The place smelled old - a combined odor of mice, dirt and moldy wallpaper. It was on this third floor that Barbie had her apartment.

Without bothering to knock, Grace pushed open the door and they went in. Rose had never seen such a place. In better days, this apartment had been the two master bedrooms of the house.

They traversed the entire depth of the building, joined together by a narrow passageway in which were wooden cupboards, formerly used for linen, and now made over into a kitchenette. There was a bathroom adjoining the room in back. In the front room two windows looked over the "El" tracks. As they came in, a train went by and it was impossible to talk for the noise of the coaches crashing past the closed window.

This gave Rose additional opportunity to look around. It was a strange room. There were heavy, dusty velvet drapes at the windows. Against the wall opposite the door stood two couches, end to end, covered with more lengths of dusty, faded velvet. Above these, on the wall, hung a fake Turkish shield with crossed scimitars, spearheads and a Persian helmet. The dust was so thick on them they looked antique. In fact, they had appeared on musical comedy stages only ten years before.

In another part of the room there was a large, expensive radio-phonograph combination which seemed out of place amid the general dinginess and disorder. The other furniture consisted of an over-stuffed chair with a dirty grey linen slip cover, several straight-backed chairs and a great many leather cushions on the floor. There was no table, but a wide shelf along the wall near the entrance door held bottles, glasses, ashtrays and other paraphernalia for impromptu parties. Above this shelf was a large crayon drawing in a natural wood frame. Rose thought it ugly. It was a Matisse original. It showed a stout, nude woman squatting on her hams, nursing the abundance of her own breasts. On the wall beneath it, some wag had scrawled in pencil:

"*Headlights. Chrysler Imperial, 1931.*"

Another hand had added:

"*Don't drown those puppies, lady!*"

There was a shouting of hello as the three girls came into

the apartment. Barbie had visitors, two young women and four boys. Two of the boys seemed to Rose very effeminate. The other two were surly-looking individuals she later learned were just ordinary young men recovering from a hangover. Of the two girls, one was pretty and the other a homely person whom Rose took at first glance for a man, until she noticed the short skirt under the masculine jacket. Her face was as hard as a man's and her hair close cut. Collar, tie and jacket were the products of a men's shop. Rose gaped at her. Once or twice she had seen women who dressed that way on the street or at Harry's in the Village, but this was the first time she had ever met one.

Barbie, in the same green silk slip she had worn when Rose first met her, was seated in the middle of the double couch. The masculine young woman sat on the floor at her feet and was rubbing her naked ankles. The other girl sat on the edge of the big couch facing Barbie, and the four young men were walking about the room.

Barbie made no attempt to introduce the new arrivals, but motioned Rose to a seat beside her on the couch.

"I've often thought of you," she said when Rose sat down.

Rose, looking at her as she spoke, felt she had never seen an uglier pair of eyes, and yet the glance and the voice were kind. Barbie's eyes, indeterminate blue, were flecked with little brown specks, and their shape was bad. Otherwise, if she took better care of herself, Rose decided on this second meeting, Barbie would not be a bad-looking girl. She had a strong, solid frame, big, soft, white hands, nice shoulders, natural blonde hair that was inclined to be stringy and always looked as if it needed washing, although Rose later found out that personal cleanliness was one of Barbie's few rules of conduct, and that she stuck to it religiously. Barbie's face looked as if it had once been pretty, but it was now too pallid and soft for true beauty.

"Have you got a job yet?" she asked Rose.

"No."

"How're you making out?"

Rose described her life with Julia.

"That's not so tough. You don't look any the worse for wear. But if things get worse, you look me up, Rose."

"I will."

Barbie turned to one of the effeminate young men, a tall, blonde youth with hair that kept falling into his eyes.

"Van," she asked, "what do you think of this girl?"

The young man, whose full name was Leonard Van Wyck, inspected Rose as casually as he would a tie he was thinking of purchasing.

"She'd go great as a nun," he finally said.

Barbie laughed.

"You've got the grandest ideas, Van," she applauded.

"Oh, don't credit me with that one," he protested. "That's from the *moyen âge*. The heroes and heroines of all their smutty stories were always priests, monks and nuns. There's something in human nature that is tickled by the sight of ascetics going through bawdy and dissolute gestures."

Rose looked from one to the other, puzzled.

"Well, if Rose here ever gets badly strapped, she'll join us," Barbie said, and then changed the subject before Rose could ask any questions.

"How is it that you're not living with Grace and Yvonne?" she asked.

Rose made a grimace.

"I like fresh air too well."

Barbie smiled.

"I know what you mean. I don't blame you. Mary, be a good child and open the window."

The pretty girl, who had sat silent ever since Rose came in, got up and opened the window. A flood of sound came in from the busy avenue below.

Van Wyck inclined his head.

"Listen," he ordered loudly.

Everyone listened intently. There was nothing to be heard but the rumble of traffic and the tearing sound of the "El" as it rounded the turn some blocks further uptown. Rose looked at Van Wyck in bewilderment. She tried again. Nothing but the usual sounds, only now a traffic officer's whistle was shrilling through the din. It couldn't have been that, for Van Wyck still bent his head in an attempt to hear something.

"Listen," he said again.

Above the sound of the traffic came a faint cry:

"Chestnuts. Red hot! Red hot!"

"Hear it?" Van Wyck asked. "The peddler's call? Hear it!"

They all nodded.

"A new note in the symphony of the machine age - a note that slides back to the cry of the first merchant. That's the depression for you, it brings back all the individual efforts of man. Look at the streets. They were drab; they are colorful. On every corner an apple vendor, a man selling trinkets or candy and *halvah* . We're returning to the old-time standard of individual effort. Look at the success magazines, they all run stories on how this man or that woman conquered her personal depression by getting out and doing something unusual. I read about one man who built up a toy business by carving out playthings from waste lumber he found in a factory yard. Initiative! Courage! Personal endeavour! That's what the depression has brought. Long live the depression!"

"Aw, nerts," said Rose. "Try going hungry for a day."

"But that's just it. We *should* go hungry. We should fast to humble our pride. Let the seven lean years come that shall blast our pride in machinery. Let us go back to the simple ages of dirt and lechery and handiwork, for in these men and women find joy and expression."

"Aw nerts!" Rose reiterated.

"Don't mind him," Barbie said to Rose. "He's a poet."

Van Wyck ambled away, his long hair, like the hair of an English sheepdog, falling into his eyes; crossing to the wide shelf which served as a sideboard, he began mixing drinks.

"I thought he was some sort of nut," Rose commented.

"He is. We all are. That's the only fun in life. Be nutty and enjoy yourself. Then you can look down on all the people who work hard and succeed. The nuttier you are, the more superior you feel. Try it, Rose, it's a good cure for the depression blues."

The masculine woman, who still sat on the floor in front of Barbie massaging her ankles, laughed.

"It's good advice, Barbie, but what about Mary? You don't let her be nutty."

Barbie looked over at the young girl, and Rose saw her ugly eyes grow soft and sweet.

"Mary," she said, "is one of the poor people who have to work damned hard and succeed. That's her curse. I have damned her to that particular hell."

"Who is Mary?" Rose asked.

"My sister," Barbie told her and added in a whisper. "Never say anything dirty or off color when she's around. She's still a good girl, and she's going to stay that way."

She turned to the masculine woman at her feet.

"I hope you heard what I said, Jean."

"I did," the woman laughed. "But I didn't need to hear. My stomach still hurts where you punched it Saturday night."

"You deserved it. Keep your hands off her."

After a little while Mary, who had been standing by the window ever since she had opened it, looking out, turned into the room.

"I'd better go for my lesson," she said.

Barbie looked at an old alarm clock on the wide shelf.

"You hurry. I don't want you to keep Miss Rada waiting."

Mary put on a smart but modest-looking coat and hat, picked up a brown antelope handbag and left the apartment, waving a goodbye from the doorway.

Van Wyck, who had finished mixing the drinks and was now pouring them, looked around.

"Let's talk smut. Mary's gone."

Barbie laughed.

"Am I that bad?" she asked.

Then she turned to Rose.

"Mary's all I've got. We were poor when we were kids in Pennsylvania and I've had a tough time. Mary's the youngest and I don't want her to go through the things I've had to go through, and am going through now. I want her to be fixed pretty - a decent person. There's only a few ways for a poor girl to get that way. One of them is the stage. I'm having Mary trained as a dancer. Miss Rada says she's very good."

Van Wyck passed the drinks and the party grew livelier. Someone turned on the radio, tuning in a jazz program.

Later in the afternoon two more people came in, a young newspaperman who sat around with his overcoat and hat on and perspired freely, and a pale young woman in a voluminous black coat and a Spanish gown who informed Rose within a very short while that she was the greatest living woman novelist, but took care to point out that her works had not yet been published, because they were too advanced, and also that she was a neurotic, that all her family were neurotics, and that she took morphine in mild doses.

Rose understood only half of what the girl said, but even that she labelled "hooey."

Shortly afterward another couple came in wearing evening dress, a fair, stout girl and a tall, splendid-looking man. Barbie told Rose the girl was a concert performer and had been judged the best harpist in the world. She was Viennese and spoke with an accent that the thin, pale girl who had described herself as a neurotic found charming, and Rose thought was funny. This couple had brought four bottles of champagne with them and a dozen sandwiches from a nearby delicatessen.

Rose had never tasted champagne before. She found that she liked it and had three glasses.

"Say, Grace," she asked, when she found herself for a moment with her friend, "does this party go on every day?"

"Day and night," Grace told her. "It never stops. Barbie never buys food or liquor. If you happen to have dough she expects you to bring something up with you. If you haven't any money just bring yourself."

"I guess she gets tired of it every once in awhile," Rose ventured.

"She never seems to get tired of it. She told me one day it was her ambition to get drunk by six o'clock every night of the year. I guess she just about does."

At seven, Yvonne and Grace had to leave and go to work. Barbie urged Rose to stay, but Rose felt she should leave with her friends.

"You've got time on you hands," Barbie said at the door, "you ought to come up here more often."

"You'll see me. I'll camp on your doorstep," Rose answered. "This is the first party I've been to in months."

Rose walked with Grace and Yvonne to the subway and then

continued down Broadway by herself. She planned to walk as far as she could before taking a streetcar. It was a nice night and what with the two cocktails, the sandwiches and the three glasses of champagne, she felt in splendid fettle.

At Thirty-eighth Street, crossing from one curb to another, and for safety's sake keeping her eye on a taxi cab coming down the side street, Rose bumped into someone and almost lost her balance.

"Trim ship," a pleasant masculine voice said in her ear as a firm hand at her elbow steadied her.

She looked up. A nice-looking young man with a clear, ruddy complexion had hold of her arm and was politely doffing his derby hat with his other hand.

"Are you all right?"

"Thanks, I'm okay."

She looked up at the man again. He was young and attractive. She felt she would like to have him walk along with her on this glorious night when she was feeling so splendid. He evidently had the same thought.

She liked the masculine timidity with which he said:

"You won't think I'm fresh, I hope. I'm a stranger in this port and I'd like to have company."

She smiled.

"So would I," she answered quite simply.

"My lord! In all my life I've never had a girl come right out and tell me a thing like that straight-off."

He seemed well pleased by the surprise.

"What do you want to do?" Rose asked.

"Have a good time. I'm a second mate on the freighter, *China Lass*. We're docked over in Hoboken. I haven't been home in the States for two years, and I'm just itching to see the sights with a nice girl."

"Want to go up and see New York from the Empire State Building?"

"No. I don't mean those kind of sights. I mean a good dinner, a show -"

He broke off.

"- that's all I mean."

It was so transparent, Rose could not help but smile. She had been excited by the cocktails and the champagne and the scores of dirty jokes she had heard at Barbie's. She felt she could fill in enjoyably the gap after the show.

The man noticed her smile and said:

"You're on?"

"Let's go!"

He hooked his arm through hers and they went off together.

Sid Nelson was his name and his home town was Tulsa, Oklahoma. He had read sea stories when he was a boy and had always dreamed of the sea, even though he had never seen any body of water much larger than a bed sheet. He had trained for his profession at the Coast Guard Academy and after two years' service as a watch officer in the Coast Guard had been dishonorably discharged for accepting bribes. He had then taken out a mate's license and gone to sea. Sid told her all this as they walked to an Italian restaurant in the thirties where he remembered one could get good wine with one's dinner.

They had supper together, drank the wine which was provided with the meal and then ordered a bottle of Burgundy. They sat, talking and drinking, until it was much too late to go to a theatre.

Rose liked Sid. He seemed a very decent fellow, and she had had nothing to do with boys since she had thrown Bill Taggart out of her room in Mrs. Feinberg's rooming house.

Without either of them speaking about it, Rose knew that

when they left the restaurant she was going to let Sid take her to a hotel. She hoped Julia would not worry about her being gone all night.

When the bottle of Burgundy was finished, Sid called for the bill. The waiter who brought it also brought two small glasses of anisette.

"On the house," he explained.

As they drank the liqueur, Sid took Rose's hand under the tablecloth and pressed it. She squeezed his hand in turn. They smiled into each other's eyes.

On the sidewalk outside the restaurant, Sid asked:

"Where do you live?"

"I live with a girlfriend."

"That's too bad. I thought I'd come down and visit for a while."

"Where do you live?"

"I'm going to bunk at a hotel."

They faced each other awkwardly a moment. Then Rose said:

"I'll come and visit with you."

"Swell! I saw a hotel on our way over here."

She remembered the place, one of the smaller side-street hotels, where no baggage is required and no questions are asked. They walked to the hotel and went in. Rose stood nervously by while Sid signed the register. A bellboy showed them to their room and, after pocketing the tip Sid gave him, turned at the door to ask if they wanted any ginger ale.

"I've nothing to go with it," Sid told him.

"I can get you anything you want."

"Never mind."

Closing the door behind the bellhop, Sid turned and took Rose in his arms. As Rose kissed him, she rubbed her cheek against the collar of his tweed coat. It was rough and masculine to the touch. There was something of the same quality in the boy himself.

She broke away from his embrace to inspect the room. She found a Gideon Society Bible on the night table. Some previous occupant had scrawled girls' telephone numbers on the flyleaf. She looked into the bureau drawers and turned the light on and off. Rose had only stayed at a hotel once before, when she was a little girl and her mother had taken her on a visit to an aunt in the west. They stopped overnight in New York and put up at a cheap hotel.

As she looked around, Sid took off his overcoat and hung it up.

"It's a nice room," Rose commented.

"Yes. It's a room with a bath."

"A bath? Where?"

He pointed to the door.

She went in and turned on the hot water. The bathroom was warm and clean. Hot water came streaming from the tap. The last bath Rose had taken was at Julia's apartment, standing on a towel and dripping water over herself from a teacup with a broken handle. The big, glistening white tub and the steaming hot water was a temptation.

"I'm going to take a bath," she told Sid.

"Aw, no! What for?"

"It's such a nice bathroom and the water is so nice and hot."

"I'll scrub your back for you," he told her, laughing.

"All right. I'll call you when I'm ready."

She closed the door and undressed as the tub filled. Then, testing the temperature first with her hand, she let herself sink gently into the warm water. She sighed with contentment.

She steeped herself, then soaped and rinsed off the soap

with a washcloth. As she tried to get around to her back with the cloth, she remembered what Sid had said. He might as well see her now as later.

"Sid," she called softly.

He opened the door a crack and put his head into the bathroom.

"Swab the decks, sailor," she said in what she thought was a very nautical voice.

Grinning, a little embarrassed, he came into the bathroom. He was in his underwear and socks. Rose noticed he had chunky, muscular shoulders. She handed him the soap and washcloth.

"Do a good job."

He scrubbed her back thoroughly, ending the operation with a kiss on the back of her neck. She twisted around so that he could kiss her mouth.

Then, evidently feeling he might offend her modesty if he stayed while she got out of the tub, Sid went into the other room, calling out as he closed the door behind him:

"Hurry up!"

She climbed out and dried herself, and then went into the bedroom, draping a towel around her. He was already in bed. Rose climbed in beside him. The sheets, clean and cool, felt delicious. Sid flung a heavy arm about her and drew her close to him.

After the brief flurry of their love-making was over, Rose stretched out luxuriously. The soft bed and the clean, well-ironed sheets were so different from her rude sleeping accommodations at Julia's that it seemed to her she enjoyed the bath and the good bed much more than she had Sid's hurried and inexpert love-making.

Falling asleep, she determined that she would take periodic vacations from the depression by going out for a night like this with Sid every once in awhile. And if not with him, then with some other man, so long as he was as handsome and attractive.

She slept marvelously well and felt gay and rested when she woke in the morning. She had breakfast with Sid and then he hurried away to Hoboken to take over his shore watch, while she went back to the apartment to mind Tommy.

THIRTEEN

The memory of that sweet sleep in a clean bed remained with Rose all the following week. She could never climb into her creaking canvas cot without thinking back to the bed she had shared with Sid Nelson. Clean sheets became almost an obsession with her. She even tried to wash the sheets of her cot in the washbasin and dry them on the fire escape. She picked a freezing cold day for the operation and her wet sheets froze hard when she put them out to dry. That night she had to sleep in her clothes on the bare canvas.

The night following this experience she let a man pick her up on the way home. He was a salesman from Ridgewood, New Jersey, and insisted upon taking her to an expensive restaurant for supper, where she felt keenly embarrassed at her poor clothing, and from there to orchestra seats at the *Vanities* before he took her to a hotel. He was not so handsome nor so attractive as Sid had been, but Rose was so tired and sleepy after the heavy meal she had eaten and the close, warm atmosphere of the theatre, that she almost fell asleep in his arms.

In the morning, as she was getting dressed, the salesman

took a sample gown from his case and gave it to her, telling her to throw her old one away. It was a good blue woolen dress and Rose was deeply grateful. With a new dress she felt almost as if she were a different person. It gave her fresh hope. With a bit of luck she could get temporary work and earn enough money to buy a new hat, new stockings, new shoes and new gloves. Smartly dressed again, she felt sure, she could get a permanent job. She was so tired of the depression. Her joblessness irked her. Going into offices to apply for a position and hearing the clatter of other girls' typewriters, she was seized sometimes with a terrible, consuming envy.

The opportunity to get money for hat, shoes and other accessories came a few nights later. She had gone to Barbie's and sat around talking with her all afternoon to get out of the cold, and then, Barbie having an engagement, she left to walk home. It was only a few days before Christmas and the weather had turned bitter. Her every bone ached with chill by the time she had gotten as far south as Thirty-fourth Street. To warm herself she went into Pennsylvania Station and sat down in the waiting room.

Turning to look at a train announcer who was calling off the trains in a deep bass voice, Rose knocked her handbag off the bench on which she sat. It opened as it fell, sending the few odds and ends she carried in it scattering across the floor.

A middle-aged man in a well-brushed black overcoat and bowler hat helped her pick up her things, then groped under the bench for a nickel that had rolled there. His face was red from exertion when he straightened up and handed her the coin.

"Thanks," Rose said. "It so happens that that's my last nickel. I'd be out of luck if I lost it."

The man seemed gravely concerned.

"Your last nickel? Have you a family? Have you a job?"

He seemed so kindly and sympathetic that Rose answered frankly.

"It is terrible," he said, "that a wealthy nation like this should let its workers practically starve."

"Oh, I guess it isn't the country's fault. It's just one of those things," Rose told him. "It just happens. Good Lord, I'd never even heard of a depression until this one came along and socked me on the nose."

"My dear, you're not the only one who had never heard of a depression before. I, too, am one of the unfortunates. Since the present economic crisis set in I have lost everything I owned."

"Gee, that's tough," Rose said.

It wasn't so easy for a man when he got that old to lose all his dough. She felt very sorry for him.

"Well, as one victim of the depression to another, my dear, would you allow me to take you to supper? It would cheer me no end to sup with a pretty young woman."

Rose felt flattered. He did seem such a nice man, so distinguished and refined.

"I'd love to go," she said, trying to force her natural voice to be soft and take on what her mother always described as a "genteel tone."

The man in the black overcoat gave Rose his arm and they walked from the station. He hailed a taxi on the street and ordered the driver to take them to a small restaurant Rose had never heard of before.

They had an excellent meal and her new friend, who had introduced himself as John Brown, was very entertaining, telling her thrilling stories of a trip to Paris and describing the country place he had been forced to sell.

"Gee, I bet you hated to lose it," Rose commented.

"My dear, it broke my heart to part with the old homestead.

I'd had it ten years, and many a jolly party we'd staged there."

"I've never owned very much," Rose said, "but I can imagine how hard it is to lose all that."

When they had finished supper, the waiter came with the bill. Rose did not notice that Mr. Brown paid it with a twenty dollar bill and got back only a few ones in change. To Rose, small restaurants were cheap restaurants; she could not imagine that this little, unpretentious place was one of the most expensive restaurants in the city.

They sat and talked for a moment more after he had paid his check. He told her about his apartment and she commiserated with him when he said he would have to find cheaper quarters.

"I'd like you to come up and see my apartment. You'll probably be one of the last persons to see it before I have to leave it and sell most of my furniture. I have some very pretty things you might like to look at, etchings and things of that sort, you know."

Rose was genuinely interested. She welcomed this opportunity to see the apartment that he was soon to lose. She thought he must feel about it in somewhat the same way she had felt when she was forced to leave Mrs. Feinberg's house.

They took another cab to get to his apartment. It was in a small, but well-kept little house on Beekman Place. To Rose, Beekman Place meant nothing. Only Park Avenue and Fifth Avenue were expensive places to live according to her notions about monied people. The apartment proved to be attractive and charmingly decorated. Mr. Brown showed her about, gave her a cocktail and let her sink down into a big, soft easy chair by a glowing coal fire.

"Say, it's a shame you've got to leave this place," Rose said.

"Isn't it though," he said, looking about as if it hurt even to think of leaving. "But let me show you some of the things I told you about. Are you easily shocked?"

Rose grinned.

"I've seen a lot," she said.

"Here is something you've never seen before," he said, and crossed the room and took up a leather-bound book.

He brought this back and opened it to the ornamental frontispiece. Rose looked down. It just looked like an old-fashioned decoration to her.

"This is a little-known book," he told her, "but it may interest you. It was drawn and compiled in the eighteenth century."

"That's a long time ago," Rose commented. "Just about Washington's time, huh?"

"That's right. The book is called *Aretin's Postures*. Look through it. I dare say you've never seen anything like it before."

Rose dutifully turned the page. What she saw made her burst out laughing. It was a steel engraving of a man and woman in close and curious embrace, an impossible posture for any human being with normal joints.

Mr. Brown was surprised at Rose's reaction.

"Does it only amuse you?" he asked. He had thought the lewd picture might arouse her desires and make her curious.

"I think it's funny."

She turned another page. There was another drawing, equally amusing to her. She turned page after page and every drawing made her laugh. This was not at all the effect that either M. Aretin or Mr. Brown had in mind when the one drew the pictures and the other presented the book.

"I didn't know they had books like this," Rose commented.

"There are many books like this."

"Got any more? I think they're terribly funny."

He brought out a book of photographs on the same order.

These disgusted her and she only looked at one or two, while Mr. Brown shook up a cocktail and turned on the phonograph.

Rose looked up from the pictures and watched him make his preparations. He wanted a party. Well, it might cheer him up. She, too, would have liked someone to be gay and happy with when she had lost her little room.

The phonograph blared out:

"Time on my hands, you in my arms

Nothing but love in view -"

Rose got up out of the armchair, put down the books that had been in her lap, and made a few dancing steps, snapping her fingers.

"That's what I like to see," said Mr. Brown. "'On with the dance, let joy be unconfined.'"

Rose danced up to him and he took her in his arms. They danced around the room. He danced very rigidly, in an old-fashioned manner that amused Rose, and she kept calling out:

"Come on - put some pep in it. Get hot! Get hot!"

"My dear child, I'm all out of breath. Shall we sit this one out?"

"Let's."

They sat down on the couch together and he opened the book of photographs and began showing her various pictures, pointing to them and asking:

"Ever done that?"

Each time she shook her head and laughed.

Mr. Brown was enjoying himself and Rose was glad. She felt that a man down on his luck should have a little amusement to take his worries from his mind.

At about one o'clock Mr. Brown suggested that she stay all night in view of the fact that it was so late and that he was too tired to see her home and, as a gentleman, he could not allow her to go home alone. Rose looked around the apartment. The bed would be warm and comfortable.

"Okay," she said.

He let her go to bed alone in a little guest room. She was just dropping off, thinking what a darling old boy he was, when he came in. When he left her she wondered why men past middle-age fool themselves by thinking they can still enjoy the pleasures of youth.

In the morning, Rose, who was used to waking with an alarm clock, overslept. It was nine o'clock when she woke up. A Negro maid, in dust cap and apron, had opened the door and was looking into the room.

"Hello, miss," she said quite casually, as if she were not at all surprised to find a young woman in the apartment.

"What time is it?" Rose asked.

The cleaning woman told her.

"Gee, I'd better get going."

She got up and dressed as the woman swept and dusted.

"Look under your pillow, Miss," she advised.

Rose looked and found two neatly folded twenty dollar bills.

"Whose are these?" she asked.

"Yours, of course."

"Say, who is this guy Brown?"

"Mr. Brown? Mr. Brown is a very rich man."

"He told me he was broke."

"No. He ain't broke. He lost a million on the market, but he's got three million more."

Rose felt herself flushing with anger. She felt like throwing the forty dollars into the waste basket, but thought better of it. With a sweeping blow of her handbag, she knocked a Sevres vase from the mantelpiece to the floor, where it smashed into pieces.

"I hope to hell that cost a lot of money," she said. "The dirty liar. I'd have had nothing to do with the rat if I had known he had money. I thought he was bust and feeling bad."

"But, Miss -"

Rose was already out of the room and on her way to the door of the apartment.

FOURTEEN

Julia was crying when Rose got home.

"What's happened?" Rose asked.

"We'll have to break up."

"But why?"

"Mr. Kleinert has found another tenant and I found something that looks like a job. We have to try to get out by tonight."

"Oh, that's all right, don't cry, Julia. We'll find something to tide us over. Where's Tommy?"

Julia began to sob anew.

"Where's the kid?" Rose asked again.

"I've had to board him out."

"What do you mean?"

Julia was crying so hard she could not answer. She was almost hysterical. Rose brought her a glass of water, then a washcloth for her tear-streaked face, and waited to hear the story.

It developed that the day before she had found a job. A religious fanatic wanted a secretary. He was writing a history of Josephus, the Jewish historian, a long-winded refutation of the known fact that Josephus was a traitor to his people.

The man wanted to prove that he was a benefactor because he had founded a school of Jewish learning after the walls of Jerusalem, through his treachery, had been torn down. It was a silly theory and the man, a retired furrier, was a silly man. He had offered Julia five dollars a week and board and lodgings in his apartment, where he lived with his wife and four grown children, in return for her work as typist and editor. His chief demand was that she "look into his soul."

Julia had planned to take the baby with her, but her new employer would not hear of it and she had thought to leave him at the apartment with Rose. Then Kleinert had told her that she would have to move. She had found a place where she could leave Tommy for five dollars a week. The job would just keep both of them alive, and no more. But even that was something.

"Well," said Rose. "I think I'll take a vacation from the depression. I'll run home to Athol for Christmas."

With the money she had gotten from Mr. Brown, Rose bought herself a pair of cheap, serviceable shoes, a new hat to go with the new dress the salesman had given her, and paid a tailor five dollars to interline her old winter overcoat with shoddy. Then she bought a handbag as a Christmas present for her mother. She packed her purchases and, in her old clothes, carrying her hatbox and a bundle, took the subway as far as it would go and walked over to the Post Road. She had completed the first stage of her trip to Athol.

From here, she traveled by rule of thumb. Three trucks, two salesmen and four young men with nothing else to do provided her with transportation home.

She found things in a sad state. Her father's little shoe store was about to go into receivership, and there was no hope in sight. The largest mill in town was about to close up and move away to Carolina and non-union labor. This would impoverish a large proportion of Athol's workers and what little chance there might have been for Mr. Mahoney's little business. This, however, was not the worst.

To help pay the rent of their little house, the Mahoneys had been forced to take in a boarder, a milkman, who believed that one of the prerogatives of a paying guest was the privilege of sleeping with the mistress of the house.

As Rose's father was away during the daytime, and the milkman home, he had taken advantage of the situation to seduce Rose's mother, a fat, slatternly woman with a weak will. Mrs. Mahoney lived in dread of her boarder, and yet could not seem to say no. This was the first time in twenty-five years of unhappily married life that she had been unfaithful, and the whole situation was too much for her. Whenever she could, she ran off to the corner grocery, operated by her crony, Mrs. Wichnefsky, to drink the liquor she peddled. Most of the time Mrs. Mahoney went about the house drunk and weeping, except when she suffered the milkman's embraces. Then Rose could hear her gusty sighing and passionate ejaculations even through the closed door.

Rose's brother, Tim, had also been hurt by the depression. In 1928 he had been expelled from the police force for accepting bribes from speeders. Since then he had worked as a brush salesman and his Irish good looks and quick tongue had won him a ready following of housewives. Brushes went best when he supplied bed service as well. But now that so many men were out of work and staying home, Tim's activities were greatly curtailed. He hung about the house all day, grumbling and cursing his bad luck.

The Mahoneys had a dreary Christmas. The handbag Rose had purchased for her mother was the only present. There was no tree, no holly, none of the traditional cheer and good will.

Mr. Mahoney spent the day itself at the dining room table, scribbling figures on scraps of paper, trying to find some way to save his business from bankruptcy. At five o'clock he gave up the task, and, crying, went off to bed. It was the first time Rose had ever seen him cry.

The day after Christmas, Rose decided that her vacation from the depression was over. It was too dreary and terrible at home. On Christmas Day, her mother being occupied with dinner, the amorous boarder had tried to put his arms about her as she passed him in the hallway.

"The hell with it!" said Rose. Packing her bag, she started to hitch back to New York. "The new year might offer better luck."

She had good luck. A big moving van picked her up just outside of Springfield and took her all the way to New Rochelle, where she was lucky again. She had hardly gotten out of the truck than a kindly-looking man in a small coupe stopped and offered to take her into New York.

He was a talkative fellow and, breezing along, told her all about himself. He was a clock salesman and, although business was poor, he still made enough to keep his wife and child in comfort. He showed her a picture of the child. It was a pretty youngster and Rose told him all about little Tommy, and how she had tended him in the days when Julia went job-hunting.

"Have you got a place to live now?"

"No."

"That's tough."

He was silent a while, a great contrast to his former verbosity. Rose watched the traffic on the Post Road. Then he said:

"Are you a good girl?"

She looked at him. He didn't seem the type that would play around with girls. She wondered why he asked.

"I'm no better than most," she said, "and I'm no worse."

"Good," he said. "I've been trying to think up something for you, to help you out. In the office there's a bunch of young fellows who make pretty good salaries. Some of them have apartments of their own. You're a pretty girl, and I was wondering if maybe you couldn't move in with one of them. Most of them are darned nice fellows."

"Say, that is a funny proposition."

"Yeah, I know it's a funny proposition. But it's one way out, and a sight better than the streets or the breadline. I know, I was bust in St. Louis once. They're nice fellows, like I said, and you'd practically be a wife to one of them if you did that. It wouldn't be a fly-by-night affair. I imagine any chap you went with would want to keep you for good. Maybe marry you."

Rose thought it over. It was a funny proposition. Yet there was a certain amount of sense to it. She could be assured of a bed at any rate.

"Okay." she said.

He drove downtown on Fifth Avenue as far as Forty-fifth Street and then turned west. In the middle of the block between Fifth and Sixth Avenues he parked his car. Pointing to a window on the second floor of the building opposite, he said to Rose:

"See that window, the Hammond Clock Company?"

Rose looked up. The Hammond Clock Company firm name was lettered in gold on the plate windows.

"You stay right here in the car," the salesman said to her, "and I'll go up and talk to the boys. I'm sure one of them will like the idea. You just wait here."

Rose waited nervously. From the corner of her eye she could see a group of men, most of them young and clean looking, office workers, come to one of the windows and look down on her. She sat still, hoping that the one who picked her would be young and handsome.

In a few moments the salesman came down and handed her a key.

"You go to this address," he said, giving her a slip of paper. "This is the key to Waldo Gardiner's apartment. A hell of a nice fellow! He's the assistant advertising manager, just a year out of Dartmouth and comes from down South somewhere - Florida, I think."

Rose climbed out of the car.

"Thanks," she said. "You're a hell of a good egg yourself. Maybe some girls wouldn't think so. Maybe they'd rather have money, or good advice or something. But you've fixed me up in the best way that either of us could think of just now."

"I was glad to do it," he said. "I hope you and Waldo hit it off."

Rose went to the address on the slip of paper, a walk-up apartment house on Lexington Avenue at Thirty-fourth Street. She found Gardiner's apartment. There was a neat card pasted on his door with his name on it.

Unlocking the door, she let herself in. It was a pleasant room with two great windows looking out onto a garden in back. There were comfortable chairs, a big studio bed, and an old-fashioned carved walnut desk with a typewriter on a movable stand. A big terrestrial globe, the varnish peeling off it, stood on the desk.

Rose walked around looking at the various pieces of furniture and at the pictures on the wall, trying to visualize the young man who lived here. She couldn't.

FIFTEEN

She took the cover off the typewriter in Waldo Gardiner's room. It was a new machine and the bright keys winked and flashed in the lamplight. She looked at it and the thought came to her that she had not touched a machine since she had left Landsman & Miller. She found a piece of paper, sat down and began to type, over and over again: "The quick brown fox jumps over the lazy dog."

She was so engrossed in her exercise she failed to hear the door open behind her. She only heard the click of the latch as it closed. Jumping up, she whirled around and looked at the young man who had come in.

He was a tall, gawky, hollow-cheeked individual with tremendous horn-rimmed goggles. He seemed astounded to find Rose in the room. Maybe the salesman had been jesting with her, but Rose decided to play the game through.

"Well, here I am," she said brightly. "Do you like me?"

The young man's mouth gaped open.

"Huh?"

"I said, well here I am - do you like me?"

"Well, I don't know you."

"I'm the girl you looked at out of the window. Here's the key you sent down to me."

"Oh! I'm not Waldo Gardiner. I'm just a friend of his. I was passing by and stopped in - the door was open. I live upstairs."

Rose sighed with relief.

"What's your name?" she asked.

"Andy Miller."

"Tell me something about this fellow Gardiner."

"Waldo is a good egg. He tries to write short stories. It's his only fault."

"What do you do?"

"I'm a doctor."

"A real doctor?"

"Yes."

"Well, I never saw a doctor as young as you are."

"I've been practicing three years and getting poorer every year. But I'd better run along now. Tell Waldo I was in to see him, will you?"

Rose nodded and the young man left, closing the door securely behind him. Rose took the paper out of the typewriter, crumpled it, threw it away and replaced the cover on the machine.

She searched the room for a cigarette. Finding one in a black lacquer box with a snow scene enameled on the top, she settled herself in a big easy chair. Leaning her head back as she exhaled, she found a hollow in the stuffing of the chair back. It must have been made by his shoulders, but it reached her head. He must be tall.

He was neat; she could see that by his room. The whole place was clean and orderly. In the bathroom his shaving things were laid out on a shelf beneath the mirror. In the closet his clothes were neatly hung. The drawers of a maple lowboy were well packed with shirts, underwear and socks. Even the desk top was orderly, the paper and carbons piled neatly.

He was tall and he was orderly. That was as much as she could find out about him from the place. But she did not have long to wait before she saw him. Hardly had she finished snubbing out her cigarette butt when she heard a key in the lock. A second later the door swung open and a young man, taking off his hat, came smiling into the room.

"Miss Mahoney?"

"Yes. Mr.Gardiner?"

They were very formal with each other.

Waldo Gardiner was a handsome man. He was tall, square-shouldered, and had a round open face with ruddy, clean-shaven cheeks that always smelled of soap. His hair was brown, straight and slicked back smoothly from a part on the side. He had blue eyes that opened wide in a childish stare whenever anything surprised or embarrassed him. They were wide open now.

"I like your place," Rose said to ease his embarrassment.

"I'm glad you like it," he said. "Now, I'll just get washed up and change my shirt and we'll go out and get supper. As we eat, I can explain the conditions on which you're here."

He seemed relieved to get that off his chest.

"Okay," Rose agreed.

She knew, or thought she knew, the conditions under which she was to occupy the apartment with Waldo.

He picked out a clean shirt and a fresh tie and went into the bathroom. She could hear him whistling as he splashed water on his face. It reminded her a little of her brother, Tim, when he was younger and nicer.

Waldo looked shining clean when he emerged, buttoning his vest.

"Ready?" he asked.

"As soon as I get my coat and hat on."

They walked down the stairs sedately. Crossing the street, Waldo took Rose's arm and made the chivalrous pretense of helping her across. She liked that. Bill Taggart never helped her, not even to clamber onto a bus.

They went down the street to a little tearoom. Nice girls and bright-looking young men were eating there. A little candle flickered on the table between them and Rose was glad, because she knew it would flatter her complexion. Waldo looked especially attractive and charming in that light.

He made her choose what she wanted and then gave the order to the colored waitress. Evidently he ate there often, for Rose noticed that the girl called him Mr. Gardiner.

Then, lighting a cigarette, he began:

"Ours is a rather unconventional sort of arrangement, and I think we ought to talk it over and know just exactly where we stand."

"That'd be fine."

"All right; here's my proposition: you can stay at my place as long as you want, and I'll take you to breakfast and supper. Luncheon you'll have to get yourself any way you can. As long as you're friendly and companionable, and don't make any trouble, you can have the run of the apartment. You can save me a little money by cleaning the place once in a while. I have a girl come in now, and she's none too good. She charges fifty cents an hour. If you clean up for me it'll just about pay for your meals."

"That'd be fine," Rose said.

"Now, here's the point," Waldo went on. "I don't want you to think you have to do anything you don't want to do. That's up to you - or rather - it depends on how we get on. You see what I mean?"

Rose grinned.

"No necking unless I want to, eh?"

"That's right. I think it's the only fair thing. After all, it would be a lousy way for me to take advantage of your hard luck."

"You're too good to be true."

Waldo flushed.

"No. It's just the way I feel about it. I tried to see the whole business from your point of view as I walked down here."

"Then why did you have me come?"

He shrugged.

"Just one of those things. I thought it would be nice to have someone around. You're pretty and I liked your looks when I saw you from the window. That probably had a lot to do with it. You might call it an optical yen for you, if you want to label my emotion."

Rose looked at him. She could hardly believe he was telling the truth, that he was actually giving her a choice over whether she sleep with him or not.

He went on explaining his reasons:

"I'm not entirely unselfish about this. This business of making love entails responsibilities for the man as well as the woman. Perhaps I don't want to take on those responsibilities until I know you better. That may be my reason."

She looked at him closely.

"I don't think so," she said.

"What do you think?"

"I think you're just nice."

The she grinned and added:

"Your mamma must have brought you up well."

He laughed at that, and his laughter broke the ice of their strangeness. They had a gay time during the remainder of the meal, laughing and joking and telling each other their simple life stories.

Waldo's was the conventional one of the well brought-up young man. His father had a thriving fruit farm in Florida near St. Petersburgh. He had sent Waldo to Exeter for his preparatory schooling and then Waldo had chosen Dartmouth as his college. After graduation he had come down to the city and, through a family friend, had obtained without any difficulty a position as assistant advertising manager at the clock company.

After supper they made a leisurely return to the apartment, smoking as they went along the street. Back in his room Waldo picked out a magazine and handed it to Rose.

"I work four hours every night;" he explained, "from eight to twelve. You'll have to amuse yourself as best you can while I work."

He saw the look of disappointment on her face. They had been having such a nice time.

"Oh, it's not as bad as all that," he said quickly. "I take two nights off a week, and we can go to a movie or go dancing somewhere and have fun."

"I'll be as quiet as a mouse," Rose assured him, sitting down with the magazine.

He crossed the room and sat down at the typewriter. Rose looked at the magazine for a minute, glancing at illustrations and reading the captions under them. Then she heard the rattle of his typewriter. He typed slowly. She looked over to see what was wrong. He was working the hunt-and-peck system, using only one finger of one hand. She watched him for several minutes. It was painful to see.

"Waldo," she said softly.

"Yes?"

"How many pages can you type in four hours?"

"Five," he told her. "Why?"

"I'm a typist, you know," she answered. "Why don't you let

me sit at the typewriter and you dictate to me? I can take it on the machine. We'll have five pages done in an hour."

"Say, that's an idea!" he said enthusiastically. "Let's try it."

She got up and took his place. They worked splendidly together, Waldo dictating the draft of a short story, she writing it down as he spoke. They wrote fifteen pages in two hours. He was overjoyed.

"Say," he exclaimed, "this is grand. I can do just about twice as much work in about half the time. It's only a few minutes after ten, and I've done more than I usually do in two nights."

Rose clapped her hands together, delighted.

"And gee, I'm tickled too," she said. "Now I can pay for my keep. I'll retype these papers tomorrow and make a good clean copy for you. That's the way we can work together all the time."

"Swell!" he rejoiced.

Waldo passed her a cigarette and lit it for her.

"Say, we ought to celebrate your coming here," he said. "Let's light a fire in the fireplace and drink some wine. I have a bottle of Rhine wine in the closet that a friend brought me from Canada."

"Where are the glasses and the wine? I'll set it out while you light the fire."

He told her where to find the various things. When she got down the wine bottle from the closet she saw a box of sweet biscuits on the same shelf. She arranged these on a plate and poured the wine into two whiskey glasses.

When she had finished doing all this, the fire was already roaring and crackling on the hearth. Waldo drew up a big chair and then started to move a smaller chair to the fire.

"Don't bother," Rose told him. "I'd rather sit on the floor."

"No. You sit in the big chair and I'll sit on the floor."

"Oh, let's not fight about it. Let's both sit in the chair."

He made Rose sit down and perched himself on the broad arm of the big, over-stuffed armchair. They drank slowly, enjoying being quiet in front of the warm fire.

"Gee, I could sit this way all my life," Rose said. "I don't feel as if I had ever been cold or hungry. You forget these things so darned quickly. It was just this afternoon I was freezing to death walking along the Post Road."

"And it was only this morning that I felt so damned lonely."

Rose looked up at him, her eyes bright and brimming with happiness.

"You don't have to be lonely," she said. "You're too nice. Any girl would go nutty about you."

"You?"

For answer, she put up her arms and embraced him. He bent down and kissed her.

She moved over to one side of the chair and made room for him.

"I'll crowd you," he protested. "You'd better get up and sit on my lap."

Sitting on his lap, Rose kicked off her shoes and let her feet grow warm before the fire.

"Gee," she said, "I suppose married life is like this - peaceful and sort of sweet."

Rose hurried across the room. She could hear Waldo's footsteps on the stairs, and she liked that first greeting, when his cheeks were cold and frosty and smelled of fresh, clean air.

She opened the door and threw her arms about him even before he had a chance to take off his hat or lay down his briefcase. With a little pang of dismay she noticed that his embrace was lax.

"Waldo, what's the trouble?" she asked, afraid, looking up into his face.

He released her and hung his head.

"I've just lost my job."

"Because of me?" she asked anxiously.

He embraced her, fiercely reassuring.

"You sweet! Of course not. They just let me out because the company's been losing money and they felt they had to get rid of the dead wood. I suppose I come under that heading."

"No, you don't. How silly! Everybody's being fired nowadays."

"I know, but that doesn't help much," he said, peeling off his overcoat. "What'll we do for money?"

"Sell some of your stories."

"Well, we'll try," he said slowly, the doubt of many disappointments in his voice.

"You can't get a job now," Rose argued. "Why not devote all your time to doing stories? You sold one."

She looked down at her dress and fingered the material, then repeated, smiling:

"You sold one."

He had bought her the new dress, some stockings and a new hat with the proceeds of the sale. That had been the week before last, two weeks after Rose had come to live with him.

"I think you're right," he said seriously. "I don't think I will look for a job. You take care of my money - this week's pay - and we'll try to make it stretch for a month, until the rent is due again. I ought to be able to sell something by then to pay the rent and carry us for another month."

"Oh, I can make your pay stretch for a month and a half," Rose assured him, "if you'll buy a gas ring. I can attach it to the connection in the bathroom and we can eat our breakfasts and luncheons here, and just go out for one meal a day. Then we can work all day here undisturbed, and you can take a nap in the afternoon while I retype what you've dictated. We can turn out lots and lots of stories."

Her optimism renewed his hopes. He became enthusiastic.

"I bet we can even make enough money to go up to Provincetown for the summer," he said.

"That'd be swell. We could hang around in bathing suits all day long."

So it was decided that Waldo stay home and work on his short stories instead of making futile efforts to find another job. The first month of this arrangement went off very well except for one particular: he did not sell any stories.

Aside from the worry about the future, they were happy. Rose was pleased to have something to do. It gave her a great satisfaction to take his dictation, do his typing and cook his breakfasts and luncheons. After the months of unemployment and loose ends, work gave her a feeling of measured peace and security. Although she herself might not have put it that way, she was in love, very deeply in love, with Waldo.

On his part, he had a strong affection for her, and as the weeks passed, and she became more and more useful to him, he became dependent upon her for many things. Despite the fact that his affection was less intense than her love, theirs was an ideal relationship of its sort.

To make her even more happy, Rose found that Waldo's friends liked her. Young college men in the main, they found Rose a pert and refreshing person unlike anyone they had ever met before. Her frankness and her calm acceptance of her unusual relationship with Waldo appealed to their sense of Bohemianism. They prided themselves on their liberal viewpoint on such matters, but found few girls who would accept their theories and put them into practise.

Rose and Waldo banked heavily on the two stories, adventure yarns, which he had written since his discharge from the clock company. At the end of the month, with a little mock ceremony of God-speed, they sent them off. The week following Rose ran down a dozen times a day to check the mail box. Bills came, many of them, and a threat from the 'phone company to shut off service unless one of these bills was paid, but there was no envelope with a magazine's name on it and a check inside.

Two weeks after they were sent, both manuscripts came back with curt rejection slips. The rent was a week and a half past due. The telephone had been taken out. The laundry refused to return the wash until back bills were paid. With the return of the manuscripts, Waldo, always easy-going and cheerful, became despondent and morose.

Rose, sick at heart with the fear of losing him, made pathetic efforts to cheer him up, to give him a little of her own stubborn courage.

One afternoon he went for a long walk, and when he came back, he was especially silent and moody. She knew something definite had happened, but dared not ask him until after supper. Then he broached the subject himself:

"You like me pretty well, don't you, Rose?"

"I love you," she said simply, and he could not doubt the truth of it when she said it that way.

"That makes it very hard."

"Makes what hard?"

"Leaving you."

Rose began to cry, silently, the tears running unchecked and leaving little shining paths down her powdered cheeks.

"Waldo," she said, "you don't have to leave. We still have some money left. We can go to a cheap room somewhere. We can sell your furniture. Maybe I can find a job to help out until you can sell some stories."

He shook his head apathetically.

"But, Waldo, I'm sure we can do it."

"No. It wouldn't be fair on either of us. I've just sent a wire to my Dad for money. I'm going home."

It was on the tip of her tongue to ask:

"But what about me?"

She remembered Mildred, whining when they had to leave Mrs. Feinberg's, and kept still.

Waldo's arrangements were soon made. He sub-let the apartment to a friend, Fritz Howard, a hard-drinking young fellow from an advertising agency, who also made a dicker with him for his furniture. Waldo gave the twenty dollars he received for this as a parting gift to Rose.

In the nicest sort of way, it was part of the agreement between Fritz and Waldo that Rose would stay on in the apartment. They did not make this agreement in so many words, nor did Waldo mention it to Rose, yet she understood that this was to be the case. She was so stunned, so apathetic at the break-up of her life with Waldo, so cruelly hurt by his plans to leave, that she hardly thought about it. Life would just go on with loud-talking, hard-drinking Fritz in Waldo's place. She would have to put up with it as best she could. It would be better than the streets and a hopeless search for a job that never materialized.

When it was time for Waldo to go, Rose went with him to the station. At the train gate they said goodbye.

"Good luck, Rose," he said. "Your coming to the apartment was the nicest thing that happened to me during my whole stay in New York."

Rose bit her lip. She felt like crying. She knew she would never see him again.

"You've made me happy, too, Waldo."

"Goodbye."

"Goodbye."

Both wanted to kiss, but they only shook hands at parting. Waldo felt it would seem stupid to kiss a girl when it looked so much as if he were running out on her. Rose remembered Fritz would probably be waiting for her at the apartment. She wanted the kisses of the two men as far apart as possible.

She watched Waldo as he walked down the platform. He turned twice to look back at her and each time her heart leaped. There was still the little hope that he might stay. She felt no animosity toward him. He had been good to her. He had made the months she had lived with him the only bright and happy ones of her depression. And she saw how he looked at it: it was not pure selfishness on his part. He could have stayed, and he knew she would have stuck with him no matter how badly fortune treated him; but that, he felt, would be working a greater hardship on her than by turning her over into Fritz's care. He thought he knew Fritz. He was a man's man, and Waldo felt certain that after a time, when she had a little chance to forget him, Rose would be happy with the other boy. His reasoning was kindly as he saw it. As he did not love her, it was hard for Waldo to understand the depth and strength of her love for him.

Rose hung about the train gate, peering in at the platform until long after Waldo was settled in his Pullman seat. When the train started she turned away and walked out of the station and across town to the apartment. Fritz would probably be installing himself now in the room she had grown to love. It would hurt her, she knew, to see him sitting in the big armchair in which Waldo had sat when he dictated to her. For a moment the thought crossed her mind that she had twenty dollars, that she might leave Fritz and live on this until such a time as she could find a job. Find a job? Every new edition of the newspapers carried headlines about the depression. More and more people were finding themselves out of work. Hopeless! She put away the thought.

"The hell with it."

Fritz might not be so bad after all. She had never given him much thought. She had been too wrapped up in Waldo himself to pay much attention to his friends.

By the time she reached the building, Rose felt weary. It was the first time since she had come to live with Waldo that she had had that strange, dragging, hopeless weariness which had been her constant companion in the days when she lived with Julia.

As she climbed the stairs to the apartment, it all came back to her. Happy with Waldo she had forgotten all about her other friends. She'd have to go and see Julia and find out how Tommy was getting on at the place where she had him out to board. She'd have to see Fanny. Perhaps Fanny was a little more happy; time and long usage might have blunted the edge of her tragedy. And Mildred. It was an almost foregone conclusion that Mildred had gone to the dogs. And she felt like seeing Barbie, too, for Barbie had always appealed to her as a strange, but good-hearted person. She remembered the everlasting party at Barbie's. It might be fun to take Fritz up there. She would never have thought of taking Waldo. She had always wanted him all to herself.

Rose hesitated for a second at the apartment door, and then she swung it open and walked in cheerily, a smile on her lips.

"Hi, Fritz!" she called out.

Fritz was already sitting in Waldo's old armchair, slumped down, one leg negligently thrown over the arm. He was smoking a little, thick-set pipe and he had a highball in his hand. Another young man, a slim, oval-faced fellow with blonde, close-curling hair and a short, upturned nose was unpacking a suitcase, throwing the things out of it onto the bed without noticing where they fell. Rose thought he looked like the Prince of Wales.

In a corner of the room stood a big brown paper bundle about four feet high and three feet in width. Rose wondered what it might be.

In response to her greeting Fritz turned his head and grinned.

"Hello Rosie," he said without bothering to get up. "What's the glad word?"

"Are there any left in this depression?" she asked.

He grinned again and Rose saw he was almost drunk. His grin

had a vacant, fatuous quality which she could easily recognize.

Rose took off her coat and hung it up, tidied her hair before the mirror and then put on a little house apron she had bought at the five-and-ten-cent store in the first days of her stay with Waldo.

"Can I help you unpack Fritz's things?" she asked the slim, blonde fellow who was now trying to sort out the odds and ends on the studio bed.

"His things are over in that bag across the room. These are my duds."

"Oh."

"Hey, Fritz, you might introduce me to the young lady," the boy called across the room.

"What for? You'll get to know each other soon enough," Fritz said in a surly tone.

The other young man only grinned.

"Don't mind him," he said to Rose. "He always gets that way when he's been drinking. It's one of his most charming traits."

"Aw, shut up!" Fritz shouted.

"My favorite pastime: baiting Fritz when he's drunk," the other boy said, addressing himself to Rose.

"But what's your name?"

"I'm Alfred Newland, Fritz's roommate."

Rose looked puzzled.

"But where do you fit into this picture?" she asked.

"I've roomed with that rogue elephant over there ever since we were Freshmen at Penn State. You don't think I'd relinquish such an honor just because there happens to be a chit of a girl in the way."

"You mean you're both going to live here?"

"I've come with bag and baggage."

"All three in one room?"

"I hope you're not uppity about such things. I assure you, I'm the most modest of persons myself and yet I don't mind in the least. Why should you?"

Rose was angry. She had not counted on anything of this sort, and she did not know just how to take what Alfred had said. His glib, fast line was puzzling. She sat down on a corner of the bed and lit a cigarette. Fritz was pouring himself another drink.

"Is he always like this?" Rose asked.

"Drunk? Oh yes, most of the time. He's an advertising account executive and that's their chief business - getting drunk with clients. He's just practising now. You should see him when he really extends himself."

"I can imagine."

Alfred bustled about industriously, chattering and putting away his things. Rose talked to him and, after a while, when she saw that Fritz made no move to unpack his belongings, she opened his two bags and put his things away. While she and Alfred worked around the apartment, arranging things and setting up the new bed, a folding affair that took quite a bit of ingenuity, Fritz remained slumped in the big chair. After a time he stopped mixing highballs for himself and began to drink the whiskey straight, gulping down one glass after another.

Rose looked at him sitting sunk in a drunken stupor in the chair Waldo had always occupied. She could almost see Waldo sitting there, his elbows on the arms, his hands joined together, a long-stemmed pipe in his mouth as he dictated, brows drawn together in concentration, alive, earnest and young in spirit. Fritz was only a year or so older than Waldo, but he had the set, disillusioned maturity of a man who had seen much and found all of it bad.

Looking at him as he sat there, breathing heavily, and gazing fixedly at the floor, Rose thought Fritz ugly. As a matter of honest fact, Fritz was not bad looking. He had a sort of surly good looks that attracted little goody-goody girls who had been brought up in sheltered homes. He looked, although he was not, as if he were venturesome and devil-may-care. To Rose he seemed a disagreeable person. They had not spoken more than two or three words together since she had come into the apartment. She felt she was unwelcome.

Rose put the last of Fritz's shirts into a drawer and then took down her little hatbox with the rose lithographed on its cardboard sides. It was a symbol of hardships to her, a sign of fresh and uncertain wanderings. She had hidden it on the top shelf while Waldo had been in the apartment. Now she took it out and opened it, putting it on the bed. She went to the bureau and, from the separate drawer Waldo had allotted her, took out her things and began carrying them over to the bed.

"What are you doing?" Alfred asked her, pausing to look at Rose as he hammered a nail to support a picture.

"Your little boyfriend over there doesn't seem to want me around. So I'm getting out while the going is good."

Alfred put down the picture and came over to her, wiping his hands on a handkerchief to remove the dust that had been rubbed off on them as he puttered around the molding to find a place for his picture.

"Where are you going?"

"Just going."

"But don't you think that's a bit unfair to Fritz, running out on him while he's drunk? Why not wait until he's sober?"

"That all sounds very good, but where am I going to sleep tonight? I don't want to bunk with a stinking old drunkard."

Alfred smiled.

"If I were chivalrous and less loyal -" he began.

"Oh, pipe down."

"He won't bother you," Alfred told her, seriously, looking at Fritz. "A couple of more drinks and he'll sleep like a log. We'll roll him over to the wall so that you'll have plenty of room."

"No. I'm going. He'll be doing this all the time and I'm not so fond of drunks that I'll put up with one unless I'm married to him - and not even then."

Alfred lit a cigarette and stood silently watching her pack.

"Where are you going?" he asked again.

"I don't know and if I did it would be my business."

"I'm not just asking from curiosity," he said. "I don't like to see you leave here. It's almost as if we were putting you out. You make me feel like a hard-hearted landlord evicting a poor tenant."

"I should worry about how you feel about it," Rose said. "That's none of my business."

"Wait a minute," Alfred laid his hand on her arm. "Let's talk this over. I don't want to see you go. Not for any of the reasons you might imagine, either; you're Fritz's girl. That's out. What bothers me is what's going to become of you. You can't have very much money and I know darn well you're not going to get a job in a hurry. I've heard your story from Fritz, who had it from Waldo. Now listen to some good advice from your Uncle Alfred."

"Go on. You have a sweet singing voice," Rose cut in.

"Thank you. I've been complimented on it before. Now listen: I know Fritz isn't the finest person in the world, but in his own way he's a gentleman. He won't beat you and he won't let you go hungry. And I doubt very much if he'll bother you in other ways a great deal - he's too pie-eyed most of the time. If he ever does get rough with you, I'll be around, and I won't stand for it. Be sensible. You may not find Fritz as good-hearted as

Waldo, nor as easy to get along with, but he'll be a sight better company than the men you have to accost on the street to make your living if you leave. Or, of course, if you'd rather go to a flophouse and eat in breadlines -"

Rose shuddered. She had been too close to all that before. He was right. She turned the little hatbox upside down on the bed, dumping out everything she had packed.

"Okay," she said. "I'll stick around. But don't expect me to reform him."

Fritz fell asleep in his chair after a little while. Rose and Alfred undressed him and put him to bed, rolling him over to the wall so that Rose could sleep beside him without touching him.

"He'll stay that way all night. Now I'll hike into the bathroom and put on my pajamas," Alfred said. "You can undress in here, and when you're decent again, you rap on the door. I won't come in until you do."

"Thanks."

Alfred heard Rose sobbing herself to sleep that night. Once, he was moved to whisper across the darkness separating the two beds:

"Steady, there! Steady!"

He could hear her make an effort to control her crying. A little later she fell asleep.

"Poor kid," Alfred thought, turning over on his right side to sleep. "I guess she liked Waldo pretty well and Fritz is no prize."

SEVENTEEN

The alarm clock's insistent buzzing woke Rose. She jumped out of bed. Her movement roused Fritz. He turned over on his back and looked at her.

"Where the hell did you come from?" he grunted, voice thick and quaking.

Rose did not bother to answer. She looked over at the other bed. Alfred had evidently not heard the alarm. He was sleeping sweetly, half his face buried deep in the pillow.

She decided not to wake him until after she had dressed.

Fritz started to get up, lifted his head from the pillow and then let it fall back with a groan of pain.

"Good God!"

"What's wrong with you?" Rose asked, pulling her coolie coat on over her pajamas.

"A head."

"Go soak it somewhere."

Fritz half sat up, supporting himself on his elbows.

"Who the hell are you?" he asked, peering at her.

"Just one of the fixtures here; I go with the lease," she told him.

"Oh, yes. I forgot. Sorry."

"When do you have to be at work?" Rose asked him.

"At nine. What time is it?"

"You've got time to get another half hour's sleep while I fix your breakfast and make some coffee."

"Breakfast? I don't want any breakfast. I can't eat anything. Just give me some tomato juice."

"There isn't any. We never kept it."

"Well, are you a cripple? Go out and get some."

Rose put her hands on her hips.

"Get up," she ordered. "I want to talk to you. You and I ought to know just where we stand. I'm not here to run errands for you unless I want to run them. Get it?"

He sat up.

"If you want to stay here," he said, "you do as I tell you. I don't expect you to run errands, but I do want you to know that I'm the boss of the joint and that I can run you out whenever I want to."

"I'll go now."

Fritz got himself painfully out of bed. He felt as though a heavy knife blade were pressing into the center of his skull. At his every move it bit deeper into his brain.

"Listen," he said in a conciliatory tone, "when I've got a head, I'm liable to be a little bad tempered. Don't mind it. I'm sorry for what I said. Stay here. I think you and I will like each other."

Rose bent down to pick up a slipper. She was facing him, and as she bent he could see her little breasts through the low-cut neck of her pajamas.

He grinned.

"Yeah, I think you and I could like each other a lot," he said again.

Rose put on one slipper and groped for the other.

"You'd have to change a lot before I could like you."

"I'm not such a bad guy when I'm sober."

"I can't tell about that until I see."

He put his feet to the floor.

"Where are my slippers?"

"Look for them."

"Aw, hell, girl, let's not fight."

"Then don't order me around."

"I wasn't ordering you around. I just asked you a civil question."

"And I'm telling you that I'm not your nigger valet."

He got unsteadily to his feet.

"All right, now that we understand that, let's be friends."

"I'm willing enough to be friends, if you'll meet me halfway." Rose said. "I've got to be friends, I haven't any place else to go. But if you make it too darn hard for me, I'll go anyhow. With me, it's a matter of the worst of two bad choices."

Fritz tottered unsteadily toward her.

"All right. Let's be friends."

She put out her hand. He disregarded it.

"That's no way to make friends," he said. "I'll show you how -"

Fritz moved forward clumsily and tried to put his arms about Rose. She evaded him.

"Hey, none of that. That's worse than taking a drink before breakfast."

"That reminds me," he said, and shuffled bare-foot across the room to the bottle of whiskey he had left on the hearthstone the night before. He poured himself a generous drink and downed it in four gulps.

"Ugh!" he shivered as the whiskey burnt his throat and warmed his stomach. "Now I feel more like myself, Rosie."

"Good. I'll start breakfast."

"Wait a minute," he said and started towards her, his arms outstretched.

She turned to him and said with disgust:

"Can't you wait? I'm willing enough for all that hooey - but not now. Wait until you're sober and look decent. The morning's no time for muzzling around anyhow - you've got to get to work in a little more than an hour."

"Aw, come on. Work can wait."

"So can a guy wait for a job these days," Rose warned him.

He thought that over for a second.

"You're right. I'd better get ready to go to the office. I'll take coffee if you've got some. No sugar. No cream."

"Condensed milk's what you'd get here anyway. I don't buy cream."

"Ah, Waldo didn't care for luxury, eh?"

"Oh, shut up," Rose cried, going into the bathroom and slamming the door behind her.

On the little gas ring in the bathroom Rose made her coffee. While it was percolating, she took down some five-and-ten-cent-store dishes and filled them with prepared cereal and milk. Then she got out spoons, sugar and the can of condensed milk and put these on a tray. Last of all she squeezed orange juice and poured it into glasses.

Steadying the big breakfast tray against her stomach, she carried it into the other room.

Alfred had gotten up while she was gone and both young men were partially dressed. They sat on the edges of the beds in their trousers and undershirts, talking.

"Come and get it," Rose sang out, putting her tray down on Waldo's old desk. Fritz shambled over and looked at the food with disgust.

"Lord, I can't eat. I'll go get shaved."

Alfred grabbed a glass of orange juice, drank it down, and said:

"Thanks, Rose. That's all I ever have for breakfast."

With the two boys in the bathroom, shaving and finishing dressing, Rose sat alone at Waldo's desk and ate her cereal and drank her coffee. She had a second cup, although this was unusual for her, just so that too much of the coffee she had prepared would not go down the drain.

She remembered breakfast with Waldo. He always bathed, shaved and dressed before sitting down with a good appetite. Rose loved to watch him eat his cereal, one spoonful following another with precise regularity. He had broken the rhythm only to say a few words to her now and again. When they drank their coffee, Waldo always lit a cigarette after the first sip, and smoked as he finished the cup.

She sighed.

Fritz left immediately after he had dressed, calling a careless goodbye to Rose over his shoulder as he made for the stairs. To her surprise, Alfred put on a tattered silk dressing gown over his shirt and trousers, pulled a chair to the window and sat down with a heavy book in a blue cloth binding.

He had hardly made himself comfortable when he jumped up, rummaged through some odds and ends on the desk and produced a small piece of chalk. Squatting down beside his chair, he drew a circle about eight feet in diameter around it.

"Don't pass this line," he warned Rose, "when you go about cleaning up. You won't bother me so long as you don't cross this line. And don't ever talk to me when I'm in this circle."

Rose laughed. Alfred started to step into the charmed circle he had made.

"Wait a minute," Rose called out.

He paused, one foot suspended beyond the chalk boundary.

"What do you want?"

"What are you doing? Don't you work?"

"I'm working," he told her.

"What do you mean? You're just sitting down to read a book."

"Sweet innocence! Isn't that work enough?"

"I mean work you get paid for doing," Rose insisted.

"Yes, I get paid for reading these books. Not much, to be sure, but I get paid, and it helps keep food in the old bread basket."

"They pay you to read a book? What for?"

"I review them."

"Oh," Rose said as if she fully understood, although she had never seen a book review.

"And is that all you do?" she asked.

"No. But I haven't a regular job. I used to work on the Hartford *Courant*, but they fired me and I came on to New York. I bunked in with Fritz because we'd lived together in college, and when I couldn't find a job, I just began going around picking up odd bits of writing to do. I write brochures, leaf -"

He was going on to enumerate the types of writing he did for a living, when Rose interrupted him.

"Oh, you're a writer!"

Waldo had been a writer and she was pleased to know Alfred was another writer, no matter how different the sort of work. It made her remember Waldo more vividly. Perhaps she might be useful to Alfred, too. She had grown to hate idleness.

"Oh, you're a writer!" she said again, thrilled.

Alfred looked at her in wonder. No one had ever made such a fuss about the fact before.

"You might call me a writer. That is, I do book reviews and I've written brochures for perfume houses and for a vitreous products corporation. You should read my pamphlet on "Beautiful Toilets in the Beautiful Bathroom." It's a masterpiece of its kind. The most insidious attack against sales resistance that this old world has seen in many a year."

"Waldo was a writer."

"Yes. I knew Waldo. But he wasn't much of a writer. The only time he ever really seriously worked at it was the last month or so when he was out of a job."

"But he was a good writer," Rose protested.

Alfred smiled. He saw here was no use arguing that point with her. He started to step into his charmed circle.

"Wait," she called again. "There's something else I want to ask you."

He walked over and sat down in the armchair, reaching into the pocket of his dressing gown for cigarettes and matches.

"Well?"

"You seem a good egg; tell me something."

"I'd tell you almost anything."

"Tell me what the arrangement is between you and Fritz about this apartment."

"A purely business arrangement," he told her. "It's cheaper to live two in an apartment. I like to live with Fritz. He's always out somewhere and doesn't roll home until early in the morning. Then he's too drunk to talk, anyhow. I like that. It gives me plenty of time to myself, to read, write and loaf around. I especially like to loaf around. That all you want to know?"

"No. What about me?"

"Well, it's this way. Fritz pays three-fourths of the rent. He's able to pay it. He has a good job. I have very little money. I pay only a fourth. Figure it out for yourself."

"I'm Fritz's girl?"

"I believe I told you so last night."

Then he laughed.

"In fact," he went on, "I've already been warned off the master's preserves. He told me this morning not to talk to you unless I needed to ask you something. He's jealous, very jealous indeed, that new lord and master of yours Rosie."

In the ensuing two weeks Rose was to find that out for herself. Fritz was rarely home. He went out a great deal, and when he did come home, he was usually so drunk Rose and Alfred had to undress him and put him to bed. When he was home, in the mornings before going to work and one Saturday afternoon when he stayed in the apartment because he had a bad cold, Rose noticed that Fritz watched her and Alfred closely, trying to find signs of an intimacy which he grumbled about when he was drunk, and which did not exist.

Her obligations to Fritz, she discovered, were none too arduous. He disgusted her physically, and she disliked sleeping in the same bed as him, but that was the extent of their relationship. She never did know what was wrong with Fritz, but several drunken attempts to make love to her were squelched by her merely saying "no." She could not understand that. He did not seem to be lacking in vigour, and yet the tiniest, whispered "no" ended his most arduous attempts.

Despite his scarcely lukewarm efforts at love-making, Fritz's jealousy of Alfred was passionate and ever-present. It seemed to prey on him that, of the two, Rose liked Alfred better.

Alfred and his work served to remind Rose of Waldo. By typing his manuscripts and repairing his worn shirt-collars, she could recall her former happiness. After a little time she began to look upon Alfred as something of a weak successor to the boy who had left her.

Fritz paid three-fourths of the rent, it was true, but as he was always away drinking and roistering with his boon companions from the advertising agency, the burden of taking Rose to luncheon and dinner fell on Alfred. He never seemed to mind and never made any attempts to force himself upon her with the argument that he helped support her.

She had bought her own luncheons and dinners at first, until the twenty dollars Waldo had given her was gone. Then she had to accept kindnesses from Alfred. The very fact that he never used this to his advantage endeared him to her; never in the way that Waldo had been dear to her, but she respected and liked him.

Alfred worked harder and faster than Waldo had and used up less of her time, and Rose began to pick up on old friendships. She called on Fanny, who made her come up for Sunday dinner at her apartment. Every Sunday Fanny entertained Julia in order that the other girl might have one day in the week when she could have her baby with her. When she saw Tommy, Rose noticed that, while he had grown, he did not look so robust and rosy-cheeked as when he had been in his mother's care. But Julia, she saw, did not notice; she was so delighted to have her baby with her that, no matter if he had been as gaunt as a skeleton, she would have thought him as cherubic as an infant angel.

Fanny seemed happy, and her husband was overflowing with joy and pride in his new wife. They were contemplating a move to Albany where he had been offered a partnership in a thriving stationery store.

Julia, still working for the religious fanatic, assisting him to write his interminable history of Josephus, was not so happy. She missed Tommy during the week and worried about him. The money she got for her services as secretary and general literary drudge was just enough to pay for Tommy's keep at a cheap boarding nursery. She looked shabby, worn out and ill, but when Rose asked her, she said she felt well and happy. Rose had to hug her when she said that. It was typical of Julia.

Alfred worked in the mornings only, and then went for long walks around New York and along the Palisades. He never asked Rose to accompany him. She grew lonesome in the apartment and several times went to Barbie's to join in the endless party that went on there. Fritz chided her one day when he smelled liquor on her breath, then flew into a perfect fit of fury when Alfred laughed at such a rebuke coming from him.

Fritz made such a storm about her drinking that Rose decided to call off her visits to Barbie. There was no sense going there unless one drank with the rest. She took to visiting Grace and Yvonne's apartment for companionship, but could not stand the fetid airlessness of their hole and always tried to induce Yvonne to take a walk in the park or along Riverside Drive.

On one of these rambles they came across Mildred. She was trying to solicit sailors on the Drive in broad daylight. She looked horrible. Both Rose and Yvonne had an impulse to pass her without speaking, but checked it and went up to her. She was overjoyed to see them, but the moment her first flush of pleasure at the meeting was over she tried to borrow money. Yvonne lent her a dollar. Then Mildred began complaining. The young pimp with whom she had fallen in after setting herself up in an apartment had beaten her, had stolen all the money she earned and finally forced her to go on the streets and solicit. Customers had fallen off badly. It was the depression, she said. But both Rose and Yvonne knew that men who would be attracted by Mildred as she was now would be poor indeed, in both purse and spirits. They were silent and frightened when they left her. Rose regretted the impulse which had prompted her to give Mildred her address.

Again life became monotonous. With Fritz drunk and

morosely silent, the apartment was not an over-cheerful place for Rose. There were times when her memories of Waldo's cheerful good-heartedness almost made her cry.

Alfred was pleasant even when he was tremendously busy and Rose grew fonder of him little by little. She found out that he had been married - an unfortunate marriage that had ended in divorce - and one reason why he had to work so grindingly hard and at such poorly paid tasks was because his alimony payments were far beyond his slender means. There were some weeks when he had so little money that he went on a diet he had invented. He ate one egg, a little rice, some tea and used agar-agar for bulk. This kept him full and contented for a whole day and the entire cost of the meal, when he prepared it himself over the gas range in the bathroom, was about ten cents. He boasted that he could live, exclusive of rent, on a dollar a week, most of which he spent on tobacco. It made Rose furious, the very same week in which he was forced to go on the diet, to see him send a twenty-dollar check to his ex-wife. He grinned at her anger and concern. Other weeks he had more money, and if he had more than five dollars in his pocket at any one time he was certain to spend it foolishly. One day, receiving seventy-five dollars for an article, he spent the entire sum on a Japanese print, a beautiful thing showing a sea wave breaking over a small boat. Then he went on slim rations for the rest of the week. Rose gave him a talking to about it, but it seemed to do no good; bills burned through his pockets as if they were made of phosphorous.

Then he received an order to do a long series of articles on tea-planting for a trade journal and he put Rose on a regular salary of a dollar a day to help him. They were necessarily together a great deal during this time and a certain fondness grew up between them. On a blowy day in March, when he did not feel like going for his usual walk in the afternoon, Alfred built a fire and he and Rose sat down before it to drink a highball as relaxation.

Sitting there it reminded Rose so much of her first evening with Waldo that she fell into a soft, relaxed mood. Alfred was also affected by it and stopped his continual patter of semi-clever conversation and remained silent. They sat for about ten minutes without speaking and then Alfred bent down and kissed her. They remained in an embrace for a long time. Then he took her up in his arms and carried her to the bed.

Afterward, sitting on the edge of the bed, he said, a little regretfully, "I suppose it had to happen."

She understood what he meant. She felt the same way about it.

Their physical attraction for one another, slight as it was, and the fact that it had reached consummation, did not escape Fritz. He accused them bitterly one Sunday morning before going off to Mass, a duty he never missed. As if by mutual consent neither Rose nor Alfred said either 'yes' or 'no' in answer to Fritz's tirade. The following day Fritz put them to the proof.

Alfred went uptown during the day to see about the tea-planting articles. To kill time while waiting for an appointment with the editor who had ordered the stories, he dropped in at Fritz's office. Fritz pulled a long face at the sight of him and said:

"Gee, Alfred, I'm in a mess. We'll have to get rid of that dame down in the apartment. I haven't been feeling well the last few days. I went to see Doc Andy and he looked me over. I'm sick on account of her."

"You mean - ?" Alfred said, blanching.

"Yes."

Alfred turned white.

Fritz set his jaw. He had learned what he wanted to know.

"Yes, I suppose she'll have to leave," Alfred said, recovering himself. "I'm sorry for you, Fritz, but you'll get over it all right."

"I suppose so."

Fritz did not want to accuse Alfred of treachery. He preferred to take his anger out on Rose. He even looked forward to the moment when he could order her out. The fact that she was penniless made his prospective satisfaction only more complete.

Alfred, however, out on the street again, thought it all over and decided there was a possibility of Fritz having lied to him. He determined to question Rose. 'Phoning the editor, he excused himself from the appointment, and hurried to the apartment. He got there before Fritz.

"How do you feel?" he asked Rose.

"Fine. Want to do some work?"

"No. I want to ask you something. You feel well, eh?"

She nodded, puzzled.

"Well, Fritz tells me he's sick because of you. Do you know what I mean?"

Rose was breathless with anger and astonishment. Finally she got out the words:

"The dirty rat!"

Alfred smiled.

"I thought he was lying to me."

They heard Fritz's key in the door. Both of them stood rigid, waiting for him to come in. Fritz was astonished to see Alfred there before him. One look at them and he knew his lie had been found out. He grinned sheepishly, then said:

"Well, anyway, I found out what you were doing behind my back."

"If you had asked decently, I might have told you," Alfred

said. "If you were a decent person, I would have told you. Rose has just called you a rat. Allow me to add the adjective - drunken."

Fritz's jaw muscles worked.

"And I thought you were my friend," he said.

"You took a great deal for granted. You were a convenience. You were never a friend. Let me tell you what I really think: you're a drunken clod, always trying to bluster and hide your inferiority complex."

It was the truth. It stung Fritz. He plunged forward, striking out. His blow caught Alfred off balance and the young writer fell over onto the studio bed. He dodged up again quickly and punched out, hitting Fritz in the eye.

They stood in the middle of the room and exchanged clumsy blows. Both were strong, but neither was a skillful fighter. After a few swinging haymakers both were winded and fought slowly, hardly able to lift their arms. When their blows landed they were too weak to be effective. They stood there silently, trading weak blow for weaker blow. It was ludicrous.

"Aw, stop it," Rose said.

Alfred let his arms drop to his sides. He saw how foolish it was to fight this way. Fritz took advantage of this to strike a vindictive blow at Alfred's jaw. Alfred staggered and fell.

"You rat!" Rose said. "It's just what I'd expect from you. You can't even fight fair."

She started to bend over Alfred to help him up, but he shook his head and, clinging to the wall, got to his feet himself. He slumped down on a corner of the bed and let his hands hang down between his knees, breathing heavily in jerky pants, as he tried to catch his wind. Fritz stood in the center of the room, head hanging. He, too, gasped breathlessly.

Rose got down her little hatbox, threw her clothes into it, put on her hat and coat and went to the door.

"Don't fight any more, boys, your penny is rolling into the subway grating - she's gone," she said, and slammed the door behind her.

 EIGHTEEN

Barbie yawned sleepily and her breath came over Rose's face, hot and whiskey laden.

"Six o'clock," she said, "and I'm not drunk yet. I hope to God somebody comes in with a bottle of gin. I sent Van out to scout around for some an hour ago."

Rose said nothing. She was embarrassed. Barbie had allowed her to stay at her place the whole week, had fed her and had even lent her some clothes, and Rose knew that the other girl was in one of her periodic states of extreme poverty when there was absolutely no money forthcoming.

"Gee, isn't it always that way?" Barbie commented. "When you're bust nobody comes to see you. When you have money to buy your own liquor they come with barrels of it."

Rose found it hard to say.

"Barbie, I think I ought to get out of here. You've spent at least five dollars on my food alone since I've been here."

"Oh, don't let that worry you. Stay. I want you to stay."

"I can't stay any longer. I'm not the kind that can do that."

Barbie patted Rose's arm.

"Silly."

"Listen," Rose said, "you once told me I could work for you. Why don't you let me work for you now, so that I could make my keep?"

Barbie looked at her closely. Her ugly eyes were kind and shrewd.

"You don't know what I do, Rose, do you?"

"But if you do it, it's all right for me," she said.

The week had passed and she had still not discovered how Barbie managed to make a living. Of course, the people who dropped in brought sandwiches and liquor and once a young broker had come in with a whole roast ham. But Rose knew that none of the people who dropped in to laugh, tell smutty stories and drink ever left cash for their hostess.

Barbie's apartment was a salon of a low order, but nevertheless a true salon. People of the most diverse sorts came there - high and low, clean-minded and degenerate, rich and poor, the dull and the talented. They came to sit and talk and meet others and merely to be with the silent yet powerful personality that was Barbie. She had an inexplicable charm. Even Rose never knew why she liked Barbie so well. It was something more than Barbie's generosity, something more than her freedom of speech and talk, something that no one could understand. Yet it undoubtedly existed.

"So you still don't know what I do?" Barbie asked.

"No."

"Ever hear of stag parties?"

"Yes. Sure."

"I suppose you know they give exhibitions sometimes, to entertain the boys."

"Yes. Strip dancers they call them, don't they?"

Barbie was scornful.

"Oh, strip dancers! That's nothing. That's just teasing."

"Well, what do you do?"

"I don't. I'm just the manager."

"You mean you manage the strip dancers?"

"Oh, no. That was just the way I was trying to explain it to you. I don't stage exhibitions for stag parties. It has to be a mixed crowd or I won't let my girls perform. Stag parties get too rough. Men without women get grabby. I don't let anybody touch my girls. Not unless the girls want to be touched. That's different. Ours is a business, like anything else."

"But what do the girls do?"

"Well - they - they perform - a sort of act, you know. Mine is the best exhibition troupe in the city. We make a regular little play out of ours. Van Wyck writes the dialogue and continuity and sometimes little verses for the girls to speak while they go through their stuff. We've got a medieval act now. I bought some old theatrical costumes for the girls, and they come out as knights and ladies and troubadors before they do their stuff. Van calls it 'The Court of Love.' They used to have things like that in those days."

Rose was still puzzled. Such things had not come within the range of her experience before and as she was never one to talk "dirt" she had never heard of such shows. She was not shocked.

"Do they - make love in front of all the people?" she asked.

"Well - yes - but it's mostly fake. We only give the show at private parties and I always fix the light so it's pretty dim."

"Girls? Girls only?"

"Yeah. That's what men and women both like to see - girls making love."

"Well," Rose said hesitantly, "if it's just faking, why don't you let me work for you?"

Barbie shook her head.

"You're not the type."

"Does Helen work for you? And Lily? And Isabelle?"

"Yes. They're part of the troupe."

"Well, I'm just as good-looking as they are."

"It isn't a question of that. You're better looking. You're just not the type, Rose, that's all."

"I wish you'd let me do something," Rose said.

The door swung open and Van Wyck came in, two strands of yellow hair hanging at either side of his face like a pair of parentheses. He had a paper-wrapped bottle in his hand.

"All I could get for you, Barbie, was some Dago red."

"Pour me some."

He did so and brought the glass to Barbie.

"Have some, Rose?" he asked.

She shook her head.

"Say, Van," Barbie began, "Rose wants a job in a show. Think you could write a part for her where she could just stand and talk and not do anything? I don't want the other girls fooling around with her."

"Oh, say!" he chortled, "I've wanted to write in a part for her. I wanted to have a little page-boy come in at the end of that first scene and then act as a sort of master of ceremonies. I could do her part all in rhyme. Rose has a pert figure. She'd look fine in page's tights."

His was the enthusiasm of the creative artist for his work.

"All right," Barbie said. "You're hired, Rose. I'll have to give you a little less than the other girls get, because you won't have to do any of the dirty work."

"Fine."

"I'll start work on your part tonight, and we can have it all ready, rehearsed and everything by the time we give our next performance."

Rose stayed on at Barbie's, eating, drinking and even sleeping in the confusion of the never-ending party that reigned there. It was a strange, hectic life in which nothing definite ever happened: endless, unexciting chaos. One could bear it, but one could not enjoy it. There was none of the clean purposeful joy of living she had felt during her time of happiness with Waldo.

She rehearsed the lines that Van Wyck had written for her one afternoon in the back room, while the other girls went through their parts completely dressed. She saw nothing very reprehensible in their postures and gestures at the rehearsal. She was to discover that these, when combined with complete nudity, made a lewd, exciting spectacle for the kind of person who enjoys such things.

That night, at a party in a sumptuous duplex apartment on Park Avenue, before a crowd of women in expensive evening dress and men in tail coats, who made a polite chatter in the big room where the show was being held, Rose conquered a little wave of stage fright and went out into the semi-circle of nude girls in various postures. Standing, her figure straight and fine in the tight-fitting page's hose and doublet, a plumed hat on her yellow hair, Rose recited Van Wyck's lines in the serio-comic sing-song which he had taught her. Then, as the girls went through their act and she watched, astounded by the difference from what she had seen at rehearsal when they were dressed, she spoke her little pieces. Most of the spectators had seen such shows before. Rose's part was a new twist and her pertness refreshing against the background of the other performers' apathetic routine.

Afterward, dressing in the room that had been set aside for the girls, Rose was surprised to see several of the women from the audience come in and look at the girls as if they were strange animals. One young matron, her cheeks flushed and her eyes bright, giggled and asked questions. None of the girls answered.

Rose's share of the night's work was fifty dollars. She gave it back to Barbie for her room and board for the month.

After that the troupe did not have an engagement for a long time, but lack of money caused no great hardship in Barbie's household. So long as Barbie had money enough to pay for her sister's dancing lessons everything was all right. Food and liquor just seemed to come into the apartment, and Barbie always paid the rent quarterly and in advance.

Rose was strangely untouched by her part in the lewd exhibition. It was just another job, a better job than prostitution. And a thousand times better than the hopeless job-hunt.

What caused her most misery was the indolence and inaction to which such a life forced her. She fairly longed to sit at a typewriter, to hear a man's voice dictating "your letter of the 16th instant -". Often she stood before a little typewriter store on Forty-second Street and looked in with avid eyes at the display of machines.

Spring came. It hardly made any difference in the murky interior of Barbie's apartment. That backwash of life's current felt no quickening in the springtime. Like Barbie, Rose found herself growing careless of her personal appearance. She no longer felt the desire to walk in fresh air, for she was still sensitive enough to be ashamed of her poor clothes and slatternly appearance.

Then Van Wyck came in one day with joyful news.

"Our depression's over," he said. "I met a fellow who wants to have us give a show at his penthouse. He's inviting a lot of his friends. We'll do it outdoors under a floodlight. The building is so high nobody can see, but it will give a bigger kick to it."

"Won't it be too cold?" Barbie asked anxiously.

"Oh, no. I'll write spring verses, give a vernal flavour to the whole business. It'll be grand! It won't be cold."

"Say," Rose commented. "I'm glad I wear tights. That air is going to feel pretty cool on a bare bottom."

"Oh, no. It'll be lovely out of doors."

"All right," Barbie said. "We'll let the girls play on the roof. But be sure that there's someplace else for them to give the show if it's a windy night, or raining."

"Oh, I'll take care of that," Van Wyck assured her. "This guy that wants the party has lots of money. He'll have some big room in the place for an indoor show. But it'll be swell outdoors."

A few days later they went up to the roof of an apartment house overlooking the East River. It was a beautiful penthouse apartment, and as they undressed and put on the costumes they were to retain for only a brief interval, the girls exclaimed in delight at all the beautiful things in the room that had been assigned to them.

Japanese lanterns had been strung on wires and the roof was aglow with soft light. The naked bodies gleamed seductively in this radiance. The night was none too warm, but it was not cold. When the show was over, the host asked Barbie if she and the girls would not stay and mingle with the other guests for an hour or so. He thought the medieval costumes would look pretty among the modern dress of his guests, and it would be a refreshing novelty for his guests to talk and drink with girls in so strange a business.

"Another hundred dollars," Barbie said.

"All right."

"All right, girls," she said to them in the dressing room, "you can do what you want for an hour or so. Try to get yourselves rich husbands. And you, Rose, you can go in with the rest but stay away from those rotten people. Imagine anybody paying to see the things we do for them!"

"I certainly wouldn't give a nickel to see it," Rose said.

With the other girls, Rose joined the people on the roof - then wandered off to lean against the coping and look at the East River below. Small boats moved on its dark surface. Only their lights were to be seen. It was an eerie sight. A cool wind came up from the river and the little Japanese lanterns swung gaily. Further up the river Rose could see the regimented lights at Welfare Island. A terrible place, she had heard from the other girls. She shuddered. One raid on Barbie's apartment during a rehearsal and she would be there.

She looked down at the river again. The darkness seemed so clean and sweet. For the first time this year, the wind brought to her that rich, good odor of soil loosened by the spring rains. It was rare that one could smell it in New York. Rose breathed in greedily.

As they had dressed for the show, Rose had heard two brokers in an adjoining room talking. They had discussed the depression.

"It ends this summer," one had said.

"Yes, the end's in sight. You can feel a quickening of the pulse already," the other answered.

"Things always pick up in the spring. People buy new clothes. They begin to think of spring-cleaning. Those who have money pay carpenters and painters and plumbers to re-do or repair their homes. I suppose it's the nest building instinct that starts it all. But one thing's sure, the spring brings new life."

"Thank God for that!" the other man had said.

Rose remembered the conversation now, leaning over the roof edge to look at the darkness, a darkness that seemed pregnant with rebirth and reawakening.

"I shouldn't waste time hanging around in Barbie's apartment," she said to herself. "I ought to go out and look for a job during the day. There must be jobs by now."

Then she remembered that her clothes were in a terrible state. To look for a job she would need money for a new wardrobe. As she was, no one would hire her, not even for factory work.

She owed Barbie all the money she was to get for the performance she had just given. That was to pay for back board and lodging.

"I'll borrow some money from her," Rose said aloud.

One of the men whom she had overheard discussing business had said that people buy new things in the spring. That would mean the stores would be taking on help. She would try for a salesgirl's job first.

This resolution made her feel happy, even a little exultant. Optimism came back to her. She already saw herself busy behind a counter all day long and going home at night to a clean, quiet room. Maybe she'd go and visit Barbie once in a while, but only once in a while. Rose liked a good party, but she was too earnest about her own life to enjoy such a continuous, depressing party as went on interminably at Barbie's. Only Van Wyck, a futile person of small talent, and Barbie, who had made her hard-boiled surrender to life, could find satisfaction in such an existence. Not Rose. She felt strong and courageous, eager for things she could not describe to herself. Decency and security, perhaps.

She breathed in deeply again. Again that fresh odor, redolent of the spring and the good earth.

She looked around at the other people on the roof, noisy, garish, useless.

"The hell with it!" she said. "Tomorrow Rosie gets herself a job."

NINETEEN

"Sure, I'll lend you the money," Barbie said. "I'll cash this check today and you can have the money tonight. Go window shopping now and pick out your stuff."

"Fine!" Rose said. "I'll run around now and take a look into the shops. Be sure and have my money, though. Gee, won't it be swell when I have new clothes and a job!"

"Swell?" said Barbie, and her ugly eyes softened. "It's just swell that you can think that way. You're lucky! God bless you."

Rose went happily along the streets, looking into the windows, trying to pick out things she would buy with the fifty dollars Barbie promised to lend her. At one large department store she saw a spring coat that appealed to her and went in to ask the price, but the salesgirl, a smiling person, kindly displayed cheaper coats.

"They're not taking on any help here, are they?" Rose asked her.

"I just got my job this morning. I was out of work three months."

Rose felt her heart leap. They were hiring again!

A little after eleven o'clock, having picked out what she would purchase on the morrow, Rose started back to Barbie's. She took a bus up Fifth Avenue and clambered up the winding stairs to the top. It was an open-topped bus and she was the only passenger on the roof. It gave her a feeling of aloofness from the crowds on the street. Before her, going up the Avenue, was a procession of covered buses, looking like a long cavalcade of elephants. The Empire State Building was shining in the sun. As the bus crested the little rise at Thirty-eighth Street, a flight of pigeons swooped across the Avenue in front of the Public Library, glimmering white in the strong spring sunlight.

Tomorrow she would have a job. There was no doubt about it. She felt like a conqueror.

That night, while a group of young intellectuals at Barbie's damned the machine age with fanciful arguments, Rose went about smiling, two twenty-dollar bills and a ten tucked into her stocking. Tomorrow she was going to get a job.

In the morning Rose hurried around the shops and bought herself a dress, new shoes, cheap new underwear, stockings and a handbag. Then, as a final gesture, she had her hair waved.

In the afternoon she applied at the department store where she had priced the spring coat. She found the store's employment department, filled out a blank and was interviewed by a shrewd-eyed young woman her own age, whose every move crackled with efficiency. She questioned Rose closely, and then decided they could use her.

"Am I going to sell?" Rose asked.

"I have a better job for you than that. One of our executives just asked me to hire the freshest secretary I could find. I think you look as though you might qualify. You look smartly dressed. He likes that - feels that it's necessary in a department store.

He wants somebody to talk back to him, and complains that the depression has made a slave of every girl that works for him."

"Oh, I'll be fresh enough for him," Rose assured her.

"You can begin work tomorrow if you want to, or else on Monday."

"Tomorrow."

Pulling on her new gloves just before stepping out, Rose heard the executive who had hired her say to another woman:

"We don't need five more girls in the book department. We need only two. But those two have to know something about books. I'll try to find someone who at least looks intelligent for your department tomorrow."

Julia was always reading books. It would be a great job for her. Rose decided to call up Fanny and get in touch with Julia to tell her about the opening.

But first, Rose wanted to pick out a room for herself. She wanted to get away from Barbie's as soon as she could. Barbie's was no place for the secretary of a department store executive, with a salary of thirty dollars a week. It looked like a fortune to her. The thought of thirty dollars a week regularly made her feel brisk and confident. She bought a newspaper and searched through the advertising columns for a room. There was one on Thirtieth Street near Second Avenue that sounded attractive from its description. It was seven dollars a week - very reasonable. She went down and looked at it.

It was a small room with one window looking out over a street that seemed clean and quiet. Rose liked it immediately. The landlady, a big German woman in a Hoover apron, seemed kind. Rose still had nine dollars of her fifty left. She paid for the room in advance and then went uptown to tell Barbie about her good fortune, Barbie was overjoyed.

"I am so glad for you," she said. "I told you you weren't the type to go about with us. You'll make good. And when you do, don't forget Barbie. I'd like to see you every once in a while."

Barbie looked around. The phonograph was blaring out a jazz tune. Everyone was laughing at a smutty story that Van Wyck had just recited.

"But not here. I'd rather see you at your place."

"I'll never forget you, Barbie. You're like a rock in the sea. That's the way I've looked at you. I knew I could always hang on to you no matter how damn rotten things went."

The two girls kissed, and Rose, the battered little hatbox on her arm, started out for her new, clean room.

Rose sat on her bed and counted her money. She had bought soap, washcloths, toothbrush and other toilet articles. There was only seventy-five cents left. She would have to live for a week before she would get her salary, and she did not want to borrow any more from Barbie. Suddenly it flashed into her mind. Julia owed her five dollars. Maybe if she was a little better off now she could pay it. It wouldn't hurt to ask. She could tell her about the job at the department store.

Rose went downstairs and 'phoned from Mrs. Landenberg's, the landlady's, telephone. She called Fanny. Fanny's voice was hurried and excited as she gave Rose Julia's new address.

"She lives on Twenty-eighth Street near Third Avenue. Don't try to 'phone her because she has no 'phone."

"I'm right around the corner from her," Rose told Fanny. "I'll run around and see her. Did she lose her job?"

"With the religious fanatic? Yes. He gave her some money and told her to go and try to write the book herself. But I've got to rush now Rose. We're leaving for Albany in about thirty minutes. I'll write you. Goodbye."

"Good luck," Rose called to her. But the receiver had already clicked down.

Rose went on upstairs, put on her hat and coat, then left for Julia's apartment. If Julia had the money, well and good. If she didn't, why then she would find some other way to get it. But anyway, it would be nice to see Julia and Tommy and find out how they were making out. Rose felt happy. As she walked along the street, she sang:

"You're my everything underneath the sun -"

Even the noise of the elevated train wheels as they rattled and banged over her head at Third Avenue seemed jolly.

It was a dark block on which Julia lived, with ash cans and garbage pails blocking the sidewalk. The houses were mean tenements. Rose decided, as she turned in at the number Fanny had given her, not to mention the fact that Julia owed her money. From the appearance of the house, Julia was still badly off.

The bells connected with the various apartments did not work very well. Rose rang and rang again the bell under Julia's name. There was no response. She pushed open the door and went into the house.

There was a rank odor of rats and dampness in the hall. On the walls evil-looking brown paint was peeling off in big, scabby patches. One tiny gas light dimly illuminated the hall and Rose fairly had to grope her way to the stairs. The banister as she touched it felt dirty to her naked hand. The stairs squeaked and groaned when she set foot on them.

She climbed to the second floor and then called out:

"Julia! Julia!"

Her voice echoed through the house. There was no answer. She waited. A door opened on her left and Julia poked her head out. She looked miserable. Her woolen dress was worn through at the elbows and her hair was straggling about her shoulders.

Her eyes were red, as if she had been crying. A light seemed to dawn in her face when she saw Rose.

"God has answered," she said passionately, throwing up her hands in a gesture of unconscious happiness and relief.

Rose became frightened. She tried to peer more closely at Julia's face in the flickering light. There was no madness there - only joy and tears of relief streaming over thin and haggard cheeks.

"What is it, Julia?"

Julia's only answer was a terse question.

"Have you five dollars?"

"No."

A look of terrible worry came over Julia's face.

"What's the matter? Are they going to dispossess you?"

"Tommy's sick. Come in."

Rose went with her into the little dog hutch that passed for a room, a damp and evil-smelling hole lit by a single paraffin candle burning in a saucer. There was no furniture, nothing but a mattress laid on four soap boxes. On this, rolled in a shawl, a blanket and a dirty rug, lay Tommy. There was a water glass with a cracked rim on the floor near his head.

"What's wrong?" Rose whispered.

"Pneumonia. They didn't give him enough to eat at the boarding place. He's undernourished. His heart may give out. I'm scared -"

"What do you want five dollars for?"

"Tommy. The doctor - a nice, kind man - left a prescription to be filled. I didn't dare tell him I had no money. I was afraid he might not take the case. I was so scared and frightened. Now I've got to get this prescription filled. I have no money. I'd go on the street to get it, but I can't leave him."

"Give me the prescription. I'll get your money for you," Rose said. "I have friends. I'll borrow from them. I'll be back in half an hour. Just keep your shirt on, Julia, and stay quiet."

"Rose," Julia said, and it seemed to breathe gratitude, "I'm sure that God must have sent you. I was just praying."

"He picked a funny angel this time," Rose said, trying to joke.

Before she left, Rose took a fleeting look at Tommy. He lay very still and his little cheeks burned with fever. As she glanced at him, Tommy shivered. Even Rose, inexperienced in such matters, could see that the child was dangerously ill.

"Please hurry!" Julia whispered.

Rose, prescription in hand, ran down the stairs and into the street. She paused a moment. Barbie was her best bet in a matter of this sort. She would get a taxi and go up there. She had enough money for that, and speed counted. It might be a matter of life and death.

She walked to the corner and looked up and down the street for a cab. There was none in sight. On the corner, however, she saw the lights of a drugstore. It might be a good idea to step in and find out just how much a prescription of this sort would cost. A stout little man with eye glasses was behind the counter.

"How much does a prescription like this cost, Mister?" Rose asked.

He studied it carefully for a moment.

"I can make it up for four dollars. There are expensive ingredients -Digitalis, other drugs."

It was good that she had stopped in to find out. She would have to borrow ten dollars from Barbie.

"All right," she said to the druggist, taking the prescription out of his hand. "I'll be back in a few minutes."

"Wait," he called to her.

"I'll be back," she shouted over her shoulder as she hailed a taxi cab.

The druggist, seeing her get into the cab, shrugged his shoulders and went back into the store. If she had money enough for cabs - well - that was a different story.

It cost sixty cents to Barbie's apartment. As she paid the driver, she looked up to see if there were lights in the windows. There was none showing.

"Probably playing rotten games in the dark," Rose thought to herself as she started to climb the stairs. It was very quiet in the house. Reaching the third landing, Rose tried the door. It was locked. She banged on it. There was no answer. Rose twisted her hands nervously together.

"It's the first time I've ever known this door to be locked," she said, and then called hysterically, "Barbie! Barbie!"

"Whoa back," came a reassuring call from the stairs. "I'm coming."

Barbie panting from her climb up the stairs, came onto the landing.

"What's wrong?"

"Julia - you remember - the girl with the baby - her boy is sick - maybe dying. I've got to borrow money for a prescription. Lend me five. I'll pay you next week."

"God damn!"

"But, Barbie - the kid is dying."

"I know, and I can't help him. I have no money."

"But Barbie - you just got money."

"I gave some to Mary's dance teacher to pay her tuition, and the rest I just spent. Helen caught the flu the other night at that damn penthouse. I had to pay in advance at the hospital. I haven't a single cent. I'd do anything to give you money for the kid, but I haven't got it."

"I know," Rose said and started running down the stairs.

Even as she ran she tried to think of someone who might give her the money. Fanny was gone. Grace and Yvonne were working. Alfred? If he had money he would give it to her. She ran to the subway, savagely forcing her way through the theatre crowd.

At Thirty-fourth Street she ran up the familiar stairs and beat on the apartment door until Alfred opened. He fell back a step at the sight of her.

"Have you six bucks?" she asked.

"I'm on my agar-agar ration. I haven't a penny. What's wrong?"

In short quick sentences she told him.

"What about Andy upstairs?" he asked. "I know he hasn't any money. I tried to borrow some yesterday. He never has any, but he's a doctor. He might help."

Without bothering to put on his overcoat Alfred ran up and got the thin, gangling young man who had surprised her on the first day she had come to Waldo's apartment.

Andy slid into his coat and went with them. They hurried down the long slope of Thirty-fourth Street to Second Avenue and then on to Third, turned there and walked rapidly, panting in their haste, to the house where Julia's little boy lay ill.

"I couldn't get the money, but I got a doctor," Rose told Julia. "He might help."

Andy examined the sick boy. Then he straightened up and shook his head.

"I'm sorry. His heart's going - if only I had -" Andy's voice trailed off as he concentrated. "That prescription you spoke about - it must be for the heart. You've got to get it filled."

Rose looked at Alfred. It was plain to see that he was deeply touched. His eyes were full of pity for the little boy on the mattress. Rose turned fiercely to Alfred, gripping his shoulders.

"If I were a man," she said, "I'd run out on the street and

knock down the first person I saw - take the money from him. Why don't you?"

He shook his head.

"Go on," she said.

He shook his head again.

"I couldn't. I'm not a man of action. I could no more do that than fly."

"You're a yellow-belly!" she shouted at him. "I'll get that money!"

She flung herself out of the room and down the stairs and ran to Third Avenue. Men were passing. Some of them must have money. She stood on the corner. A burly man in a blue reefer jacket went by. She gripped him by the arm.

"I'll do anything for four dollars," she told him, "if you'll only hurry."

"Get away, you tart!" the man shouted, pushing her aside.

A little bearded Jew in a black overcoat that reached to his heels went shuffling by. She took hold of his arm.

"I'll do anything for four dollars, if you'll only hurry."

He shrugged and walked on.

Then came a tall, thin man in a baker's white, flour-caked apron.

"I'll do anything for four dollars, if you'll only hurry."

He took her chin in his hand and turned her face up to the street lamp.

"Anything?" he asked grinning.

"Anything," she answered. "Anything, if you'll only hurry!"

"Come on down into the basement of our shop," he said, pointing across the street.

Twenty minutes later Rose, her new dress stained white with flour, came breathless, exhausted into Julia's room. In her hand she held the small bottle of medicine.

Another man was in the room with Andy and Alfred, a tall young man with a little moustache and very white hands, stooped low over Tommy.

Rose handed the bottle to Julia. The strange young man waved it aside.

"His doctor," Alfred whispered.

He bent over the child again and took the pulse beat. He frowned. They all stood silent. From his bag he took a stethoscope and applied it to the child's chest. He listened for a moment, then got up from his knees and, crossing the room, put the stethoscope back into his bag. Only then did he shake his head. The child was dead. Rose took the bottle from Julia's hand and dashed it to the floor.

"Four dollars!" she shouted.

Julia began to sob, standing still, her hands straight at her sides and the tears running over her face to fall in tiny splatters to the dust-caked floor.

Rose looked at Alfred. His eyes were wet.

The strange doctor was talking to Andy.

"Damn it! You know, doctor, I marked that prescription P.P. Why in God's name didn't they have it filled?"

"They didn't know," Andy told him.

Rose took the doctor's arm.

"What do you mean?" she asked, "P.P.?"

"It means poor patient. Poor patient! We put it on the prescription when we want it filled and the patient hasn't any money. The druggist would have honored it."

Rose clenched her fist. If she had only had those four dollars. It was want of money that had made them so desperate that she could not even wait to hear what the druggist was going to say to her. It was want of money that had killed the child. It was want of money that made all the unhappiness in the world.

Alfred put his hand on her shoulder.

"I can guess how you got that money." Then suddenly, in a choked voice, "Will you marry me? I need you. I've felt that ever since you left."

Rose laughed bitterly.

"Ask me again when you're a millionaire."

She went to the window. In the East the sun was coming up. The great black bridges over the East River were glowing pink at their edges. Behind her, Julia sobbed and kept sobbing. The three men talked in low, sad voices. But Rose, hard-eyed, looked out over the towers of the city, rose-colored in the dawn, and vowed she would never let herself be caught in the net of poverty again - the poverty that had killed Tommy.

She would be inhumanely cruel. Self-assertive, immoral, industrious - anything; whipping herself on to become rich and secure. That was what mattered. And poverty was the crime of crimes. Tomorrow the new job. She would never let it go until she had a better one.

An afterword
by Damien Love

"Years ago I wrote novels for a living, and when RKO was looking for producers, someone told them I had written horrible novels. They misunderstood the word 'horrible' for 'horror' and I got the job..." – Val Lewton.

Writing in 1957, six years after Val Lewton died at the absurd age of 46, the great movie critic Manny Farber, one of Lewton's earliest champions, observed: "Americans seem to have a special aptitude for allowing History to bury the toughest, most authentic native talents."

Farber went on to list Lewton alongside Walker Evans and James Agee (himself, in his years as film critic, Lewton's first and most fervent admirer) on a roster of "unlikely, self-destroying, uncompromising, roundabout artists" who at that point had been almost forgotten, swept into near-oblivion by an historical tide he felt was in the process of doing the same thing to such disreputable, anti-Art genre-specialist directors as Howard Hawks.

Five decades on, thanks partly to the gnawing perception of writers like Farber, the battles over whether Evans, Agee and Hawks count as great American artists have been fought and won so conclusively that it is getting difficult to imagine they ever had to be fought at all. And, while still unfairly unknown outside the ranks of film-buffery, within that charmed circle, Lewton, who made his name down among the shadows in the most disreputable genre of them all, low-budget horror movies, has long been rediscovered and revered.

As producer-auteur of unexpected films like *Cat People* (1942), *I Walked With A Zombie* (1943), *The Seventh Victim* (1943) and *The Body Snatcher* (1945), morbid, melancholy movies that shied away from monsters to emphasise ordinary lives violently derailed by their own suppressed, suggested horrors, Lewton is the key figure in introducing notes of psychology, even a nagging, bleak, pop philosophy to the genre. His dark, obsessive, occasionally bloody visions occupy a place in American sound cinema analogous to that in American literature occupied by the fever dreams of Edgar Allan Poe.

All the stranger, then, that, while Lewton the *auteur* has been pulled to safety and his work become the object of bottomless fascination, Lewton the *author* has been all but washed away by History's relentless tide, to the extent that barely any traces remain. The book you now hold in your hands, the best known of Lewton's novels, has been out of print for over half a century, and not seen in its original form since it was first published in 1932.

Lewton wrote nine novels in all, plus, as he once gleefully highlighted in a list of his own credits, two works of pornography sold under the counter in New York in the early thirties. ("I have a beautiful picture of this book taken from the *New York Daily Mirror,*" he noted of his erotic title *Grushenskaya,* "showing it being shovelled into the police department furnace.") How these books came to be lost is impossible to say. But it is not stretching a point to suggest it happened for the same reason Lewton's horror movies once seemed in danger of being disregarded: because they appear to be, and to a degree are, pure, authentic pulp, with enough whiff of salacious, sensationalist drugstore bookracks to send arbiters of taste and "serious" audiences scurrying.

Certainly, Paramount, which snapped up the rights to *No Bed of Her Own* when the book became a success, soon distanced itself from it. The idea to pair Miriam Hopkins with Clark Gable in a movie adaptation was quickly dropped - presumably around the time the studio's story department actually read the novel, and realised it was practically unfilmable.

Indeed, take a random sampling of the strictures of the Production Code then tightening its grip around Hollywood's basic instincts, and it seems almost as if Lewton wrote his story with one eye on that list of censor's commandments, checking off laws as he broke them:

> "...pictures shall not infer that low forms of sex relationship are the accepted or common thing... sex perversion or any inference to it is forbidden... sex relationships between the white and black races is forbidden... profanity is forbidden... dances suggesting sexual actions are forbidden... no film or episode may throw ridicule on any religious faith... white slavery shall not be treated... brothels and houses of ill-fame are not proper locations for drama..."

Scrapping the plan to film Lewton's novel, Paramount decided to simply retain its pulse-quickening title, for a movie starring Gable and his future-wife, Carole Lombard. In the event, the censor refused even that, and so the film became *No*

Man of Her Own, a gambling story with no relation to Lewton's book, rushed out in time for Christmas 1932.

When *No Bed of Her Own* was republished as a dimestore paperback in 1950, the lurid cover screamed, "The Intimate Story of One Girl's Behaviour When Faced With Big-City Temptations! Complete and Unabridged!" In fact, the edition was heavily bowdlerized, with many episodes, including Rose's observation of the cinema usherette's furtive prostitution in the balcony darkness, completely removed.

In the forties, when America wore its unselfconscious racism on its sleeve, Lewton stood out as one of the most genuinely liberal – as opposed to breast-beatingly Liberal – film-makers in Hollywood. Watch how actors like Theresa Harris and the calypso singer Sir Lancelot easefully banter in his films and you still see what James Agee meant when, in 1944, he argued these were "the most unpretentiously sympathetic, intelligent, anti-traditional and individualized" black characters to have been presented onscreen until that point.

Still, in 1932, the author of *No Bed of Her Own* has no compunction about having the dullard Mildred say "nigger," just as Lewton, whose family was Jewish, doesn't hesitate to have his Irish Rose call Mr Farbstein, the grifter who cons her into buying "The Silver Magic Wonder Bars", a "kike"- because, as if it needed spelling out, that's how these characters would have spoken, and thought. In the 1950 reprint, however, Mr Farbstein has transformed into "Mr Farrar," and any explicit, slangy racial slurs are gone – as, indeed, is any mention of Mildred having ever danced with a black partner at all. The differences between the two editions speak volumes about the differences between the crackling thirties and the starched fifties in general, and the painful hypocrisies of the latter period in particular. (This edition, of course, restores the 1932 text.)

Even Lewton, within whom a perpetual battle between quiet, high-minded artist and hustling, low-down showman seems to have raged, appears to have been in two minds about the exact worth of his story of Rose Mahoney and her Depression. His son, Val E Lewton, remembers his father being very proud of this novel – especially his claim that the German translation of *No Bed of Her Own* was among the books burned in Germany under Hitler's orders.

Yet, in 1973, when speaking to Lewton's biographer Joel E Siegel for his seminal study, *The Reality of Terror*, Verna De Mots, Lewton's long-term secretary, recalled:

> "The only time [Val] ever scolded me was when he came into the office early one morning and found me reading one of his novels. He blushed and became quite angry. 'Don't ever let me catch you reading one of those books again,' he shouted, and slammed the door."

✳ ✳ ✳ ✳ ✳ ✳ ✳

Very likely the most literate producer in forties Hollywood – although competition for the title was hardly fierce - Lewton first seemed destined to become a writer. After he'd stopped writing novels, he continued to seek the company of other writers. He tended to avoid the glitzier Tinseltown parties, but with his wife, Ruth, became a regular at the Santa Monica salons of the Polish actress and writer Salka Viertel, where, along with Greta Garbo, the refugee likes of Thomas Mann, Bertolt Brecht and Christopher Isherwood gathered to commiserate with each other over the sunny incomprehensibility of their new surroundings, and rekindle a faint bohemian scent of the old countries fallen under darkness back across the Atlantic.

Salka's teenaged son, Peter, became Lewton's assistant, and it was Lewton who encouraged the future *White Hunter Black Heart* author to publish his first novel, *The Canyon*, at 19. Lewton would later hire embattled LA novelist John Fante to write scripts, but his least likely literary relationship is the friendship he struck up with William Faulkner, who, while labouring through his own unhappy Hollywood years, lived opposite Lewton in Pacific Palisades. There is the exquisite story that, late one evening, Lewton was roused by Faulkner's panicking maid: Faulkner was missing, gone raging off into the night on a drunken bender. Dispatched to find his friend, Lewton eventually discovered the author several miles away, huddled in terror inside a chicken coop.

Perhaps Lewton was always so drawn to books and their writers because his own early years actually suggested the opening chapter of a novel, some turbulent Russian drama. He was born Vladimir Ivan Leventon on the edge of the Black Sea in Yalta, then part of Russia, on 7 May 1904. His mother, Nina, was the daughter of Yakov Leventon, a Jewish pharmacist of local renown and fierce temper, who had fled the pogroms and returned, who boasted of having once served Tsar Alexander III, and who filled prescriptions for the tubercular Anton Chekhov on his regular visits to the Ukrainian town, then as now a popular resort.

Nina had an older brother, Volodya, a journalist who moved to Berlin, and a younger sister, Adelaida, known as Alla, a small, dark girl with eyes like black pools, who had an increasingly difficult relationship with her father – and then, exiling herself from home, none at all.

In 1905, Alla finally left for the United States. There, as "Nazimova," she became a phenomenon on Broadway – where she introduced the techniques of Stanislavsky and the work of Ibsen and her friend Chekhov to America – and a towering presence in early Hollywood. By the 1920s, famously bisexual, she would be as well known for the swirling society parties held in her Hollywood home, "The Garden of Allah," as her revolutionary acting.

While her sister's star ascended far away, Nina found herself stuck. She had studied music in Dresden, but any ambitions for a career in the arts were cut short when Yakov suffered a stroke in 1892 and she was called home to care for her father. A cultured, fiercely intelligent woman, who had corresponded with Emile Zola on the latest rise of anti-Semitism in Europe, she grew frustrated at Yalta's provincial pace and, seeking distraction, fell for a young man of excitingly ill repute, "Maximillian," whom she married in 1898, shortly after Yakov's death.

The identity of this Maximillian, Lewton's father, has long been shrouded in mystery. Various sources cast him as a tall Russian soldier or devilish British Naval officer, but in 1997, in his biography of Nazimova, Gavin Lambert identified him instead as Max Hofschneider, son of a Yalta moneylender. All sources agree, however, that Max's reputation as a drinker, gambler and womaniser was well earned, and that neither marriage nor children – Lewton's elder sister, Lucy, was born in 1900 – improved his character or curbed his appetites.

The marriage was a disaster. In 1906, having seen her husband gamble her inheritance away, Nina took the children and left. She never used or spoke his name again. After two hard years scraping clerical work in Berlin, she accepted an invitation from her distant sister to come and work for her, and, in the spring of 1909, set sail with her little family for America.

Lewton spent his first years in the United States with mother, sister and exotic aunt in Port Chester, New York, where Nazimova had carved a tiny, stubborn patch of Russia, a wooded estate she called "Who-Torok," Russian for "Little Farm." Few male figures around, he turned to stories, his own wild inventions as well as books, for company and escape, becoming a voracious reader of near-photographic memory. His son recalls that, as an adult, Lewton could read as many as four novels a night, and retain full details of each.

The writing career started in earnest at 16, when he landed a job as reporter on the *Darien-Stamford Review* – then promptly lost it, when his scoop about a truckload of kosher chickens dying in a heat wave was revealed as something he'd invented because he was bored. He studied journalism at Columbia, and dropped out after two years, citing lack of interest. Short-lived positions at the King Features syndicate and on other newspapers, including *The New York American*, followed. Covering New York's night courts, he became friendly with Donald Henderson Clarke, the journalist, proto-hardboiled novelist and general man-about town to whom *No Bed of Her Own* was originally dedicated. Clarke helped him get a brief job on his paper, *The New York Morning World*, a favour Lewton later returned by employing Clarke to write scripts for his RKO horrors.

Clarke was a friend to New York's Jazz-Age mob boss Arnold Rothstein, and the world he revealed undoubtedly fed *No Bed of Her Own*; in 1929, when Lewton, strapped for cash, was looking to buy a wedding ring for Ruth Knapp - his childhood sweetheart, whose family disowned her for persisting in loving him – a group of sentimental, high-class Manhattan call girls he knew through Clarke banded together to help, introducing him to the jeweller to whom they pawned the trinkets their admirers gave them.

Lewton published his first book, a small-press folio of romantic poetry, *Panther Skin and Grapes*, in 1923, aged 19. Two years later, his first novel, *Improved Road* was published, bizarrely enough, in Edinburgh, Scotland (making it strangely fitting that another Scottish publisher should now revive *No Bed of Her Own*). A second novel, a rattling "Russian" potboiler titled *The Cossack Sword*, followed in 1926.

Meanwhile, under the auspices of her famous sister, Lewton's mother, Nina, had found work in the story department of the New York office of the Metro Picture Corporation, later MGM. By 1928, she was head of the department, and that year found her son a job in publicity, working under the lyricist Howard Dietz, the man who composed Hollywood's anthem, "That's Entertainment." There, it was Lewton's task to write features about, and radio and newspaper serialisations of the company's new releases. (Several of the latter, including *The Rogue Song* and *Rasputin and the Empress*, appeared as novels in his name.) In this capacity, he was required to produce over 50,000 words every week, a figure that would leave most professional writers today chewing the carpet. More remarkable still, he continued to write for himself on the side.

An odd, atmospheric, but strangely sceptical short story, "The Bagheeta," about a lonely hunter's search through dark Ukrainian forests for a fabled black cat said to transform into a woman – the often overlooked dry run for *Cat People* – appeared in the legendary pulp magazine *Weird Tales* in 1930. The following year, under the pseudonym "HC Kerkow," Lewton blasted out another novel, *The Fateful Star Murder*, in less than 48 hours over a single, epic weekend session

When *No Bed of Her Own* (Lewton's second novel of 1932, following *Where the Cobra Sings*, an adventure written under another pseudonym, "Cosmo Forbes") became a minor sensation, its publisher, Vanguard Press, offered him a contract. The deal required him to produce five novels in a year; an insane, back-breaking proposition, which at the time presumably seemed a welcome easing of pace.

With this under his belt, Lewton left MGM that year - although, lest things get too easy, in addition to his Vanguard contract, he also signed to write a thrice-weekly radio serial, *The Luck of Joan Christopher*. (Of the Vanguard books - three of them written under his most regular pseudonym, "Carlos Keith," to hide the fact that one man was writing so many books so quickly – the first, *Yearly Lease*, is the stand-out: a peculiar, layered, blasting soap-opera as curious as, and even more vigorously trashy than *No Bed Of Her Own*; in other ways, with its evocations of life as a struggling writer in Greenwich Village, the most autobiographical thing he ever wrote.)

One year later, as Lewton completed his Vanguard contract, David O Selznick contacted his mother at MGM's story office, to ask if she could find any Russian-born writers to tackle a script for a proposed adaptation of *Taras Bulba*. Among others, she recommended her son - the esteemed author of *The Cossack Sword*, after all – and so Lewton got the call to Hollywood.

His script for *Taras Bulba* was never filmed, but Lewton was there when Tara burned. The exact extent of his contributions to Selznick's movies will never be known, but it was Lewton who saw the Swedish film *Intermezzo* and persuaded Selznick to bring the story, and its star, Ingrid Bergman, to the American screen. He was the man who tried to talk Selznick out of *Gone With the Wind* ("ponderous trash"), but also the man who designed one of that film's most striking sequences, the celebrated shot as the camera rises over hundreds of wounded soldiers - and the man who suggested to director Victor Fleming that a dinner table scene in which two large grapefruit were positioned in front of Vivien Leigh's breasts perhaps be reframed.

In all, he stayed on as Selznick's story editor and right-hand man for eight years. Then in 1942, he met Charles Koerner,

RKO's head of production, at a party. With his studio deep in financial crisis following its adventure with Orson Welles – the honeymoon that produced *Citizen Kane* and *The Magnificent Ambersons*, artistic peaks and economic disasters – Koerner was looking for someone to lead a unit devoted to low-budget horror, which, as the ongoing success of Universal's monster-mashes proved, continued to turn a healthy profit. They already had a name for the first movie: *Cat People*.

****

Of all the stories told about Val Lewton, and there are many, one in particular seems to sum him up. It happened in 1944, when he was called into the office of Jack Gross, his superior at RKO. The two did not get on; Lewton, whose often painfully reticent character concealed a wicked sense of humour, had conceived a typically obscure manner in which to communicate contempt, by refusing to call his boss anything other than "Mr. Gross."

When he'd started at RKO, Lewton worked within severe restrictions: famously, his movies had to cost no more than $150,000, run no longer than 75 minutes, and satisfy the ready-made, market-tested chiller titles the studio imposed upon him. Yet within these limitations, he was extraordinarily free. Working out of sight down in the metaphorical basement, costing little, he was let alone, which helps explain the surprise of *Cat People*. On release, that first film was a word-of-mouth phenomenon, making between $2,000,000 and $4,000,000 – historians debate the figures, but all agree the movie almost single-handedly put RKO back into the black.

Even if they didn't understand Lewton's films, the studio chiefs understood those numbers, took notice, and, going by the Hollywood logic that if a thing isn't broke it needs fixing, came increasingly to meddle in his productions.

Mr. Gross had come recently to RKO from Universal, where, as one of Lewton's regular directors, Mark Robson, once put it, "the prevailing idea of horror was a werewolf chasing a girl in a nightgown up a tree." Sitting with him when Lewton was called in was a man from Exhibition, named Holt. They had news: RKO had just signed Boris Karloff, whose name more than any other was synonymous with the full-blooded Universal style, and Lewton was to make a trio of chillers with Karloff as his star.

"And remember," Holt concluded, wagging his finger in Lewton's face. "No messages!"

By the time he had stalked back to his own office, Lewton was in fury. Grabbing his telephone, he called back: "I'm sorry, but we do have a message," he seethed. "And our message is that death is good."

Sixty years on, the starkness and strangeness of that taunting statement of intent still draws you up short. What is even more extraordinary is that the first film Lewton made with Karloff, *Isle of the Dead*, a static, eerie pale fire of a movie, actually lives up to it.

So many of Lewton's films do. He professed no religion, but it is almost possible to view movies like *Cat People*, *I Walked With a Zombie* and especially his suicidal masterpiece *The Seventh Victim* as subscribing to a philosophy akin to the heresy of the Cathars, the radically austere mediaeval sect whose name, an insult handed down by their persecutors, made them the first "cat people": existence is presented as a kind of purgatorial grey hell, death a sweet relief. (It's worth injecting here that, while discussing the author photograph for this book, Val E Lewton rejected one image of his father with the words: "A great photograph - but not characteristic, because he looks happy.")

For Lewton fans, perhaps the single most surprising thing about *No Bed of Her Own*, which comes charging at the reader with the hustle and pep of a thirties Hollywood heroine, could be that it doesn't mount the tenebrous seduction nor share the morbid, pensive melancholy of his movies. Look again, though, and hints of the film-maker to come are everywhere buried. Even in a description of Rose's little rented room, Lewton will throw in a baffling moment like this:

> "Such slight inconveniences as the gas heater did not greatly matter. Rose often said: 'I don't mind it. It's almost as cozy as a fireplace, and if I ever get tired of life all I have to do is close the window and turn on the gas.'"

It sounds like a joke – until you remember *The Seventh Victim*'s suicide chamber, another rented room, furnished with only a patient hangman's noose, just in case.

Dim shades of future themes, obsessions, archetypes and even specific scenes move among these pages. Barbie, the mysteriously listless hedonist, prefigures burned–out sensationalists in *I Walked With a Zombie* and *The Seventh Victim*; the secret, baroque burlesques she stages have a counterpart in the masques Karloff's asylum keeper makes his "loonies" perform for high society in *Bedlam*. The underlying theme of the novel is the underlying theme of all Lewton's movies from *Cat People* on; how life can shift a fraction of a degree, shadows comes rushing, and people can find themselves slipping into a world whose existence they never suspected.

In other respects, the Lewton we know from the films is all

over this book: the abiding concern for female protagonists; the frank and humanist approach to society and sex; the eye for the details of character's lives; the forward-driving storytelling; the persistent literary digressions.

There is, too, the curious parallel between the circumstances surrounding the writing of all Lewton's novels and the later production circumstances of his movies. Like the films, Lewton's books had to be cranked out astonishingly quickly, and targeted a specific, traditionally downscale market. And, like his movies, they aim at achieving far more than that market usually expects. The book is for the drugstore - but any faint overtones of the naturalism of Dreiser and Zola are no coincidence.

Most importantly, and regardless of whether the reader is a Val Lewton fan or not, *No Bed of Her Own* deserves its place back in History simply because it holds up as a fantastic little read in its own right. Arresting, unpretentious, still surprising, it grabs on the surface level, yet is resonant with unexpected, sly and subtle undercurrents. Whether or not it was the first American novel to tackle what was turning into the great Depression, as has been claimed, in its own, tough, burrowing, disreputable little way, it offers a vibrant street-level urban snapshot of its times, vivid enough to remind us the Depression did not descend solely on dustbowl landscapes.

The book throws open a tiny, hidden window onto the New York of 1931, and through it that teeming city comes blaring. A place of cold, electric days, cosy little rooms and deserted afternoon speakeasies, of grumbling cigar-makers, religious fanatics, taxi-dancers, seedy photographers and polite performing bears. A city where the growing ranks of the unemployed move half-glimpsed like phantoms through the crowds and Walter Winchell still rattles off the inky dirt of the day. Where the remaining rich gather by night as a secret society on high, clandestine rooftops, to watch their fantasies enacted by bored performers, and Marxist law students put the world to rights in late-night chop suey joints. A place where the Roseland dance palace still thrums at night and, at Forty-seventh Street, the yellow dust from the Radio City excavation still hangs in the air. And ringing out amid the din, one girl's voice, undefeated:

"Go tear yourself to pieces!"

Damien Love
Glasgow
November 2005